AWAKENING TO RICHES

When Pope came to, a high wind was beating against the rain-swept windows. He suddenly remembered Dr. Klemper, the spear haft striking him in the back before darkness suddenly enveloped him.

Of Dr. Klemper, nothing was to be seen. But on the floor just in front of the instrument panel was the bone-white skeleton, lying amid a neat row of metal buttons and the two halves of a zipper, shoe nails arrayed in a neat geometrical pattern by each skeletal foot. On the floor beside the skeleton, two .45 automatics glistened in the overhead lights, as did half a dozen spent shell cases. Protruding from the spine were a flint spearhead and the time-bleached shaft of a wooden spear. To one side lay shreds of what had been a leather pouch. Among them was a pile of bright gold nuggets, enough to fill Justin Po[illegible] overflowing.

By Daniel da Cruz
Published by Ballantine Books:

F-CUBED

THE GROTTO OF THE FORMIGANS

THE AYES OF TEXAS

TEXAS ON THE ROCKS

TEXAS TRIUMPHANT

MIXED DOUBLES

MIXED DOUBLES

Daniel da Cruz

A Del Rey Book
BALLANTINE BOOKS • NEW YORK

A Del Rey Book
Published by Ballantine Books

 Published in the United States of America by Ballantine Books, a division of Random House, Inc., New York and simultaneously in Canada by Random House of Canada Limited, Toronto.

Library of Congress Catalog Card Number: 89-90751

ISBN 0-345-35167-3

Manufactured in the United States of America

First Edition: August 1989

Cover Art by Barclay Shaw

For

Linno, Doon, and the Cobra Girl,
wakadoozers all

Table of Contents

I—Two-Part Invention

I
Two-Part Invention

1. PRELUDE
23 JUNE 1996

JUSTIN POPE WAS DIVIDED INTO THREE PARTS: AMBITION, genius, and gall.

He had the ambition to be acclaimed—like the young Beethoven—the greatest composer of his age. He had the gall to pretend that he was indeed such a genius. And he had the genius to get away with it.

Pope's genius was to convince people who should have known better—his professors and fellow students—that within him burned a veritable volcano of musical creativity, which burst forth at intervals in an eruption of deafening brass and cymbals and bass drums leavened, inexplicably, by passages of simple, unadorned, and all-too-brief melody. That he was able to compose such eloquent melodies proved that he possessed a talent of the highest order. That he sandwiched them between ear-crunching avalanches of unorganized sound, his mentors solemnly explained to the unconvinced, who winced when they listened to Pope's music, was merely to enhance their beauty by contrast with the lack of harmony of what preceded and followed. Immensely proud of their student, they explained that his compositions were a logical extension of the dissonances of modern masters such as Prokofiev, Stravinsky, Holst, Poulenc, Milhaud, Cage, Hindemith, Copeland, Webern, and Glass. Not for him the outdated austerities of Bach, Buxtehude, Telemann, and Handel. Pope, genius that he was, could have written that sort of music had he so chosen, but his imagination had leapt across the centuries, and the music that the genie within compelled him to write left him no leisure to cater to the shallow tastes of yesterday. Or so they said . . .

Alas, for the kind of music that filled his hours and his notebooks there was no audience except the professors he had gulled into believing that his was the voice of the future. It was music full of complex and grating disharmonies, jerky rhythms, long silences broken by thunderous chords, arpeggios that mixed and intermingled like paints smeared haphazardly on an artist's palette. Yet sometimes, by an alchemy mysterious even to him, they resolved into stunning chromatic tone pictures, sunbursts of sound, with the sweep and majesty of a Turner battle scene. Those lyric passages convinced everyone that Pope could, had he so wished, have written the rest of his music to the same measure. Such grace notes of genius, the erudite critics of the Bay area proclaimed, would one day flower into an oeuvre that would enrapture the world.

Some day—but not today. Meanwhile, he stole. Not everything: merely most of the charming melodies that enchanted his professors; the dissonances were his own. He *had* to steal, for in no other way could he satisfy his yearning for fame while he was young and vigorous and able to enjoy it. Once he made his mark, he told himself, he would have the leisure to really learn the art of composition or, even better, use his celebrity to launch a musical career in which his natural talent for fraud could be put to good use, like conducting.

Meanwhile, he had to get on with the business of winning his doctor of music degree, the safe refuge of those who desired a musical career but had no talent.

And so, without protest from his conscience, from the yellowed, crumbling archives of the Faculty of Music at the University of California, for three years he had abstracted themes written for such extinct instruments as the *cor anglais*, *oboe d'amore*, *diplo-kithara*, *racket*, and *lira da braccio* by the unknown Renaissance composers Luigi Baptistini, Mario Mariocuti, Emil Harnishneggar, Petrus Lermontov, and others. He then spliced them into the jangling, discordant passages that so bewildered and repelled, and therefore impressed, his teachers.

In his final year of graduate school Pope was a campus phenomenon. By consensus of both teachers and his sheeplike classmates, he was easily the most gifted of them all, a composer destined for greatness in his own time. Here was a composer who would not, like the pathetic Franz Schubert, die in poverty and obscurity before his talent could fully mature.

On the other hand, Pope reflected on the night of 23 June 1996, as he trudged through the rain toward the Omar Haffar Molecular Sciences Building, his fate might be far worse than Schubert's: a life of ignominy and ridicule . . .

The note had arrived in the afternoon mail. Unsigned, it contained a single hand-printed word: "Baptistini." At intervals over eight months, he had received two others like it. The first had read "Lermontov." Nine weeks later he had received the second, with the single word "Mariocuti."

The first had elicited little reaction. Someone had perhaps detected a resemblance between one of his compositions and one of Lermontov's. A mere coincidence. It happened all the time in music. Handel had plagiarized his own works shamelessly, while Respighi had plundered those of others. Even the great Wagner had not been above borrowing a phrase that was, note for note, first heard in Mendelssohn's Symphony no. 5—in reality his no. 10—the *Reformation*.

Examples of conscious plagiarism were countless. Beethoven used a theme first written in 1800 for his "Creatures of Prometheus," borrowed it for a country dance in 1802, then for the Variations in E Flat Major, and finally in 1803 for the finale of his *Eroica* Symphony. The prolific Franz Schubert himself had not been above borrowing the principal theme from his opera *Rosamunde* later in a string quartet and in a theme and variations for piano, the Impromptu in D Flat.

But probably the most egregious case of wholesale "borrowing" had been of the theme first heard in Bach's Third Partita for Unaccompanied Violin in E Major. He himself had used it again twelve years later, rearranged for organ in his 29th Cantata, and finally in his great B Minor Mass. It was also borrowed and rearranged by Robert Schumann, Sergey Rachmaninoff, Fritz Kreisler, William Smith, and Leopold Stowkowski, among others. If Pope appropriated the music of others for his own, at least he was in the best company.

Still, the receipt of the second note, bearing the name Mariocuti, disturbed him. There was here no question of coincidence. Pope had lifted three distinct themes from Mariocuti's Missa Solemnis in C Minor, a work so obscure that according to the library checkout sheet, no one at the university had even looked at it for more than thirty years. And yet somebody obviously had, and had detected Pope's fraud. The thought gripped him like an icy hand around the throat. He began to look over his shoulder, to gaze deeply into the afternoon shadows, but to no avail: no secret watcher lurked there.

Pope's anxiety was allayed somewhat by the thought that he was in his final trimester, following which he would receive his doctorate and be free forever from the necessity to steal the themes of others. Conditional upon his receiving his Ph.D., he had already received several excellent offers from leading American conservatories. He would accept the one requiring the lightest teaching load and get down finally to writing great music, for he was vain enough to believe that the spark of true musical genius smoldered within him.

Meanwhile, however, the final movement of his major work to date, the Symphony in D Major, the *Malibu*, still had to be written, and he lacked a theme for it. Taking all precautions to avoid being followed, he went to the university's musical library late one night in mid-May and spent four hours ransacking the stacks for an appropriate theme. He finally found one by Luigi Baptistini that clashed nicely with the stolen motifs from the earlier movements. He made a photocopy and within ten days had submitted the finished symphony to his adviser, who was visibly moved and fulsome in his praise. Pope's Ph.D. was in the bag.

On May 2 Pope opened his mailbox to find a letter with the single hand-printed word "Baptistini."

No doubt about it: Somebody was on to him.

Who could it be: someone in his composition class, where students each Monday played their work in progress for criticism? A member of the faculty with an encyclopedic knowledge of obscure and dusty compositions and a taste for cat and mouse? A librarian with access to records of publications withdrawals? It could have been any of those. No more evident than his tormentor's identity was his motive. Did his nemesis plan to wait until the moment when, Pope's hand outstretched for his diploma, awarded with highest honors before thousands, he would denounce Pope as a fraud? Or perhaps he would wait until Pope had landed his professorship and force him to resign in disgrace when the truth was revealed.

After he had received the third letter, Pope briefly considered throwing in the towel, moving away from Berkeley, and starting all over in some distant country. After all, Handel had left his homeland for England in mid-career, and Scarlatti had abandoned Italy for Spain, and Delius England for an orange orchard in Florida, so why not Pope—for Paris, say? But the defeatist mood quickly passed. The well-muscled frame of the tall, broad-shouldered, wide-browed young man, brimming with self-confidence and optimism, had no room for self-doubt. Everything would work out fine, he decided. It had to: an inner voice had complacently assured him that one day he would put his mark on the world.

It was, therefore, a serene young man who sloshed through the rain toward the Omar Haffar Molecular Sciences Building, where he performed the light night labors that justified his full scholarship at the university.

Twice a week he swept the floor and dusted the furniture in the office and laboratory of Prof. Dr. Dr. Thaddeus Klemper, late of Göttingen, Distinguished Research Scholar at the Percival Coates Memorial Electromagnetic Research Facility. Pope's qualifications for the job were the ability to wield broom and dust cloth and a total ignorance of physics, for the good doctor was rabid about secrecy regarding his researches, which had something to do with terrestrial magnetism.

Pope snicked back the three Yale locks that secured the door to Prof. Dr. Dr. Klemper's domain, entered, made sure the door was locked behind him, and switched on the lights. He slung his dripping raincoat across a chair in the corner and surveyed the cavernous laboratory. It looked more like a mad scientist's attic storehouse than a research facility. It was crowded with equipment, much of it still in wooden crates, piles of electrical supplies covered with a tarpaulin, a dolly supporting what seemed to be an intricate television antenna, steel filing cabinets, a massive generator still strapped to its wooden pallet, and, along one wall, a long instrument panel with blinking lights. Spreading over all, like a web spun by some gigantic but demented spider, was festooned a maze of wires attached to glass insulators suspended from a framework of steel pylons. The wires led to banks of squat green boxes whose fronts were adorned with dials and meters whose purpose Pope—who could not tell a joule from a jewel, a coulomb from a column, a volt from a colt—did not even try to guess.

Pope opened the door to the broom closet and took out a feather duster, which he flicked abstractedly across whatever piece of equipment lay in his path as he leisurely walked the length of the lab. His mind was far away, on the Baptistini theme of the *Malibu* Symphony. Insensibly he began beating time with the duster to the music pulsating through his mind. Then, without warning, another melodic line intruded, blotting out the Baptistini. The notes racing through his mind were truly sublime, and he realized with a sudden flush that the music was entirely original, that *the inspiration was his own.* His beat became more agitated as he pursued the theme, deep in wonder, ready to follow wherever it would lead. Mesmerized by the unprecedented melodic invention coming from him—Justin Pope—he marveled at its transcendent beauty as it unrolled before his unseeing eyes like a brilliantly hued magic carpet of interwoven sound. When the theme abruptly ended and the music returned to the movement's familiar dissonance, Pope threw down the feather duster, pulled his notebook from his hip pocket, and began to transcribe the music he had just heard before it could escape his memory. He wrote standing up, his notebook resting on a filing cabinet, page after page, and when he had written down the melodic sequence, he went straight back to the beginning, orchestrating the entire sixty-four-bar passage just as he had heard it in his mind's ear.

The first sullen glow of another sodden day had filtered through the clerestory windows when Pope, exhausted, finally returned to the world. Rain still hammered down on the low building's roof. Wearily, he had switched off the lights and reached for his raincoat, when fatigue said the hell with it. He lay down where he stood, behind the filing cabinet, tucked the wadded raincoat beneath his head, and promptly drifted off to sleep in a velvet sea of unaccustomedly rich dark harmonies.

He was still afloat on waves of silent sound when Prof. Dr. Dr. Klemper stumped into the laboratory and double-locked the door behind him. He was a short, swarthy, powerful man in his late forties with the granitic weathered features of a seaman. He turned on the floodlights and from the locked drawer of his laboratory desk took out the neatly typed operating manual he had been writing and rewriting during the past eight months. He placed it on the lectern next to the computer before the instrument panel. From time to time double-checking with the manual, he began to punch in the commands that, he had calculated from ceaseless experimentation, would project him three thousand years into the past, plus or minus fifteen years. It was a vast improvement on his first efforts, which had been accurate only to within two centuries. The reentry program was more precise by many orders of magnitude: it would bring him back to the moment of departure, plus zero to seventeen hours.

Only slight adjustments to the program were necessary. When he had entered those on the computer, he switched on the big gasoline-driven generator on its concrete platform in the center of the lab. The generator ticked over with a steady pulsating hum. Klemper watched the dials on the instrument panel swing up to critical levels. Then he pulled the master control lever to the ''Engage'' position and straightened in his swivel chair. He took a cigar from the breast pocket of his suit coat, carefully cut it in two with scissors, and lit one of the halves. When it was going nicely, he tucked the other half in his opposite cheek and began chewing contemplatively. When the cud was well masticated, he took an engraved silver box from his waistcoat pocket and deftly put a dollop of snuff between lower lip and gum. Thus fortified, he punched the word ''Run'' on the computer keyboard, hit the return, and leaned back in his chair for the long quick trip back to prehistoric California.

The lights in the laboratory dimmed momentarily, then a purplish electric haze began to fill the room like smoke in a poolroom. Sunlight shone brightly through the skylight for a minute or so, faded into darkness, then again flashed into the laboratory. The oscillations between light and darkness sped up until it seemed that the laboratory was being illuminated by a scarcely flickering stroboscopic light. The walls dissolved, to be replaced by a canopy of trees that alternately shrank and swelled and from time to time briefly gave off the acrid fragrance of burning wood. The racks of instruments, the bookshelves, desks, filing cabinets, growling generator, and the naked bulbs dangling from their cords were bathed in an unearthly light that slowly turned from purplish to red, held steady for some minutes, then turned slowly back to purple. About the overhead wires a multihued aurora crackled like northern lights in miniature. The two men—one still asleep—were frozen in the positions they had found themselves in when Dr. Kemper had set the time-transference machine in motion. Their minds and bodies were in a state of suspended animation, unbreathing, not even conscious of the thread of life that was being stretched thin but had not yet snapped.

Suddenly there was a fearful jolt, and it was light. The laboratory—everything that stood beneath the framework of overhead wires—had been transported intact to the crest of the wooded hill on which, three thousand years hence, the Omar Haffar Molecular Sciences Building would rest. Around them the hill was carpeted with sweet-smelling wildflowers. A mule deer, frightened by the sudden apparition, fled for its life with a clatter of hooves. Dr. Klemper laughed in triumph, stood up, and drenched a wild daisy in a well-aimed jet of tobacco juice.

He went to a metal locker, unlocked it, and changed into a leather jacket with a fur collar. Zipping it up, he donned leather gloves and a flier's helmet with goggles. Around his hips he buckled a web belt with a brace of .45 automatic pistols and canteen. From the locker shelf he took a leather pouch, which he tied to his belt, and an aerial map. Spreading the map out on his desk, he verified the course that would take him to his destination, a little more than an hour's flight away.

Justin Pope, who had been awakened by the jolt of the laboratory coming to rest, watched in stunned disbelief as Prof. Dr. Dr. Thaddeus Klemper removed the padlock from the huge mover's crate that occupied the opposite corner of the lab and trundled out a one-man helicopter, its blades folded back. He quickly locked them into position, stepped into the tiny open cockpit and fastened his seat belt, and switched on the engine. While the main rotor windmilled, Klemper adjusted his helmet and goggles. He gunned the engine. The craft rose into the air, canted forward, and curved up and across the trees in a wide arc, heading east toward the valley where Sacramento would one day rise and nearby Sutter's Creek, where nuggets of gold lay strewn on the sands, ripe for the plucking.

The tiny helicopter shrank, became a dust mote dancing on the horizon, and finally disappeared. Justin Pope stood up and stretched his aching limbs. What had happened was obvious enough if totally incredible. He had heard about time travel but had never believed it was possible. Even now, with the evidence before his eyes, he was inclined to suspect that he was the target of some monstrous practical joke, the victim of a powerful hallucinogen injected into the air—that purplish vapor perfectly fit the bill—which gave him the the illusion of traveling forward—or was it *backward*?—through time.

Whichever it was, he was in another era, for sure. Of the campus and Berkeley there was no sign. Oakland and San Francisco, he knew without looking, would have vanished as well. The contours of the land around him seemed vaguely familiar, so if he had traveled in the three linear dimensions, it had not been very far. But without question he had been transported to another time. The future, or the past?

Probably the past. Had it been the future, Dr. Klemper would have armed himself with more sophisticated weapons than the Colt .45, which dated all the way back to the Philippine insurrection in the early 1900s. Moreover, if they were in the *distant* past, as seemed likely, the noise and killing power of the brace of pistols would suffice to put an army of Indians to flight.

Pope stepped out into the meadow that surrounded the laboratory, now standing roofless in the sunshine. It was absolutely quiet. Well, not quiet, really. On the contrary, the air was seasoned with the scents of summer, the humming of insects, the warble of birds, and the warm whisper of the wind, the lullaby of nature that all but blotted out the memory of the familiar noises of civilization—the rumble of rush-hour traffic, the howl of distant sirens, the amplified wail of rock music, the slamming of doors, the inane chatter of nasal human voices. He was in another, saner world. It suddenly came to him that the sounds around him blended to perfection with the tranquil harmonies of Telemann, Haydn, Mozart, and Schubert, redolent of a less complicated age. Pope's music, by contrast, filled with frenetic dissonance and discord, reflected his own confused culture and perilous, war-threatened times. Were he to dwell in a place like this, the music he wrote would be gentle and rhythmic, sweet and soothing.

He sighed.

On the crest of the hill he sat in the shade of a spreading black walnut that must have been five centuries old, inhaling the fragrance of the wildflowers around him and surveying the vast solitude that spread in all directions. Beyond the line of trees to the west lay the empty sea, while to the landward side rose a light blue haze from purple valleys. Looking closer, he perceived a dark gray smudge filtering through the blue.

Smoke! An Indian campfire, or perhaps the smoldering remains of a recent lightning strike. He longed to investigate, to be the first white man ever to set eyes on an American aborigine, but prudence held him back. He had no idea where Klemper had gone, or why, or when he would return. One thing was certain: he did not intend to be left behind when the good Prof. Dr. Dr. turned ahead the hands of time.

Justin Pope had scouted a fairly substantial area of the immediate vicinity of the time-transported laboratory when he heard the distant drone of the returning helicopter. In the time it took the sun to ascend to its zenith, he had found the remains of a number of campfires, some shards of broken pottery, and the bones of freshly slaughtered game. He had also sampled wild fruit and berries that only faintly resembled the modern varieties in size and taste, drunk from a spring of clear cold water he had discovered on the hillside, seen dozens of rabbits, squirrels, quail, and deer—none particularly alarmed by his presence—and briefly followed trails that crisscrossed the hillside, on which the prints of both animals and barefooted humans were visible. But of Indians he saw none.

Until now.

Squinting toward the sound of the approaching helicopter, he discerned movement on a neighboring hill. Looking closer, he saw a file of what seemed to be naked men heading in his direction at a dead run, in hot pursuit of the helicopter that had just passed over them at treetop level. Pope felt his throat tighten as he calculated the odds. The chopper was flying four or five times the speed of the running men, but by the time Klemper landed, disengaged himself from his harness, folded the main rotor, and pushed the machine back into the lab, they would be upon him.

Either Klemper did not perceive his peril, or with his arsenal of modern weaponry he was unafraid. He settled his craft softly on the hillside in a vortex of dust and dry leaves, switched off the engine, and unbuckled his harness. Without apparent haste he climbed out of the tiny open cockpit and walked across the meadow and into the lab. He crossed the littered floor to the computer keyboard and punched in the appropriate commands for positive time-transference. Then he turned to face the wave of Indians who had just appeared on the crest of the hill, a hundred yards away, and with chilling war whoops and spears upraised were running at full speed down upon him.

The first volley of spears impaled the sheet-metal fuselage of the helicopter. If it had been the bird they thought it was, it would have died instantly. At the same moment Dr. Klemper let fly with both barrels, half a dozen shots aimed at the mass of Indians who, with shouts of triumph, were doing a war dance around the strange but now very dead flying beast. Three of the Indians fell, and the noise and the sight of their bleeding comrades scattered the rest.

Klemper grunted. He waited until the survivors had all retreated beyond the crest of the hill, then turned to punch the "Run" button on the keyboard. At that instant one of the apparently dead Indians rose silently from where he lay, with blood spurting from a severed artery in his lower leg, took three faltering steps toward the unearthly dwelling place of the evil spirit that had suddenly appeared there, and launched his spear at the back of the part-man-part-bird that inhabited it.

Klemper fell forward, his chest striking the keyboard. As a purple haze began to fill the lab, Dr. Klemper's lifeless body slumped to the floor. Pope cowered behind his filing cabinet and tried desperately to think of a prayer. Time dissolved.

When Pope came to, wedged between two filing cabinets, a high wind was beating against the rain-swept windows. According to his watch, it was nine thirty-seven, and from the darkness outside, it had to be night. As he stretched his cramped limbs, the events of the past hours—or perhaps it had been several thousand years—slowly came back to him. He suddenly remembered Dr. Klemper, the spear haft striking him in the back before darkness suddenly enveloped him.

Pope threaded his way between the packing cases and racks of equipment to where Dr. Klemper had been standing when the spear had struck home. Of Dr. Klemper, nothing was to be seen.

But on the floor, just in front of the instrument panel, was the bone-white skeleton of what had been a man, lying amid a neat row of metal buttons and the two halves of a zipper, shoe nails arrayed in a neat geometrical pattern by each skeletal foot. The professor's brass belt buckle glistened in the overhead lights, as did the two .45 automatics on the floor beside the skeleton and half a dozen spent shell cases. Protruding from the spine was a flint spearhead and the time-bleached shaft of a wooden spear. To one side lay shreds of what had been a leather pouch. Among them was a pile of bright gold nuggets, enough to fill Justin Pope's rain hat to overflowing.

2. RIVERS
26 JUNE 1998

"YOUR NAME JUSTIN POPE?"

"That's right," Pope said, opening the door wide as the lanky, neatly dressed man with pale, tired eyes showed him his badge.

"I'm Detective First Class R. B. Rivers. I'd like to ask you a few questions."

"Sure," Pope said, stepping aside. "You'll have to forgive the mess, but I—"

"I'm not here to inspect your housekeeping, Mr. Pope," Rivers said, inspecting the large room strewn with music manuscripts, a tattered poster of a white beach and palm trees on the wall, books, free weights, dirty socks, empty beer cans, a baked potato on the bookshelf impaled by a fork, the remains of last night's dinner on a footstool, and other evidence of bachelor bliss. Along one wall stood an electronic piano/harpsichord/organ, half-buried under sheet music. On the stove in the efficiency's kitchen was a pan containing a fried egg of indeterminate antiquity, staring at him unblinkingly. Rivers withdrew his gaze. "I just want to ask you some questions about your work."

"By all means. Have a chair." Pope swept a pile of manuscripts off the room's only chair and invited the policeman to make himself comfortable. "I've heard some criminally unkind comments about my *Malibu* Symphony," he began, "but I didn't expect it was the sort of thing that would interest the police."

"It doesn't," Rivers assured him, dusting off the chair with his handkerchief before sitting down. "I'm interested in your other work, in Professor Klemper's laboratory."

"Oh."

"I understand you are the—ah—custodian of the lab."

"No need to be delicate about it, Inspector. Poverty is a hallowed tradition among composers. Yes, I am its janitor. There I janit twice a week, sometimes thrice. What's missing that you think I might have stolen?"

"Prof. Klemper is missing, and although I doubt you stole him, you might be able to shed some light on his disappearance."

"I can try. How long has he been missing?"

"Five days."

"Maybe he took a trip."

"In which case he would have taken his car, which we found parked in front of the Omar Haffar Molecular Sciences Building. Or a taxi. But none of the local companies' log sheets list any pickup which might have been Dr. Klemper. He might have taken off on foot, of course, but we regard that as unlikely. Nobody has seen him in nearly a week. He's missed several important appointments, and the university has asked us to look into it."

"How about his wife?"

"He has none. Lives alone. We've asked his neighbors, his colleagues, his students. We've drawn a blank. You're about the last fish in the barrel."

Pope scratched his head. "Well, Inspector, I wish I could rise to your bait, but frankly, I've rarely set eyes on the man myself. I'd recognize him if I saw him, of course, but he insisted I do my cleaning late at night so I wouldn't interfere with his researches."

"Which are?"

"Don't ask me. Wires and dynamos and short circuits—things like that."

"So, when was the last time you saw Dr. Klemper?"

Pope frowned. "Two—three weeks ago. Saw him crossing the campus, papers stuffed under his arm."

Detective Rivers rose and snapped his notebook shut.

"Would you mind opening up his laboratory for me to take a look around? It seems you and the professor himself are the only ones with the keys."

"Sure."

The lab presented a very different aspect from what it had been that stormy night a week before. The crazy spider's network of wires crisscrossing the lab floor had been taken down, chopped into short lengths, and dumped into a waste bin. The pylons on which they had been suspended were no longer upright but were leaning against one wall. The green boxes had been disconnected from the instrument panel and packed into the huge crate from which Dr. Klemper had removed his one-man helicopter. And there was not a notebook or scrap of paper anywhere. It was just as Pope had left it.

"Notice anything different?"

Pope rubbed his jaw and pretended to examine the premises. "No, I don't think so."

"Is this the way it was the last time you were in here—which, by the way, was when?"

"Night before last. Yes, it was," Pope replied truthfully.

"Doesn't look like much was happening," Rivers said casually.

"No, I guess not. But that's the way it was with Dr. Klemper. He'd set up his equipment and play around with it for a couple of weeks, and then one day I'd come in to find it completely dismantled or rearranged for another experiment. But as I said, I'm a musician, and I don't understand these things."

"Where do you suppose he kept his notes?"

"In his desk and those lockers, I suppose."

Rivers took out his leather lock-pick kit and went to work like a movie detective. After five minutes he said to hell with it and pried open the locks with a crowbar he found on one of the packing crates. All were empty.

"Nothing missing, you say?" he asked Pope.

Pope shrugged and showed him empty palms.

"Tell me something, Mr. Pope—did Prof. Klemper ever mention the name Skardon to you? John K. Skardon?"

Pope shook his head. "No, why?"

"It was just a thought."

As far as Rivers was concerned, that wrapped up the case. He had touched all the bases and come up with a handful of nothing. Maybe the professor had developed amnesia, or run off with a pretty graduate student, or jumped off the Bay Bridge, or all three. Sooner or later a sighting, a withdrawal from his bank account from some distant city, or a tip-off from somebody with a grudge who did not want him to stay disappeared would bring the case back to life. But as of now, it was dead.

Pope hoped it would stay dead. He had done everything he could to make it so.

The three nights after his journey back through time he had spent dismantling the laboratory so thoroughly that nobody could possibly have reconstructed what had been going on there. He had bought a Polaroid camera and photographed the equipment from every conceivable angle. He had measured the length of each wire he disconnected. He had plotted the arrangement of the wires between the pylons and made diagrams of their connections to the instrument panel. He had copied the specifications and model numbers of every bit of equipment and its physical relation to all the other pieces of equipment. The notebooks, equipment manuals, and reference books he had packed in two big wooden boxes, along with the laboratory's floor plans and his other diagrams and photos, and nailed them shut. He had put them in a ministorage on a two-year lease under a fictitious name. To the best of his knowledge, no one had seen him come and go while he was carrying his loot to his old jalopy in the hours just before sunrise. Now that the police had investigated Prof. Klemper's disappearance and found nothing, no suspicion could possibly fall on him.

* * *

"I think we've got your man, Rivers," said Captain Gordon Catlin, chief of detectives, some two weeks later.

"Which man's that, Chief?" Rivers had been on missing-persons detail for three months, and the list of the missing he had not been able to trace was as long as the odds against the losers he habitually picked at Santa Anita.

"Professor Klemper."

"Do tell. Where is he?"

"Right here," Catlin said, reaching down and pulling a large cardboard box from beneath his desk. He put it on the squad-room table and opened it. Inside was what seemed to be a disjointed human skeleton. Catlin guffawed.

"Yeah," Rivers replied. "On the other hand, it might be Judge Crater, or maybe my great-aunt Lizzie. Where'd you get it?"

"Student at UC found it. He'd been shagging his girlfriend in the bushes up in the hills behind the amphitheater and, when she complained of a pain in the neck, found it wasn't him she was bellyaching about, but what turned out to be this skeleton's heel prodding her between the third and fourth cervical vertebrae. He dug up enough to realize it was a human foot and called us."

"So it isn't Klemper, after all?"

"Actually, at first I thought it might be, having been found on the campus and all that. But then I got to figuring. The bones are picked clean, which would take months if not years under normal conditions of burial. The lab says no corrosive chemicals were used, and no bone-scarring occurred from sharp instruments to cut away the flesh, so that argues natural processes. Also, look at this." He picked up one of the vertebrae.

Rivers looked closer. "I'll be goddamned! An Indian arrowhead."

"Too big for an arrowhead," Catlin dissented. "More like a spearhead, but it's flint, all right. I want you to run these bones over to the physical anthropology department at UC and see what they can make of them. They seem perfectly preserved and complete, real museum quality. We just may have discovered the first Spanish conquistador ever knocked off by local redskins.''

At the following week's staff meeting, Lieutenant Rivers reported his results. ''The anthropologists are about evenly divided,'' he said, ''on whether to line us up against the wall or ask the Pope to canonize us. It seems, gentlemen, that we have discovered a specimen of early man—they carbon-14 dated it, and the score comes to around 1000 B.C..''

''So?''

''Well, they're peeing in their pants with delight for having come across a specimen totally intact, except for three molars and a bicuspid, which are missing. But what *really* gets their gun off is their finding that the physical type is anomalous with that of local Indians of that era. In fact, especially considering the brachycephalic morphology of the skull—it has a cephalic index of 83, to be precise—*it very closely resembles that of a contemporary northern European.* Compounding the mystery is their discovery that the gentleman in question—it *is* a man's skeleton, a man in his late forties—had a compound fracture of the right tibia earlier in life. Now, such a fracture is almost invariably fatal from the resulting gangrene if not treated with antibiotics. Yet it not only healed but healed as well as if it had been set by a modern orthopedic surgeon. That indicates a degree of surgical sophistication that no one thought existed until this century. That discovery alone will cause an upheaval in the history of medicine. And truly revolutionary is the implication that a northern European, a member of a race with advanced knowledge of medicine, somehow got to California 2,500 years before Columbus discovered America. If that theory proves out, all the world's history books will have to be rewritten.''

"That takes care of our sainthood," Captain Catlin said dryly. "Why do they want to whistle up the firing squad?"

"Because we disturbed the remains. Though there is no doubt whatever that their dating is correct, they would like to have the confirmatory evidence by stratigraphy—digging down through layers of sediment they can date. They threaten to protest our methods to the police commissioner."

"Screw 'em," Catlin grunted. "Let 'em protest. They can't have everything. We gave them the skeleton. If there's any squawks, we'll say the rains were so heavy that all the overburden simply washed away, leaving the bones exposed. It may be the truth, for all I know. Anyway, in case anybody asks you, that's what you tell them."

When his name was announced as having been awarded the doctor of music degree with highest honors, there was a tremor in Pope's stride as he mounted the stage to receive his handshake and diploma. Any moment, he felt sure, a voice from the crowd would cry out, accusing him of theft and fraud. He would of course ignore the interruption as best he could but not linger to engage in any debates. As a matter of fact, now that he had Klemper's time-transporter designs, his hard-won degree was superfluous, but dropping out of the university on the verge of receiving it would arouse unnecessary suspicion. He had decided not to chance it.

But no ringing denunciation came from the crowd. On the contrary, he received a round of warm applause as he accepted the skeepskin with his name on it in gold letters and a standing ovation when the university symphony orchestra concluded the graduation ceremony by playing the scherzo from his *Malibu* Symphony.

The next week he spent unwinding from the strain of the months that had passed since Professor Klemper's disappearance and making plans for the future. The search for Klemper had come to a dead end, to no one's great sorrow. Pope had not seen or heard from Detective R. B. Rivers again, nor had anyone put him under surveillance, he was sure. It would now be safe to reconstruct the time-transporter and put it to some useful purpose. From Professor Klemper's notebooks and manufacturers' catalogs he had already ascertained that he could cover the costs of the equipment involved by melting down and selling the 251 ounces of gold nuggets the professor had picked up the day he was killed. But first he had to understand just how the damned thing worked.

Unfortunately, Klemper's notebooks and manuals turned out to be of no use at all. They were written in scientists' language, full of mathematical symbols, esoteric abbreviations, and long stretches of German, and most of it was illegible. None of it made any sense to Justin Pope. He would have to go back to school and study mathematics and the physical sciences before he could put the machine together and make it function. And his sinking heart told him that while deep within Justin Pope ran a current of musical talent—perhaps broad, perhaps narrow—the well of scientific knowledge was hopelessly dry.

In short, he had to share his discovery with someone who could make it work. But if he did, what assurance would he have that his collaborator would not cut him out? The man he needed would have to be extremely knowledgeable in the physical sciences, particularly the field of electromagnetism, totally discreet, and someone whom he could control. Mulling it over, he could not think of anyone he could trust who fit a single one of those imperatives.

Then a name Detective R. B. Rivers had mentioned floated to the surface of his memory: Skardon—John K. Skardon.

3. SKARDON
15 SEPTEMBER 1998

SKARDON LAUGHED.

If that's how he looks when amused, Justin Pope thought, I'd better not make him mad. Skardon's laugh issued from a mouth whose downturned corners registered perpetual contempt and loathing. His eyes, dark and sullen and shrouded by thick black eyebrows, smoldered with a generalized hatred of all that came within his line of vision. His tall, lean frame, with muscles that bulged beneath his blue denim shirt with the number stitched across the pocket, testified that he could, when he wished, translate his animus into action.

"The warden tells me you're a composer," Skardon said, pronouncing the word as if it were a sentence of death.

Pope admitted the accusation.

"And that you're a recent graduate of the University of California."

"I have a doctorate in music."

"And that you have read up on my case and decided I was the tragic figure on whose life you thought you could base a libretto for your first opera."

"Well, that's what I told the warden, anyway. Had to tell him *something*."

"You certainly didn't tell him the truth," Skardon growled, "or you'd be in here with me. How did you manage to kill the son of a bitch?"

"What son of a bitch?" Pope said. No doubt about it: Skardon had brains. He had definitely come to the right man.

"Don't play games with me, sonny. I'm talking about *Herr Professor Doktor Doktor* Thaddeus Klemper."

Pope was going to have to watch his step. Skardon did not have the temperament to play second fiddle. One false move on Pope's part and Skardon would end up with all the marbles. But if he wanted Skardon's cooperation, he had to be completely candid. And why not? In here Skardon could not hurt him. On the outside it would, of course, be a different story. "Actually," he said, "I didn't kill him. Some Indian did." And he proceeded to tell Skardon the story of that remarkable rainy night back in June when Klemper, unaware of Pope's presence in the laboratory, had transported them both back a thousand years before the birth of Christ. Pope had no fear Skardon would turn him in, for not only would the authorities laugh at such a ridiculous story, Skardon had a lot more to lose than he did. And he was certainly bright enough to realize that Pope was his ticket out of the maximum-security facility at Las Chipas, just as Klemper had been his ticket in.

According to the newspaper accounts Pope had read of the murder, Skardon, then a brilliant physics researcher in his late thirties, had been having an affair with an equally brilliant lissome professor engaged in the same line of research. The project, whose details had never been revealed, was under the supervision of Prof. Klemper. As the lady was married, Skardon and his inamorata indulged their sexual fancies after hours in the laboratory, more convenient and more discreet than a motel and immune from interruption since, as it was a top-secret project for the Department of Defense, they could lock the door. They customarily performed their erotic experiments on a stout wooden workbench, making up in safety in a lab filled with high-voltage equipment what it lacked in creature comforts. Even so, Professor Fonteneau, Skardon's lady friend, had managed during an intermission between intromissions to touch a live condenser coil with an outflung hand while her feet were propped up against a metal filing cabinet, which unfortunately happened to complete the electrical circuit. She died in a shower of sparks and a blaze of glory, her final primal scream of agony bringing half the student body in the Omar Haffar Molecular Sciences Building bursting in to find a stunned Dr. John Skardon, caught literally with his pants down. His defense had been that it was all a macabre accident, but the circumstances and the later discovery of an unobtrusive switch under the workbench convinced the jury that they were dealing with the premeditated murder of a woman of whom Skardon had tired. The jury, regretting that California did not have an electric chair to make his punishment fit the crime, had sentenced him to death in the gas chamber, but his sentence had been commuted by California's lady chief justice to life imprisonment.

"An Indian spear," Number 11281 mused with a sardonic laugh. "Well, it's about time somebody gave him the shaft. Poetic justice. You see, Klemper thought Fortuna and I were briefing him on all the formulas governing time-transference we had spent four years together researching, but, hell—we were feeding him a lot of bum dope along with elements he could verify on his own. Why should we share our work with *him*? So when he thought he had gathered all the threads in his hand, he rigged up his homemade electrocution device, knowing from a hidden television monitor, probably, just where we were conducting our hanky-panky. Then, when I got up to get us a cigarette, the miserable bastard, sitting in his office next door watching the action on his screen, threw the switch. After they took me away, he did a little quick rewiring, planting the switch underneath the workbench for the police to find and removing the television camera. Pretty simple, really. One flick of the switch, and he kills one threat to his monopoly on time-transference and sends the other up for life."

"Very clever, if true. How do you know it is?"

Skardon shrugged. "I can't be sure of the details, of course, but it had to be something like that. I didn't love Fortuna enough to marry her, maybe, but I had much too high a regard for her, personally and professionally, to kill her. She was as indispensable to my work as she was to my private life. Besides, if I'd wanted to get rid of her, I'd have simply dumped her off in 1880, say. Anyhow, that clod Klemper proceeds to try to put together the time-vehicle, only to learn, to his doubtless considerable chagrin, that he'd been had. He knew me—knew I wouldn't talk about the machine, that I'd bide my time and try to escape, which I did twice without success. Before I could, he figured, he'd be lost in the mists of some past or future time. Might have done it, too, if his brain hadn't been loaded down with so much academic baggage that it took him the six years I've been in here to get the time-transference vehicle running. Which brings us to the purpose of your visit, Dr. Pope."

"Make a guess."

"I don't have to guess: I *know.* You managed to steal the vehicle's plans and notes from Klemper, but you don't know what to do with them, not knowing a damned thing about physics. You've come to me in hopes I'll help you—as indeed I shall."

"For your freedom."

"And—" Skardon began, a crazy gleam coming into his eyes. Then it faded, and he forced a smile. "Yes, that's it—for my freedom."

"What do we do first? I've got all the notes intact. I suppose I could bring them in on visits, a few at a time."

Skardon laughed. "Don't be an imbecile, my boy. I have the plans and specifications right here," he said, tapping his temple. "The way you describe it, Klemper's device occupied the entire floor space of the laboratory. Typical Teutonic overkill. The whole thing can be installed in an ordinary pickup or van."

"How long will it take?"

"Three or four months, depending on how long it will take to get the components and instruments from the manufacturers and how well you can follow my instructions. You say Klemper brought out some gold. How much?"

"A little over 251 ounces. On today's market, at $840 an ounce, it would fetch something like $211,000."

Skardon shook his head. "The man had no imagination."

"What do you mean?"

"He wanted money, and that translated into gold in Klemper's commonplace mind. No wonder it took him so long to work out the details."

"Really?" Pope said. "What would *you* have done?"

"Any number of things. If I'd wanted gold, for instance, I could have taken a sniper rifle and half a dozen rounds of ammunition and knocked off Hannibal for Quintus Fabius Maximus when Hannibal was marching on a cowering Rome. The Carthaginian invasion would have immediately petered out without its leader, and the grateful Romans would have made me a demigod, given me the choice of the vestal virgins, and as much gold as I could haul away.

"That would be more dignified, and a lot more interesting, you'll admit," Skardon said, "than scratching around for nuggets in Sutter's Creek. Well, Klemper's $211,000 should cover our costs, providing you can locate a compact generator that can handle the load. The first thing you do is to buy a covered van with at least nineteen cubic feet of cargo space and install heavy-duty shocks. When you've got it, come back and I'll give you a list of manufacturers to contact for their latest catalogs. They've miniaturized a lot of the gear during the past six years, so except for the generator, there shouldn't be any heavy lifting. Once you've got all the components together, all you'll need is a garage to work in undisturbed and know how to use a few basic tools and a soldering iron for the assembly.''

''You make it sound pretty elementary.''

''All the greatest ideas are, my dear Watson.''

Justin Pope nodded gravely. ''I'll remember that.''

4. BREAKOUT
22 JUNE 1999

IT TOOK LONGER THAN EITHER SKARDON OR JUSTIN POPE expected.

Pope proved so inept at things mechanical that he had to take a crash course in shopwork at a local vocational school, followed by private tutoring by a retired watchmaker, merely to follow the instructions that John Skardon so meticulously provided. Then, once Pope began to assemble the components, Skardon realized that Pope's level of mechanical aptitude was so low that it would have been insane to take his word that the work had been done right. So Skardon had to devise a testing procedure to ensure each subassembly's integrity and conformity to specifications before allowing Pope to proceed to the next item on the list. It was frustrating work for them both.

Furthermore, the warden's suspicions were aroused when Pope's visits became ever more frequent—as often as twice a week—and ever more lengthy as Skardon indoctrinated him in the basics of electricity and magnetism. To allay them, Skardon wrote what, by the time it was finished the following summer, amounted to a substantial autobiography. It was kept in the desk drawer of his cell, easily accessible to the warden's stoolies. Its detail and frankness about what had been a very colorful life were meant to convince the warden that John K. Skardon was indeed the ideal subject of a tragic opera. Meanwhile, the plans and specs for the time-transference device, which Skardon had dubbed the *Fugit*—short for *Tempus Fugit*—were written on tissue paper and concealed in the tongue of his shoe for delivery to Pope at his regular visits. What with those two jobs, plus eight hours a day sewing mailbags, John K. Skardon had never worked so hard in his life.

Justin Pope worked at three jobs, too, but never mentioned two of them to Skardon. Besides spending his mornings and early afternoons in the garage puzzling out and executing Skardon's instructions for assembling the *Fugit*, he went every afternoon to classes in spoken German at the university, while the evenings he spent as a nurse's aide at a downtown hospital. On weekends he read history books and studied maps of nineteenth-century Vienna. At the university's medical library he boned up on the latest advances in pharmacology, with particular attention to the treatment of typhoid fever and syphilis. When spring finally rolled around, he sent an order to a survivalist supply house and eventually received a shipment containing several devices for crowd control.

To the letters from university departments of music that came to him offering interviews for junior teaching positions in the autumn following his graduation, he replied that, though flattered, before he made a decision he wished to spend the year exploring new approaches to composition. He told the exact truth.

At the end of May 1999, Justin Pope paid one final visit to Dr. John K. Skardon, who was beginning to have doubts about Pope's intentions. If he had been in Pope's place, he would have tested the *Fugit*, made sure everything was in working order, then left the machine's inventor safely in jail. After all, what further need would Pope have for him? Moreover, if Pope had had all his marbles, he would have observed from Skardon's autobiography—which he now with regret realized was unnecessarily candid—that Skardon was not the man to share his brainchild with anyone, even the man who had commuted his life sentence to life. Skardon, in fact, had not yet made up his mind about what to do with Pope once he was liberated. The young man *had* been the instrument by which Skardon would regain his freedom, and he would owe him much. On the other hand, the secret of time-transference was unique and simply too valuable to be shared. Skardon had no ambition to rule the world—although that possibility was now within reach—and he certainly harbored no malice toward the useful young musician. Quite the contrary: Pope was a most amiable, attractive young man. But the demands of life and self-preservation had priority: he would have to remove Justin Pope from the scene.

Those unpleasant but inevitable thoughts were passing through Skardon's mind as Justin Pope sat on the bench opposite him in the prison's outdoor recreation area, waiting for that week's quiz on the *Fugit*.

"I know you've had two complete run-throughs," Skardon said, "and you must be getting sick of all my precautions, but we have to get this right the first time. We mustn't have a situation where you appear on the grounds in the *Fugit* and then, for some reason, we are unable to get out again. All that would accomplish would be to put you behind bars with me."

Pope nodded. "You want me to do another set of component checks."

"Yes."

"I'm willing, but I really don't think they're necessary."

"You're not a very good judge of such things."

"That's true. But photographs, they say, don't lie."

"And what's that supposed to mean?"

Pope unbuttoned his shirt, lifted the shirttail, and removed an envelope stuck with adhesive tape to the small of his back. He opened the envelope, took out a Polaroid print, and slid it across the table to Skardon.

Skardon picked it up and examined it without comprehension. "All this proves is that you're as lousy a photographer as you are an electronics technician."

"Don't you recognize the Golden Gate?" Pope asked.

"That isn't the Golden Gate: there's no bridge."

"Exactly." He handed Skardon a second print. It was smudged and indistinct, but plainly a waterfront with many of the buildings afire. He smiled.

"I don't believe this," a dumbfounded Skardon said. "You wouldn't dare try such a stunt on your own. You faked this."

For an answer, Pope slid a third photograph across the table. It was a picture of a barefoot five-year-old boy, smoke-smudged, hawking newspapers. Behind him was an out-of-focus horse-drawn tram and the blur of women in long dresses and men in derbies and shirtsleeves, moving in haste. The 72-point headline of the newspaper in the boy's hand read "SAN FRANCISCO DESTROYED BY EARTHQUAKE!"

"At 0400 yesterday morning," Pope said, "I drove into the hills and set the dial for 19 April 1906. When the purple haze cleared, I locked the *Fugit* up and went into town on foot. I even helped out the firemen for an hour or two dynamiting buildings. And when I got back to the *Fugit*, I merely hit the "Return to Baseline Time" button, and suddenly it was 0401 of 21 June 1999." Pope allowed the implication to sink in: the *Fugit* was working precisely according to specifications. More important, Dr. Justin Pope was there only because he wanted to be.

"I see." Skardon studied his work-roughened hands. He looked up and smiled his tiger-shark smile. Control had shifted to Justin Pope. "Any suggestions?" he said quietly.

"I'm ready to move when you are."

"How about tomorrow?"

"Tomorrow it is. What's the plan?"

"You see those oak trees beyond the fence bordering the baseball field?"

"I see them."

"They are just about two hundred feet apart. If you joined them with a line, bisected the line, and then projected a perpendicular 420 feet in this direction, that is, northwest, you'd arrive right about on second base. As a trusty, I have ground privileges until nine o'clock in the evening. Be at second base at exactly eight-fifty. According to the forecast, it's going to rain from late afternoon on, and the visibility will, as usual when it rains here, be poor. Nobody will see you, and they certainly aren't going to see me. Got that?"

"I think so."

"Better repeat it."

Pope repeated it, then added, "What time should I set the time-transfer dial? And forward or back?"

"I've done a bit of research on that," Skardon replied. "We don't dare set it forward. We don't know what conditions here will be in the future. For one thing, they might cut the trees down, and your reference points would be gone. So here's what you've got to do: drive up the dirt perimeter road tomorrow night at, say, about 8:30 P.M. Figure out your coordinates, line everything up, then set your time-transfer dial to around the year 1875, when this area was still forested. When you're back in 1875, drive the 420 feet to where second base is now. But be careful and don't lose your bearings, because the whole place is likely to be filled with trees. At exactly twenty minutes after the time you've made the time-transfer, you'll set your dial to 2050, 23 June 1999, and execute. I'll climb behind the wheel, and off we go. Nobody will ever know what happened."

Nobody ever did.

Pope followed Dr. Skardon's directions to the letter and arrived at the rendezvous on a dark, stormy night. The door to the passenger seat was locked. In a flash of lightning, Skardon saw Pope gesture toward the rear of the van. It was no time to argue. Skardon sloshed to the back of the van, climbed in, and slammed the door behind him. On hands and knees he scrambled forward. His way to the driver's compartment, he observed with consternation, was blocked by a clear plastic shield. The broad smile that had animated his face as he realized he was on his way to freedom at last faded as his fingers searched in vain for a latch to open the transparent partition. "Open up!" he ordered.

Pope, busy with setting the time-transference dial, did not reply.

"Open up, goddammit!"

Pope paid no attention.

Skardon pulled from his waistband a hammer he had brought along for another more deadly purpose and dealt a mighty blow to the plastic barrier. The blow did not even scratch it. Skardon pounded it again and again and was raising the hammer to strike once more when time froze him in place. When he awakened, it was 1875.

Paying as little attention as he could to the thudding on the shatterproof plastic panel between him and Skardon, Pope put the van in gear, followed his tracks back through the forest, and pulled up to a stop between the two towering oaks. He consulted a notebook, then drove several miles through the woods, guided by a compass and a tachometer, to a wooded knoll, and stopped. He switched off the engine and reset the dials. He punched the "Run" button. Once again their minds and bodies subsided into suspended animation. When consciousness returned, it was late afternoon of a sunny, cloudless day. He turned to Skardon, who regarded him venomously. "I'm afraid this is where you get off, Dr. Skardon," he said through a speaker in the ceiling of the rear compartment.

"You don't think I'm going to let you get away with this, you double-crossing bastard?" Skardon shouted back.

"Don't waste your time, Professor. Where you're going—well, your chances of catching up to me are just about nil."

"That's your idea of gratitude, is it?"

"Actually, it isn't," said Pope, "but I studied your autobiography, you see, and learned just how ruthless you really are. You claimed that Klemper stole your idea for the *Fugit*—as I have no doubt he did. But you've committed a few deeds of violence and very questionable morality yourself in your forty-four years, as you related *con brio* in your life story. I decided it wouldn't be very bright of me to bank on your brotherly love. Your bringing that hammer along seems to vindicate my judgment."

"It's true," Skardon said unapologetically. "I *was* going to bash your brains in. Why not? What have you done to earn the right to profit from my invention?"

"I got you out of prison, for one thing."

Skardon waved that aside. "I'd have found a way, eventually. I was working on it."

"And now," Justin Pope said, "you've got something else to work on." He pointed to the town shimmering in the afternoon sun a few miles away. "You can begin at Las Chipas down there."

Skardon followed his gaze. He could not tell what year it was, but at least it was the twentieth century, for he could discern in the distance the pylons of a high-tension line. He laughed nastily. "And what if I decline your gracious invitation to leave the *Fugit*? With that shield between us, you can't force me out. Wherever you go, *I* go. And when we get there, we shall see what we shall see."

Pope shook his head sadly and touched a button on the dashboard.

Skardon heard a faint hiss from above his head, as of a coiled rattler about to strike. Instinctively he shrank back, then got a whiff of the spurt of gas Pope had injected into the compartment. He knew it well, having inhaled it during the prison riots that periodically erupted over conditions at Las Chipas prison. Two gulps of air impregnated with that gas would have him vomiting for the next twenty-four hours.

"Okay, okay," Skardon said, feeling his dinner already rising to the occasion.

"If you'll open that steel locker behind the seat," Pope

went on, removing his finger from the button, "you'll find a change of clothing which will be less conspicuous than the soggy pinstripes you have on. You'll also see a metal toolbox. Take that, too, and be careful you don't mislay it."

"What's in it?"

"For one thing, $100 in silver dollars of the late 1890s. That'll do for walking-around money. There's also $10,000 in 1903 golden eagles. I went to a great deal of trouble to get them."

"Ten thousand dollars isn't going to go very far," Skardon observed sourly.

"Farther than you think. A lot more important are the other contents of the box. Have a look." He switched on the overhead light.

Skardon opened the box and inspected its contents. "And what year, pray tell, is this?" Skardon asked, his hopes rebounding.

"Today is 25 September 1928."

"You know something?" Skardon said, for the first time with eyes that matched the smile of his lips, "you're not quite such a miserable son of a bitch, after all. I'll remember that when I catch up with you. I promise your suffering will be short." He collected his clothing, checked the contents of the metal box, and stepped out of the *Fugit*. A soft mild breeze off the distant desert caressed his cheek. He changed his clothes and turned for one last look at *Tempus Fugit*.

But time had already flown.

In the months past, a myriad of exciting prospects had opened up before Justin Pope, so many that he had had to talk sternly to himself to avoid spreading his gift of time too thin.

He could have transported himself to the banks of the Rhine and learned the art of warfare from Julius Caesar in his masterful campaigns against the Germanic tribes—if he had known Latin. He could have attended the Academy in Athens, listened to the orations of Socrates, Plato, and Demosthenes, attended the dramatic productions of Euripides, Sophocles, Aristophanes, and Aeschylus—had he known Greek. With a Xerox machine he could have saved the priceless works destroyed in the burning of the library at Alexandria. With a tape recorder he could have traced the origins of the Basque language or the sound systems of the Sumerian and Cretan tongues. With an M-22 Mark II service rifle and several thousand rounds of ammunition he could have single-handedly repelled Genghis Khan's invasion of Europe, or turned back the hordes of Hulagu Khan descending upon Baghdad, or the Ottomans at the gates of Vienna, or battled the Persians with the heroic three hundred at Thermopylae. He could have listened to the teachings of Jesus, studied the path to enlightenment at the feet of Gautama Siddhartha, or accompanied Muhammad on his *hegira* from Mecca. He could have been the intimate of Leonardo da Vinci and Michelangelo, the lover of Cleopatra or Poppea, Catherine the Great, or the Empress Josephine.

Each of these prospects, and dozens more, had its own special allure, but Justin Pope was not really that interested in lusty adventure, or scholarly research, or money, or the embraces of noted courtesans. Ever since he had first been plunked down on a piano stool and heard the strange and wonderful sounds that striking those black and white keys would produce, he had decided that one day he would be acclaimed the composer of the most magnificent music ever written. So far, his successes at the university had produced but the smallest of ripples. Justin Pope now yearned to make waves. The means was finally at hand—not on the eighty-eight keys of the piano, but on the flashing dials of *Tempus Fugit*.

5. FRANZ
10 OCTOBER 1828

FRANZ PETER SCHUBERT LAY ON HIS DEATHBED.

To this once effervescent, sweet-tempered, and immensely talented man of thirty-one, now racked by syphilis and typhoid fever, his friends were paying their last respects. He could die at any moment, the doctor said. And so they gathered in the small salon of the humble home where he lay, recalling his many kindnesses to fellow musicians, his jokes, his gallantries with the young ladies, and the abject poverty that this unrecognized genius had for his few years on earth borne without complaint.

Schubert was dying, but Vienna was dead—at least during these predawn hours of darkness. The streets were empty, and the flickering gas lamps that cast their dim light here and there did little to relieve the overpowering depth of night and gloom that had settled over the capital city of the Austro-Hungarian Empire. The quiet conversation of his half dozen friends had long since faded away, and they were slumped uncomfortably on the salon's two straight-backed chairs and single long bench against the rough-plastered wall, waiting for their friend's expiring breath. A sputtering candle on the trestle table provided the room's only illumination.

The front door eased open a few inches, and a black-clad arm placed a metal canister beside the door jamb, then withdrew. A thin pink gas began to issue from the canister. A moment later, the people in the room were jolted awake as their lungs began to cry out for air. They clutched at their throats and tried to rise, but their muscles failed to respond, and they were frozen in their seats.

The front door was flung open wide, and there, silhouetted against the glowering murk of the sleeping city, was a form that inhabited nightmares—a tall figure clad in a long black cloak, with two enormous shiny, glassy eyes, a black face without nose and lips, and, protruding from the forehead, two black horns. Satan himself. He stood for a moment, framed in the doorway, then strode past the terrified mourners into the bedroom. Screams of horror that rose in their throats were stifled by the pink mist that spread upward from the floor in the devil's wake, and they could only watch in mortal dread as the figure returned, carrying Schubert's wasted body in his arms, looking neither to right nor left as he swept through the open door, bearing the composer off to the fires of hell.

By and by the room cleared of the devil's vapor, and they could breathe again. The horror of the apparition they had just witnessed left them silent as they struggled to comprehend what had just occurred. Everyone knew, of course, that dead souls were carried down to purgatory, but very few had observed Old Nick in the act. People who claimed to have done so were often accused of consorting with the devil and paid for it with their lives at the stake. Such punishments did not occur in these modern times, of course, but it was still dangerous even to speak of the devil, much less see him. What course to follow now merited the most serious discussion.

It was nearly midday, and much beer had been consumed, many signs of the cross made, and God's blessings invoked by the time the mourners decided on that most popular of possible courses of action: silence. They would do nothing. They would not inform the civil authorities. They would not notify the parish priest. They would, to be sure, pray for the immortal soul of Franz Peter Schubert, pray for its early release from purgatory, and pray that it would ascend to heaven, where it could make celestial music to rival that which Schubert had composed on Earth. Should anybody ask, they would say that the unfortunate man had died at dusk the night before and that the putrefying body had been hastily buried to avoid contaminating the survivors.

Nobody asked.

For Justin Pope, it had taken considerable organization. He had studied the street maps of Vienna of the early nineteenth century and pinpointed Schubert's last residence, a hovel in the city's poorest section. The geography of today's Vienna, on the other hand, was of no immediate consequence, although he provided himself with the latest *Guide Bleu* to help him get to his ultimate destination. He stocked up on antibiotics, syringes, intravenous kits, and other necessary medical paraphernalia. He removed the shatterproof glass partition between the driver's and rear compartments of the *Fugit* and installed a mattress and bedding. He laid in a six-month supply of dehydrated, condensed, and canned foods, along with vitamin and mineral supplements.

At a local music shop he bought the latest electronic keyboard, which could produce, at the flick of a switch, the tones of the piano, harpsichord, or organ. A further refinement allowed the musician to build up, layer by layer, the voices of every instrument of the orchestra so that, properly programmed, the keyboard and its electronic memory could reproduce a fully scored symphonic work.

His last purchase, from a costume shop, was the black cloak, horns, and tail of the devil. He supplemented the costume with a standard war-surplus gas mask to neutralize the fumes of the CX Mark-II crowd-control canister with which he would immobilize the mourners-to-be.

The van, now equipped with heavy-duty shocks and loaded to the gunwales with equipment, he shipped on the same aircraft that took him to Vienna. He glibly explained away the esoteric equipment installed in the van by treating the customs inspectors to a story about a geological survey, focusing on the magnetic properties of the Tyrolean mountains. In the city, he rented garage space for a fortnight in a former stables that had been constructed, he was careful to confirm, as far back as 1777.

Justin Pope then wound the *Fugit*'s clock back to 8 October 1828, concealed his van beneath half a ton of straw, and set out to explore the town. His strange clothing and, to the Viennese of the early nineteenth century, great stature—although he was only six feet two inches tall—aroused considerable comment. But he good-naturedly explained to polite inquiries that this was the way people dressed on America's frontier, and his execrable German convinced them that indeed he must come from some such wild and uncivilized part of the Earth.

He scouted out Schubert's neighborhood and stayed in an inn that was on the same street as the composer's home. The local food seemed wholesome enough, but he took his meals out of cans alone in his room rather than risk picking up some exotic Viennese intestinal bug that could lay him low just when he most needed his strength. From the window he watched the comings and goings of Schubert's friends. Then, early on the evening of the ninth day of October, he set his wristwatch alarm for one o'clock the following morning, the day Schubert was said to have died, and went to bed.

Rising as Vienna slept, he trudged the mile and a half to the stable where he had concealed his van and, with lights extinguished drove it through the empty streets to the alley behind the composer's house. He donned his fright costume, took the CX Mark-II canister in hand, and played the very devil.

Back in the stable, he left the nineteenth century and glided smoothly into the last year of the twentieth with his precious cargo, now writhing in delirium on the sweat-soaked bed. After giving Schubert a shot of sedative to still him, Pope inserted a heparin lock in a vein of his forearm and started an intravenous drip. He estimated Schubert's weight at 135 pounds, and injected into the IV the 3 ml of beta-siltyphocide to bring the typhoid fever under quick control and 0.5 ml of atropocillan for his syphilis.

The sun was just coming up as Justin Pope rolled back the garage doors and drove across the cobbled streets toward the highway leading west to Salzburg, Innsbruck, and Zurich, less than six hundred kilometers away. Stopping only for a sandwich at a drive-in at Kitzbühel when the sun was high, he pressed on steadily toward Liechtenstein, which he reached at nightfall. Then, instead of continuing due west toward Zurich, at Vaduz he turned south, passed through Chur, and followed the Rhine to Brig, in the shadow of the towering Jungfrau.

According to the 1998 edition of Jane's *All the World's Civil Defense*, only Sweden and Switzerland had, properly speaking, any effective defense against the nuclear war that would one day engulf the world. Sweden had hollowed out whole mountains and supplied them with reservoirs with millions of gallons of fresh water, food, medical supplies, living quarters, air scrubbers, libraries, and, indeed, almost all of life's immediate requirements. Switzerland had gone Sweden one better by providing immense caverns hewn from its mountains with similar amenities for its population as well as others in which were stockpiled war matériel including fighter aircraft, tanks, and artillery, enough to repel any war-minded survivors of a nuclear holocaust.

Jane's had pinpointed one such subterranean complex just eleven kilometers north of Brig, and it was there that Justin Pope headed his van with his still-unconscious passenger.

Why Switzerland? Simply because it was the one place in the world Pope believed might survive a nuclear war. He needed Schubert's services but could not very well keep him under lock and key. Even if he cured him of his ailments and turned him loose, his gratitude would be short-lived, and Pope would lose all control over Schubert's destiny—and his own.

On the other hand, Pope realized as well as anyone that nuclear war was coming, that it would be infinitely more catastrophic than the politicians dared let their people know, and that there would be few survivors, and those not for long. A white nuclear winter would engulf the world, and those who escaped the first onslaught of missiles would live only to die a more miserable death by starvation, for not a blade of grass would grow on the ice sheet that would cover the world. Sometime soon, perhaps as early as this or the next century, the rain of bombs would begin, and mankind would end. How long it would take for the radiation to dissipate to bearable levels was a moot question, but he had an answer.

Playing the part of a fear-crazed survivalist crank, he prevailed upon a physicist at UC to calibrate the readout on a Geiger counter so that even he could comprehend its meaning. When the needle on the dial was in the red, the radiation it detected was lethal for any protracted exposure. When the needle was in the white, it was safe. Pope himself, having through experience learned the rudiments of electronics, then rigged the Geiger counter to the time-transference dial, so that whenever the needle rested in the red the time-lapse phase would automatically be extended until the needle drifted back into the white.

He then set the time-lapse dial for the year 2100 and pushed the "Go" button. When the purplish mist finally cleared, the dial read 10 July 3386.

He climbed down from the driver's seat and looked about him. The mountain slope looked very much the same as when he had last seen it on a trip to scout the area the previous spring, except that now there were no houses in sight or the slightest sign of humankind or its works. The fields were virgin with tall grass, and on the lower slopes of the Jungfrau grew gnarled bushes with pale green leaves of a type he had never seen before. It was day, but the sun was masked behind clouds so dense that he was unable to tell from what quarter of the sky its dim rays came.

Pope walked to the scar in the side of the mountain where the huge bombproof reinforced concrete doors had been when he had last beheld them, thirteen centuries before. They were still there, weathered and spalled, but they now stood ajar. Weeds had grown through the concrete threshold, but of the birds of the meadow that he hoped had survived, there were none. All was as still as the grave. He got back into the van and drove up the leveled approach and past the doors into the cavern. He reached for the time dial . . .

According to the dial, it was the year 3918. Pope drove through the entire tunnel complex—some four and a half miles—inspecting every darkened corner under the beam of his spotlight.

All seemed in order, if terribly depressing. Of evidence of a human presence there was none. The aircraft and tanks that had been hangared in chambers closest to the huge concrete bunker doors were now but heaps of rusting metal. What water there had been in the immense reservoirs had been exhausted, but a leak in one of the rooms produced clear spring water. In an adjoining chamber Pope set up housekeeping.

He removed the unconscious Franz and his bed from the van and deposited him on the floor. He replaced the IV bags, took Schubert's temperature, and noted with satisfaction that it was coming down to normal levels, thanks to the antibiotics. His boxes of canned, condensed, and dehydrated food and the rest of the provisions he had brought he stacked on the room's empty steel shelves. These supplies constituted the bare necessities of life, but he had resolved to make Schubert's existence, now that he had been brought back from the dead, considerably more than minimal.

Leaving the composer for a few minutes, Justin Pope

drove several hundred meters beyond the gates of the cavern and went back in time to the year 1999. Then he made the first of what was to be a whole series of trips through time and space between the cavern and Brig, between the years A.D. 3918 and A.D. 1999. He brought a commodious bed, a comfortable chair and table, kitchen utensils, cutlery and china, a gasoline generator and enough fuel to power it for several months, clothing, carpets, a large selection of books in German, three dozen digidisks, a player and videomonitor tile, a complete lighting system, and a large supply of music manuscript and felt pens. When he finished supplying the cavern room with the amenities, which required several days, only ten minutes had elapsed from the time when he had first left.

For the next two weeks Justin Pope nursed Schubert back to life and health. His recovery, once the diseases that afflicted him had been struck down with antibiotics, was remarkably swift. In the nineteenth century, only those poor people with excellent constitutions survived to be weaned, and had it not been for drinking contaminated water and consorting with unwholesome women, Schubert might have died a very old man.

That he was alive at all, and in such strange surroundings, and in the company of a pleasant young man who spoke halting and execrable German were matters of unceasing wonder to him. When asked for an explanation of what was happening to him—was he in hell, where he had resigned himself to going during his last moments of consciousness, or was he in heaven? If the former, where was the blazing furnace he was consigned to stoke throughout all eternity? If heaven, where was the Almighty, and the streets paved with gold, and the gates made of pearls? Pope temporized and assured the young man that all would become clear once he had regained his health.

Approximately two weeks after they had come to the cavern, Schubert was well enough to take short walks.

Together the two men went beyond the gates and out upon the green valley. The only sound was the stirring of the wind and the flutter of wings as bees made their rounds, fertilizing the wildflowers that grew in profusion on all sides.

"But where *is* everybody?" Schubert asked for the thousandth time. "Where am I, and who are *you*?"

It was time to tell the truth. Pope told it—or at least as much of it as he thought the nineteenth-century mind of Franz Peter Schubert could assimilate—plus, of course, a few bald lies.

Schubert listened in a daze. Finally he said, "Do you mean to tell me that we are the only two human beings alive in the whole world?"

"So far as I know. There might have been pockets of humanity which survived, perhaps in South America. But yes, I think we are."

"And the world was destroyed by a great explosion?"

"*Many* great explosions."

"But how could man be so stupid? In my time, we had wars—yes. Yet in those days war was a relatively bloodless affair, of armies posturing and maneuvering, and of actual fighting frequently only because of accident or bad judgment. The soldiers took their chances voluntarily and were paid for their risks by being allowed to loot, if victorious. Civilians were usually spared, if you discount a little good-natured raping and pillage."

"Well," Pope replied lamely, "that's life."

"That's *death*," Schubert corrected him, "and I want to know why I was spared—and you."

"Pure selfishness, I must admit. You see, I had—have—this tremendous urge to be a great composer, though I fear not the genius it takes to become one. Then, by a fortuitous accident, I came into possession of this time machine." He did not go into details of the "fortuitous accident" that had made him its sole possessor. "I saw the opportunity to observe and study under one of the greatest composers who has ever lived."

"Me?" Schubert scoffed. He put his head back and roared with laughter. "You've made a big mistake, my friend, although," he added quickly, "I thank you for your bad judgment with all my soul. Not that I don't share your excellent opinion, mind you. But while I have reason to think well of my compositions, what can you know of them? Most of what I wrote perished before the ink was dry."

"Perhaps, but not all. Enough survived to convince the world that you were a man who would die before his genius could fully flower."

"And how would you know that? I was known in my native Vienna, to be sure, but so little esteemed that I went to bed hungry nearly every day of my life for want of pupils to instruct, or artists to perform my works, or audiences to listen."

"True, but more of your works survived than you realize, and they are among the most loved in the musical literature."

Schubert was skeptical. He shook his head and felt the unfamiliar weight of the long-billed baseball cap. He looked down at the coarse blue jeans and rough wool shirt and wondered how a culture that was supposed to have advanced so far could produce not only wars in which nations slaughtered each other wholesale but clothing that was little improvement upon the caveman's uncured skins. What could such a world know of his music—or care?

"Come on back to the cavern," Justin Pope said, "and I'll show you something."

Back in the room, which on the inside now resembled the self-contained dwelling of a trapper in the far north, with every necessity of life near to hand, Justin Pope took the electronic synthesizer from its case and placed it on the table. At the sight of the keyboard Schubert, like a small child with a new toy, ran his fingers in an arpeggio up and down the keys. But no sound issued forth. He looked in puzzlement at Pope.

Pope plugged the instrument into the outlet powered by the generator in the adjacent room, sat down before it, and flipped the switch. He then launched into Schubert's Sonata in A. He was halfway through the first movement before Schubert emerged from his trance.

"Black magic," he murmured.

"Nothing of the sort," Pope said. "When I have time, I'll tell you how this all works." Remembering that he himself did not know how it worked, he hastily corrected himself. "I'll bring you some *books* that tell you how it works." He played one of the écossaises, followed by the Allegretto in C, then a piano arrangement of the *Trout* Quintet and enough of the *Wanderer* Fantasie to prove that he was well acquainted with the work, then went on to passages from Schubert's symphonies, operas, song cycles, and even a long portion of the *Easter* Cantata. "You see, Franz, you're regarded as one of the greatest composers of all time. Had you not been cut off by sickness, I have no doubt that you would have put Beethoven, Dvořák, Brahms, Rachmaninoff, and the rest very much in the shade."

"Beethoven I know," Schubert responded. "But who are those others?"

"Later. Would you like to try the keyboard?" He unobtrusively touched the switch that would record all that was played both as sound and as a sequence of notes on digidisk.

For an answer, Schubert took his place before the instrument. His eyes dreamy and focused somewhere beyond infinity, he began to play.

It was the simplest of themes, the simplest of rhythms, but it grew from a slender root to a full-blown sequoia of sound, a massive edifice from which branched out variations that explored every tempo and texture of which the keyboard was capable. Enraptured by the music he was improvising, Schubert was loath to bring it to a close. But like all worthwhile compositions, it, too, had to end. He was driving toward the coda, after no fewer than fifteen distinct and surpassingly lovely variations, when Pope, anticipating his intentions, reached over his shoulder and pushed the button that converted the sound to that of a harpsichord. The sudden shift in tonal quality set Schubert off at a tangent, still improvising upon the same theme but with a treatment reminiscent of the seventeenth century. Once again he approached the finale, and again Pope touched a button, and the rich burnished strains of a pipe organ filled the chamber. Schubert could hardly contain his excitement but played on and on, switching from one instrument to the other, until at long last the stream of invention ran dry. He leaned back in his chair, tears welling up in his eyes.

Pope said nothing.

Finally the trembling of Schubert's hands ceased, and he looked up at Pope. "It wasn't bad, you know. What a pity that I'll not be able to remember half of it."

Justin Pope pressed a button on the digidisk recorder and set the gain control on maximum. The sound nearly blew them both out of the room. Franz Peter Schubert, not an ardent churchgoer, wordlessly thanked God for the gift of preserving the music that had poured out of him with such passion. He did not know why his music had been chosen for God's particular mercies and did not much care: he was alive, and the music could continue to flow.

That night, after introducing Schubert to frozen pizza, Justin Pope told him many wonderful things. It was late, and Schubert was exhausted, when he put *Gone with the Wind*, dubbed in German, on the VCR. But Schubert, after overcoming his initial wonder at the mechanism, drifted off to sleep, muttering that it was all very interesting but the synthesizer would leave him very little time to enjoy it.

For the next six weeks, Schubert wrote ceaselessly, and when he fell into exhausted slumber, Justin Pope got busy with his camera, making copies of the scores of quartets, trios, songs, and the melodic lines for an entire opera. Meanwhile, he saw to it that Schubert wanted for nothing, that he ate the best food the caterers of Brig could provide, that he took moderate exercise, and that he did not learn enough about the time and place from which Pope had come to want to see it firsthand. For the moment, free to compose what and when he wished, he was as close to heaven as he had ever dared hope.

One day Pope said to him, "Franz, tell me about your Eighth Symphony, the one in B."

"If you know it, what is there to tell?"

"Well, for one thing, why was it never finished?"

"What do you mean, 'never finished'? Of course I finished it."

"That's odd. Only the first two movements ever came down to us. They call it the Unfinished."

"What nonsense. The last two movements must have been lost. People were always borrowing my music, always losing it."

"Could you reconstruct the last two movements?"

"Certainly. But why bother? That's water under the dam. Going back to that period of my life would be like a mathematician reciting his multiplication tables."

"I'd really like to hear what they sounded like," Pope said wistfully.

It took some persuasion, but Schubert eventually yielded, for after all, he owed his life to Pope. He spent six days writing the complete score of the last two movements as easily as if he were copying it from an open book, which his memory, in a sense, was to him.

That afternoon, Pope went to Brig of 1999 and brought back a cage of canaries, two German shepherd puppies, and a pair of calico kittens. They were not much of a substitute for human company, but they would do until he thought of something better.

That night, as Schubert slept, Justin Pope climbed in the *Fugit* and was gone.

6. FAME
10 OCTOBER 1999

JUSTIN POPE'S RECITAL ON THE NIGHT OF TUESDAY, 10 October 1999, in Symphony Hall in San Francisco was such a spectacular success that it would have been the culmination of a meteoric career for most musicians, but he managed to top it with the press conference he held immediately afterward.

In his dressing room, he had just managed to shuck his clawhammer jacket and undo his tie when the door burst open and the room filled with critics, reporters, and the enthralled power brokers of San Francisco's musical community, all trying to get the first word in. When he finally managed to still the uproar, he sat with his back to the mirror with the nonchalance of a veteran performer and genially volunteered to answer any questions he might be asked, provided they came solo rather than in chorus.

The *Chronicle*'s music critic thrust himself forward and asked Pope how he had come to write the centerpiece of his recital, the Brig Variations, and what the name stood for.

"The name?" Pope replied. "Actually, I was inspired by a square-rigged two-master I saw sailing in the bay some years back. It was battling a tempestuous gale and had to tack furiously for what seemed an eternity before it managed to get the storm on its quarter, which brought the battered, weary vessel safely into port. My variations were like that ship, carried forward on a medley of contrasting airs, which drove it to every point of the compass before a willing wild west wind brought it safely home at last."

His audience sighed with ecstasy. The man's words, even like his music, were pure poetry.

"But the *form* of the Variations," said the stringer from *Newsweek*, which had not judged the recital worth the time of its regular critic, "was so—so—"

"Traditional?" Pope supplied.

"Yes, traditional," the stringer sniffed, as if he had detected an overripe fish. "Suggestive of the early nineteenth century, so unlike the *Malibu* Symphony, which I had the opportunity to hear a year ago when it was performed by the university symphony orchestra. It's almost as if the two pieces of music had not only been written by different persons, but at different periods. Of course," he added nastily, "I don't mean to suggest . . ." He let his voice trail off.

Justin Pope paused. For a long while it seemed to the expectant throng that he was undecided whether to throw a punch at his critic or confess that he had indeed uncovered a forgotten work by some master of the last century. Then he said solemnly, "It is premature to confide my ambition, but you force me to do so, at the risk of the opprobrium of the musical world, which may well laugh at my hubris.

"You see, after I had written the *Malibu* Symphony and seen it through rehearsal and its first—and last—performance, I realized that it was much too avant-garde for today's musical tastes. I spent the next twelve months in quiet introspection, writing little, wondering how to make the musical world understand what I was trying to do. And then, suddenly, it came to me: I would have to go back a hundred and fifty years or so, to the days of Schubert and Beethoven, who wrote music which, though frequently ahead of its time, is today understood and loved by everyone. I would, therefore, write in the style, and with the musical materials and instruments, of that day.

"The Brig Variations, as well as the other works—the sonatas and occasional pieces I played tonight—were written in that spirit. If you found them derivative, I am not surprised. They *are* derivative. I wrote them in a musical language that would require no long program notes, no learned interpretation, no painful indoctrination of a hostile public. Music, in short, of a style familiar to all. Music—pure music—was what I sought to write, and I am vain enough to think that I succeeded."

"That you have, Dr. Pope," came a voice from the rear. "And brilliantly! It was a tour de force, and I for one feel that I have witnessed the musical birth of a composer of the first magnitude, who will set a standard by which all composers of the twenty-first century will be judged."

Pope recognized the speaker as the staunchest traditionalist of them all, the chairman of the San Francisco Opera, a man who considered Puccini somewhat radical, a man who dictated musical taste west of the Mississippi. Once he had spoken, all the rest would fall into line.

"A quaint conceit," the *Newsweek* man persisted, hoping to goad Pope to anger and perhaps get a really inflammatory quote out of him, "but are you going to reside permanently in the early nineteenth century, the safe and sane nineteenth century, or do you plan to take chances on new, unexplored forms?"

Pope was thoughtful. "A good question. Let me answer it this way: let's say you hand a Kurd from the Anatolian highlands a compact disc recording. He would be unimpressed. A shiny, mirrorlike, perfectly round object, but good for nothing unless one sharpened its edge, whereupon it could be skimmed through the air at the inviting throat of a Turk. But if you demonstrated to him how the human larynx vibrated, and how those vibrations could be made to excite a microphone's diaphragm, and how the diaphragm's motion could be translated into a weak electric current, and the current amplified by transistors powering a laser, whose beam burned microscopic indentations into the record, which could be converted back to sound by reversing the process, he would have a better idea of the marvel he held in his palm, especially if you played it, and the voice he heard was that of a mullah reciting the Holy Koran."

"I fail to appreciate the pertinence of the example," the *Newsweek* man said.

"Then I shall put it in concrete terms. I hope to recapitulate the entire history of music of the past two centuries in my own individual style. You have heard the benchmark, so to speak, from which I will work. I shall proceed from that foundation forward through the nineteenth and twentieth centuries, drawing those who listen to my music ever forward, until the time comes when they will apprehend that the *Malibu* Symphony and works like it I shall then write are nothing but a logical, seamless extension of what has gone before."

The audacity of Pope's ambitions silenced the crowd in his dressing room. Here was a man who, not content to write for one period, would undertake to encompass the musical heritage of two centuries, then use it as a springboard to explore ideas that at that moment only he could comprehend but that he intended to make the new language of musical thought.

His idea was so revolutionary, and his confidence so steadfast, and his magnificent compositions so breathtaking, that he received unprecedented coverage in the nation's media, including all of an inch and a half on page 4 of *The New York Times* and a thirty-second segment on ABC television as a run-in for an advertisement for All-Bran.

The following morning, luxuriating in bed in the three-room furnished apartment he had rented on the strength of his anticipated successes, he was awakened by the doorbell. A reporter, no doubt, although on the evening before he had said all he wished to say to the press for some time. They could come listen to his music and write what they damned pleased. He put a pillow over his head and tried to go back to sleep. To no avail: the bell kept up its insistent din—in an annoyingly flat B natural, at that. He struggled out of bed, knotted a bath towel around his bare waist, and put the coffeepot on the fire on his way to open the front door.

There stood a young woman who seemed vaguely familiar, although he was sure he had never met her. Had he ever met her, *he* would have been familiar even if she had not. She was of medium height and medium weight and had natural blond hair of medium length. Those were the only medium things about her. She was, she said, Angelica Hunter.

He was, he said, delighted. He opened the door and bade her enter.

He padded to the kitchen, with Miss Hunter following in his wake, and got out two cups. Without asking, he spooned out two heaping spoonfuls of powdered coffee into each cup, added boiling water, and shoved one across the kitchen table to his guest.

"Angelica Hunter," he mused. "I don't think we've met. I'd remember."

"That's what I'm here for—to help you remember. Now that you're famous, you'll need somebody to help you remember things—appointments to break, autograph hunters to dodge, checking accounts to balance, appeals for money to ignore, publishers to scorn, stuff like that."

"You want to *work* for me?"

"That's what I'm here for."

"But I don't have any money to pay you."

"Don't worry. You're going to have plenty, and you'll have me by your side to help you keep it."

"Just for the sake of argument," he said, surveying her legs, about which there could be no argument, "what kind of qualifications do you have?"

"Well, I have a master's in information science, and as an undergraduate I majored in far eastern studies, with a minor in Japanese. I know the tea ceremony, and I've been told I look good in a kimono."

"And better out of it, no doubt, but a far eastern tour

is pretty low on my list of priorities. As for information, I get all I want in the *Chronicle*."

"Well, how about this: I run a mean Xerox machine."

Pope frowned his puzzlement.

"You don't get it yet, do you, you big lunkhead? I'm here to protect you from yourself."

Pope picked up his coffee. "What the hell are you talking about?"

"About a lot of things, but let's just start with Lermontov."

"Huh?" Pope grunted, spilling hot coffee on his bare leg.

"Then we can go on to Mariocuti and Harnishneggar and, for a grand finale, make a bow in the direction of Luigi Baptistini."

"Oh." Justin Pope's voice was faint. "*You're* the one."

"I am, indeed, the one."

They looked at each other.

"Why did you do it?" Pope said, finally.

"Send you the words of warning?"

"Yes."

"Would you believe in love at first sight?"

"No."

"Then how about a strictly mercenary motive?"

"Maybe. But you appear to have too many brains in that beautiful head ever to think me capable of earning enough to interest a woman interested in money. After all, when you sent me the notes, I was nothing but a poor graduate student, working as a janitor."

"True," she admitted, "but you had possibilities."

She had detected those possibilities while doing a term paper on plagiarism in graduate studies. With access to the university library's checkout records, she had compared a random dozen doctoral candidates' dissertations in progress with the sources cited in their bibliographies and footnotes. That had provided a baseline of authenticity. She discarded such material, then examined what she had left, comparing texts with the references checked out by the students. She found that a preponderance of what seemed to have been original conclusions had been copied verbatim and wholesale from those references, without citation—brazen plagiarism. And only rarely, her own term paper reported, was the culprit ever caught.

"You were one of my two musical plagiarists," she went on, "making prints on the photocopy machine. Never a whole score, like the other fellow. That was interesting. Everyone else in my dirty dozen copied whole passages, but you were content to use a stolen musical idea merely as a launching pad. This piqued my curiosity. I was pretty confident that, in trying to pound seventeenth- and eighteenth-century themes into a modern-music matrix you'd fall on your face and be exposed, and I wanted to see the fun. So I became an auditor at your weekly critique sessions."

Pope snapped his fingers. "*That's* where I saw you."

"It was. I listened to your work in progress, waiting for the professor to denounce you as a thief. I'm not much of a musician—I studied the cello for only eleven years—but it seemed obvious to me that he'd catch on. But, to my everlasting astonishment, he swallowed it all. Pretty good performance, Mr. Pope—or was it just plain dumb luck to copy the Lermontov theme for your *Malibu* Symphony and get away with it?"

"I still don't get it," a bewildered Pope said. "You could have blown the whistle on me. Why did you send me the note—the notes—instead?"

The young woman crossed one shapely leg carefully over the other, smoothed the skirt down, and gazed at him with guileless eyes. He had not believed the stark truth the first time, so she risked nothing in repeating it. "Would you believe it was because I fell in love with your warm, brown puppylike eyes the first moment I saw you and wanted to warn you against jeopardizing your musical career should the truth come out?"

"Of course I don't believe it," Pope said firmly. Love at first sight was something that happened in storybooks. And even in storybooks luscious young women who fell in love at first sight certainly did not proclaim it openly to the targets of their affections. Nor had Angelica Hunter, although had not Pope been so wrapped up in his music, he would have noticed the girl in his composition class who cast shy, longing glances at him and once even had the temerity to ask him about a cello passage, a question he had brushed off as unworthy of his notice.

Well, he was noticing her now. "How about this, then: I saw you getting away with murder. You were deceiving your professors and your fellow students, without half trying, into believing you were some sort of musical genius. Anybody who could deceive the musically sophisticated with such ease would have no trouble at all in bamboozling the public. That ability, with your good looks and air of little-boy helplessness, could fill concert halls. With my little billets-doux, I put you on notice that you were going to have to share your ill-gotten gains with somebody else, should your promise bear fruit. Well, my dear Justin Pope, last night it bore whole orchards full, and I'm here to squeeze myself a little juice." *Now* he would think he divined her purpose: money was a motive even somebody as immune to her charm as Justin Pope could not fail to understand.

Pope pondered. That Angelica Hunter had his number was beyond question. She could demonstrate the provenance of the *Malibu* Symphony's lyrical passages with a few choice words dropped to the *Newsweek* stringer, for instance, who would be only too glad to crucify him for plagiarism and thus win his spurs as a full-time staff media assassin. Would it matter? Or would the shadow his proven plagiarism cast be dispelled by the brilliance of the works he had played the night before and the dozens of major pieces yet to come? It could go either way, but it would be dangerous in the extreme to allow suspicion to fall upon himself at this juncture in his career. Ever after, each composition he presented would be ripped apart, dissected, analyzed, and put through the musicologist's meat grinder until the uncanny similarity in style between it and the later style of Schubert became apparent. And from then on his jealous contemporaries would watch his every move, perhaps even discover some relation between his trips abroad in the van with wings painted on the sides and his premier performance of new masterpieces shortly thereafter. He did not dare chance it.

"I must confess," Pope sighed, "that it wouldn't suit me to have you warbling sweet nothings to the press. Also, as you point out, I *will* need assistance in arranging my programs, my travel, my press conferences, my publications and my—"

"My, my," Angelica said. "Giving up so easily?"

"Just exploring the concept. What salary would you expect?"

"No salary—just half of the net."

Pope felt an icy draft on his neck. "You must be out of your mind!"

Angelica smiled seraphically. "Have it your way. But man is a creature of habit, and I'll bet anything you want to lose that you haven't broken yours—of stealing compositions from real composers. Give me a reason to do so and a couple of months, and I'll find out who really wrote those Brig Variations."

"When do you wish to start?" Pope said coldly.

"How about today?"

"Very well."

Angelica Hunter drained the rest of her coffee and stood up. Without a word she went to the door and let herself out. He heard her footsteps on the stairs. He poured another cup of coffee and wondered what he was letting himself in for. He had not taken two sips when the doorbell rang. He answered it.

It was Angelica, carrying two suitcases.

"What the hell's this?" Pope demanded.

"My belongings. I'm moving in. I believe in living close to my work."

7. FORTUNE
17 NOVEMBER 1999

THE MANAGING EDITOR'S DESK WAS A VAST TROPICAL rain forest of memoranda, galley proofs, reference books, computer readouts, paper clips, dried-out felt pens, letters from an irate readership, and the remains of yesterday's pastrami sandwich, yet somehow he managed to dig out the publisher's summons on the very first try.

"Here we are," he said triumphantly to Philipa Dedeny, who collapsed into the chair opposite his desk and lit a thin black cigar.

She did not really like the taste of the thing and approached the semiannual chest x-ray with trepidation, but it fit the image she tried to project of herself as the hard-boiled reporter. The image helped cool off the office Lotharios whose hot breath was always on her neck, improved her bargaining position when the time came to negotiate next year's salary, and formed a shield against a cynical world that would have laughed at the romantic, sentimental, sensitive spirit that lay just below the surface.

It was quite some surface. If only two adjectives were allowed, long and luscious would have sufficed. She had long slim legs, long black hair, long red fingernails, a long patrician nose, and the habit of long silences that made her respondents so uncomfortable that, they later realized to their dismay, they filled them with revealing details they would never willingly have revealed to one of the best reporters in the business. As to the rest of her, her full red lips and wide dark eyes and sculptured breasts could only be described, as they frequently were, as luscious.

Philipa Dedeny was the senior correspondent in the politics section of *Time* magazine, but she hated the job, the more so because she was so good at it that she was never considered for another. Her greatest strength, beyond writing clear, concise, literate English—an attainment abandoned by most of her fellow reporters as an impossible goal—was an unerring ability to expose frauds. This led naturally to national politics, where she had stormed Capitol Hill with the vigor and success with which Colonel Teddy Roosevelt had stormed San Juan Hill—and left even more casualties in her wake.

Still, she loathed her work: it was without challenge because it was too easy. The corruption of congressmen was so blatant, so pervasive, so constant, so naked that the edge of the muckraker's knife had long since become dull. The grim satisfaction of watching them bleed when she skewered them with the pointed record of their peculations had paled, and her work now only made her weary and heavy-hearted.

She yearned for a different world, a world of gentleness and beauty and love, a world she inhabited in her dreams. There, she painted masterpieces in the morning, set them to music in the afternoon, and made love by the light of the moon. No man had yet come close to her uncompromising standards, nor had her artistic accomplishments, although she had immersed herself in painting and music since she had been old enough to carry a paintbrush and a tune. Despite her devouring passion for the arts, however, by the time she had graduated from Smith she realized she did not possess enough talent at either calling to make a living at it. She drifted from one job to another until she landed on a newspaper, where her talent for exposing fraud got her an offer from *Time* and a place among its galaxy of stars. After three years, though, the luster had dimmed, and it showed in the drawn lines around her mouth, the dull eyes, the droop of her shoulders.

She took the paper the managing editor, Murray Stein, thrust across the desk at her, read it, and handed it back.

"Well?" Stein asked. "What do you think?"

"About what?"

"About the idea of making Justin Pope our man of the year."

"Why ask me?"

"Because I respect your viewpoint."

"I'm a political reporter, not a music critic."

"I know. But our music critic is a cretin. He can't play the piano half as well as you can, and—"

"That's why he's a critic."

Stein leaned forward in his chair, his hands outspread. "It's a simple question: what do you think about Justin Pope for our man of the year?"

"Why do you ask me?"

"Frankly, because you know something about music. Also, you have a fine nose for fraud, and I've been getting some vibrations from our San Francisco office to the effect that this guy's too good to be true. I can't afford to be out on a limb on this one."

"Oh, now I see."

"Well?"

"Pick somebody else—*anybody* else."

"I would, if the publisher hadn't gone bonkers for the guy. She thinks he's the greatest genius to come down the pike in five hundred years. She compares him to Berlioz and da Vinci, and in unguarded moments even to John Lennon."

"I see your problem."

"Well, what do *you* think? I gather you think he doesn't belong on our cover," Stein said.

"He belongs is jail."

"How do you figure that, Phil? Everybody in the shop says he's the most magnificent composer since—since—well, Rachmaninoff, certainly. And he's only a very young man. Give him a few years, and he'll certainly rank with the B-boys. That's what they're saying, anyway,'' he said lamely.

''The only B's that fit him are bandit, bullshitter, and bastard. He's a thief,'' Philipa Dedeny replied. ''As for rank, that perfectly describes the odor given off by his pretensions to greatness. He's a goddamned fraud,'' she added in case Murray had not caught her drift. ''Mind you, all this is my personal opinion. It's just a feeling I've got about the guy. Probably all wrong.''

''But what about his Brig Variations?''

''Yes, I've been listening to the Brig Variations. They're magnificent. But they're not his.''

''How do you know?''

''I know they're not because I've heard his *Malibu* Symphony. The two pieces weren't—couldn't have been—written by the same person.'' She crushed her cigar viciously, wishing it were Justin Pope.

Stein studied his pudgy hands. He looked up and sighed. ''Frankly, that's what I hoped you were going to say. *Newsweek*, after a little diplomatic backing and filling, has anointed him the New Messiah of Modern Music, and if you can actually prove he's a phony, we can stick it to 'em—and good. What do you say?''

The banked fires in her eyes suddenly blazed forth. ''When do I start?''

''Right now. This is a 'must-run' assignment, and you're going to have to run like hell to meet the deadline. He's going to be our cover boy either way it goes. If the guy is on the level, we canonize the son of a bitch. If not, we document the hell out of his scam and we steal 100,000 circulation from the girls down at 444 Madison Avenue. You can take Carney, Gibbons, Fleet and Rosenberg, and anyone else you need, but get the story.''

''I'm on my way,'' Phil Dedeny said, rising.

''One thing: stick with the facts. I can live with facts. Speaking of which, the guy seems to have parted with

very few since his concert last month in San Francisco. I want a preliminary report in forty-eight hours."
"Can do."

So far, there was not a lot to tell. Justin Pope had held two other concerts in quick succession to debut major new compositions, both of them quite as brilliant and melodic as the Brig Variations. They had been given in Chicago and New York, where he had played to SRO audiences at vastly inflated ticket prices. Attempts by the press to interview him were thwarted by his new press secretary, business manager, and all-around live-in factotum, one Angelica Hunter, who kept him so completely under wraps that no one had even been able to locate his local hotel once she whisked him away from the concert hall into a waiting taxi.

The facts Phil Dedeny had been able to scrape up from *Time*'s library on the life and times of Justin Pope were meager and mundane. He was the son of a widowed practical nurse who had spent every penny she could afford on music lessons for her son, whose talents, though considerable, did not approach his ambition. He had won an undergraduate degree with distinction but had not shown enough promise to win one of the three full scholarships available for graduate students and had been obliged to work as a janitor in a physics laboratory to meet expenses. Then, in his final year, his work began to match his expectation. The *Malibu* Symphony was a large, powerful, but very uneven piece of music whose melodic passages enchanted all who heard them but whose other sections seemed strangely out of tune. That two such disparate elements could be present in the music written by one man Philipa Dedeny refused to believe. He had obviously stolen the lyric elements, although it might take a long time and an enormous effort searching the literature to find out whence they had been filched.

So far, Justin Pope's celebrity had been mostly confined to the cognoscenti. They had flocked to his concerts, been enchanted by his rugged good looks and pleasant demeanor no less than by his music, and vied in outdoing each other in their praises. His name had not yet percolated to the mass of Americans, but the music publishers, envisioning the miraculous appearance of another Beethoven in their midst, had stumbled over one another in their quest to sign him to exclusive recording contracts. Angelica Hunter had made some shrewd choices among them, driving hard bargains and insisting on six-figure advances for permission to make the first recordings. She had even managed, on the strength of the instant popularity of his later music, to squeeze Columbia Records for $150,000 for a first pressing of the cacophonic *Malibu* Symphony. Phil Dedeny computed his minimum advances against anticipated royalties so far at more than $2 million. Not bad for a recently minted Ph.D. in music.

As she listened to the Brig Variations on her portable CD player while winging to the West Coast that evening, Phil Dedeny marveled. In her notebook she jotted down phrases that she would use to describe the music in her cover story, if it ever came to that: sprightly invention . . . subtle chromatics . . . delicate tonal shadings . . . bold phrasing . . . unpredictable pralltrillers . . . sensuous power . . . ribald wit . . . quasi-fugal extravagances . . . tormented tutti and dazzling ritornelli. But the more she listened, the more obscure and meaningless became her music-critic chichés. Her mind floated away on the music. Whoever was the author of the music—and she was more convinced than ever that no contemporary of hers could have written it—he was indeed the towering genius the musical world had acclaimed Justin Pope. The man who could write music like that—this was a man worthy of what she had never bestowed on mortal man: her body and her heart.

Other reporters kept vigil in the lobby of the apartment building, the Santorini of Nob Hill, into which Angelica

Hunter had moved him after his Chicago and New York successes. His apartment, the penthouse, had a magnificent view of the bay, a luxuriant balcony garden, an Alsatian *Cordon Bleu* chef, a Mexican couple to keep house, and a private elevator to which only the occupants had the key. Other reporters maintained a vigil in the lobby of the building, but they never so much as got a glance at Justin Pope. They had not yet discovered that he and Angelica Hunter, always by his side, would descend directly to the underground garage at odd hours and leave the building in a chauffeured Rolls with mirrored windows.

Philipa Dedeny was not inclined to wait for the reclusive genius to show himself. She sublet the apartment directly below Pope's from the owners, who were vacationing in Florida, and installed her staff of five. One she ordered to the Faculty of Music at the University of California to dig up every available fact on Justin Pope. Another was detailed to find and interview his friends, acquaintances, and former lovers. A third she sent to the library's music section, there to dig out every piece of music Justin Pope had ever signed for. A fourth was to interview Pope's teachers and classmates and to determine, if possible, whether he had ever let drop some hint of where his music might have come from besides his own fertile mind. The fifth was used as driver and courier, keeping the New York office informed with daily progress reports, ordering food sent in, and washing dishes.

Philipa Dedeny had little expectation that her coworkers would find anything useful, except as background to flesh out the exposé she intended to write. An article in praise of Justin Pope—well, *everybody* was writing those. *Her* story, by contrast, would rip away the veil of ignorance, expose him as a fraud, and, she devoutly hoped, unearth the true composer of the music for which Pope was getting such fulsome credit. Hers was the direct approach: when all her subordinates were out on their various assignments, she brought in a surveillance specialist, who rigged the ceiling with button and spike mikes. All conversations taking place in the apartment above were picked up by the receiver and tape recorder in her bedroom, which she kept locked at all times.

Four days of patient listening brought Philipa Dedeny no hint of anything but innocent activity. Justin Pope practiced a number of delightful piano pieces she had never heard before but spoke very little. She had to filter out a great deal of servant chatter in Spanish, was subjected to interminable business discussions between Angelica Hunter and concert-hall managers in Europe and American music publishers, and blushed like the maiden she was when once she heard stirrings in Angelica Hunter's bedroom that could have had only one interpretation. Not until the fifth day did she hear something that brought a gleam to her luminous eyes.

"I think I'll go out this afternoon for a while," Justin Pope said, his voice casual.

"Very well," Angelica Hunter replied. "I'll be with you as soon as I make two or three more phone calls."

"No, don't bother, Angelica. I need a bit of solitude to think about my next composition."

"Of course. I guess you must get the feeling that I'm always underfoot." Her voice was contrite. "But I'm only doing it for your sake. You *know* that, don't you?"

"Sure, sure."

"I'll phone Benson to meet you down at the car."

"No, don't bother about that. I'll take the van."

"Well, if you insist. I guess nobody can tell who you are behind all that tinted glass. Hurry back, darling."

Philipa Dedeny heard the squishy sound of a kiss, then the soft closing of a door. For a moment all was silent in the room.

Justin Pope had a van. Now, that was interesting. Why would he drive a van when a chauffeured Rolls was waiting to take him wherever he wanted? The explanation, obviously, was that he wished to be completely alone, without even the presence of a hired hand. Not so obviously, she corrected herself, as she heard the receiver of a telephone being lifted in the room where Justin Pope was now alone, a number punched in, and his voice whispering into the receiver.

"Swissair . . . You have a flight to Geneva at 1330 this afternoon, I believe . . . Good. I want to reserve a first-class ticket in the name of J. Pope for that flight, and space for my vehicle . . . Oh, you don't? Well, then, what is the earliest flight you have which will take both me and my vehicle? Your 1730. I see . . . Well, book me on that. My vehicle is a van. Don't worry about that—its papers are in order, as I've taken it to Europe before. Thank you very much." He hung up.

Philipa Dedeny looked at her watch and made some quick calculations. If she left now, she could catch the 1230 shuttle to New York. From there, she knew, she could catch one of the hourly flights to Geneva and arrive comfortably ahead of the Swissair flight Justin Pope would take. She could safely have flown on the same plane Pope was going to take, since he had never laid eyes on her, but she had foolishly left New York without her passport. She called her secretary in New York, told her to bring the passport to JFK and book her on the 2145 flight to Geneva, and packed an overnight bag.

It was still dark when Philipa Dedeny's flight landed in Geneva. She checked the arrival time of Justin Pope's Swissair flight over the North Pole, decided she had time for a shower and a couple of hours' sleep, and booked a sleeperette at the airport. At 0825, when the Swissair flight landed, she was waiting in a rental car just outside the cargo terminal. Although she had never seen the van, she had a full description of it and the number of its license plate from *Time*'s San Francisco office, which had checked police records.

At 0910 the van rolled through the cargo terminal gate,

heading northeast. Philipa Dedeny kept well behind. The van, its glass opaque, its solid panels painted a plain gray except for a pair of flamboyant wings on either side, was easy to keep in sight. It drove at a sedate pace around Lake Leman, through Montreux, and along the valley of the Rhone for some 150 kilometers before it finally stopped in front of a *boulangerie* in the alpine city of Brig.

Brig, she mused. Now, *that* was a coincidence.

Pope stepped out and went into the shop to buy half a dozen flutes, the long French bread, and several boxes of pastry.

Philipa Dedeny pulled up and parked next to the van and got out. Pope was talking with the pretty young clerk in the shop, his back to the street. Philipa flipped a mental coin, decided the confrontation was bound to occur soon anyway, and quickly climbed into the van through the unlocked rear doors. Much of the cargo space was occupied by a large steel box fitted with two padlocks. She made herself small behind the box and waited.

A few minutes later Justin Pope opened the door on the driver's side, put his purchases on the passenger seat, and drove off.

The road was smooth, bordering the northern rim of what a sign said was the Aletschhorn Glacier. As Pope shifted to a lower gear to negotiate the hairpin turns and steep ascent, she briefly glimpsed another signpost out the back window: "Jungfrau, 4158 m—20 km." Though she tried to keep alert to her surroundings, the warmth of the heater and the monotonous singing of tires on asphalt proved soporific and Philipa Dedeny, still leaden-lidded from jet lag, dropped off into troubled slumber. Half-asleep, she felt the van weave up the side of the Jungfrau, and after an interval whose length she couldn't guess, slide to a gentle stop. All became deathly still, and she slipped smoothly off the ledge of consciousness into deep sleep.

She slept on until she felt a sudden jolt, as if the van

had run into the granite mountainside, and awoke to find herself enveloped in a purplish haze. She caught herself just in time, before the scream that was forming in her throat had a chance to split the silence. Justin Pope still occupied the driver's seat, his hands folded behind his head, apparently not at all alarmed by the vapor. A few minutes later he opened the door and stepped out.

Philipa waited until he had disappeared, then followed. The moment she stepped down to the concrete pavement, she realized that something was seriously amiss. They had been driving over roads whose banks were still piled high with winter snow. But of winter there was now no sign. On the contrary, wildflowers bloomed everywhere.

Everywhere, that is, except directly ahead of her, where the mouth of an immense concrete cavern built into the mountainside had swallowed Justin Pope. She shook her head, wondering how she could have slept so long that Pope had regained the sunny, snow-free lowlands. She looked around for signs of life. Finding none, she shrugged and entered the cavern. She walked some distance, toward a light shining dimly from the interior. She heard voices speaking what sounded like German.

She came to a branch in the corridor and, halting on the threshold of the room, which was brightly lit, saw Pope and a strange young man—strange yet somehow hauntingly familiar—in blue jeans and a T-shirt bearing the legend "Redskin Fever—Catch It."

"I sensed that of my company you were tiring, Franz," Pope was saying in German. "So I thought for you that of someone else to enjoy. Assuredly, German she doesn't speak. But some means of communications, comprehensible mutually, you will certainly find." He paused, listening intently. Then he walked with swift steps toward the door and seized the surprised Philipa Dedeny by the arm. He led her gently into the room.

"Miss Dedeny," he said in English, "I'd like to introduce to you the composer of the Brig Variations—and other enchanting works too voluminous to enumerate: the legendary Herr Franz Peter Schubert."

8. FATE
25 NOVEMBER 1999

PHILIPA DEDENY STARED IN DISBELIEF AT THE SMALL, scruffy man in the blue jeans and Redskins shirt. Yet she believed.

It was against all reason, of course. Schubert was dead—had been dead for nearly two hundred years. He had died a well-documented death from syphilis and typhoid fever and had been almost instantly forgotten by Vienna and the musical world. Nevertheless, there stood a man whose face too closely resembled drawings and paintings of Schubert to be a coincidence, who spoke German, and who had been introduced to her as Franz Peter Schubert by Justin Pope. Only the latter circumstance raised a doubt in her mind—Pope was such a liar and con man.

Still, it all fit with what she already knew, namely, that a man of genius had written the Brig Variations and the other music the world had attributed to Justin Pope, with the notable exception of the *Malibu* Symphony, and that this genius was not Justin Pope. Had she died somewhere along the highway out of Brig, and was she now experiencing resurrection in the company of angels? No, certainly not, for Justin Pope was no angel. The only other possible explanation was that she had been transported back to a time before Schubert had died. And yet, that did not make sense either, for there on a table scattered with sheet music was an electronic synthesizer.

"Play something," she said, the first thought that popped into her head.

Schubert looked questioningly at Justin Pope.

Pope translated and pointed to the keyboard.

Schubert smoothed his muttonchop whiskers, smiled broadly, and sat at the keyboard. He began to play. It was something Philipa Dedeny had never heard before. Nor had Schubert, for that matter. She thought it divine. Schubert, nodding to himself from time to time at the pleasure of discovery, could not disagree. It was beautiful music inspired by the totally unexpected presence of a remarkably beautiful woman, a woman of delicate features and long silken legs such as he had never seen before, a woman from another planet.

She listened enraptured. Justin Pope listened with consummate satisfaction, for he knew the digidisk had recorded every note. None of the three was even vaguely aware of how long the music went on. Only when Pope glanced at the counter before rewinding the tape did he realize that the marvelous improvisation had lasted a full twenty-five minutes. He would call it, he decided, the Berkeley Impromptu.

When Schubert finally raised his hands from the keys, Philipa Dedeny sank onto the bed, emotionally wrung out. Through glassy eyes she gazed at the beaming Schubert, who plied Justin Pope with urgent questions.

"He wants to know who you are, where you came from, and how long you're going to stay," Pope said finally.

"And what did you tell him?" she murmured, her mind still reeling from the music.

"I told him you are a writer for *Time* magazine, which means as little to him as it does to me; that you came from New York City, which means even less; and that you intend to stay more or less permanently, which means a great deal."

Philipa shook her head, which suddenly seemed to be filled with cobwebs. When it cleared a little, she sat up. "How did you know I'm from *Time*? How did you know my name?"

Pope gave a self-deprecating shrug. "My nanny done

told me. You know Angelica Hunter, I believe. You'd *better* know her, having bugged our apartment for the past week and overheard every conversation we had, in and out of bed. Too bad you couldn't have heard the conversation we had when *you* were moving in, when the infinity mikes we'd installed in the phones in the apartment below us betrayed your eavesdropping plans. Angelica thinks of things like that. Couldn't live without her, as she frequently reminds me."

"You set me up with that call to Swissair!"

Pope nodded.

"You knew I'd follow you."

Pope grinned. "Well, I *hoped* you'd follow me. Once we heard that you had suspicions that I didn't write the music I've been presenting to the public as my own, we knew we'd have to do something about it. Sooner or later you'd have found evidence to confirm your suspicions, and the game would have been up. I'm not quite ready to call it a day, you see.

"I intend to leave you here in Franz Peter Schubert's warm and welcoming embrace, which will make him very happy, I assure you, and I get rid of you, which will make *me* very happy."

"And what will make *me* happy, or doesn't it matter?" Her eyes were bitter.

"Oh, yes, indeed. While you were doing your research on me, Angelica was doing some research on you. She discovered that you are a failed artist, sort of a female Justin Pope, but without the imagination to do something about it. You are in love with what you don't have, namely, genius. *Voilà!* I give you genius of the first order, one of the greatest of all time. If his fuzzy hair and chubby physique don't quite measure up to the standards of male beauty to which you aspire, well, you can't have everything.

"On the other hand, you'll have a great deal. Franz assures me he was quite the devil with the women—remember, he didn't contract lover's catarrh from a toilet seat—and the gleam in his eye every time he looks at you indicates that he'll give his all, however much that may be. And he'll compose some of the greatest music ever yet unwritten to please you. Who could ask for anything more?"

Philipa Dedeny knew better than to protest. However he had done it, Justin Pope—or Angelica Hunter, more probably—had obviously thought everything out. The best thing for her to do was play along, not act the outraged maiden, and bide her time. If Pope was convinced she would yield with minimum protest to whatever he had in mind, his guard would come down. By then she would have some plans of her own.

Meanwhile, the prospect of spending some time with the youthful Schubert was anything but unpleasing. Justin Pope had described him as fuzzy and chubby, but those were a man's superficial criteria. What mattered to her was the beauty within, and the music he wrote was proof that there was beauty within him to overflowing. She had read much about this man, and it was all favorable. He had a bubbly, fun-loving nature, was kind and generous to his friends, and enjoyed to the hilt the few pleasures that life had thrown his way. She always knew that she was saving herself for someone unique; now she realized that that man was Schubert. Fate had ordained it.

That settled, she got down to practicalities. "I don't have a thing to wear," she observed. "I hope you don't expect me to stay here without clothes, shoes, makeup—everything a woman must have. I simply won't do it."

"Make a list," Pope advised. "I'll bring everything back on my next trip."

"It would be a lot easier if you told me how to get to town."

"There *is* no town. Today is the tenth of November 3919. Some time ago a nuclear war destroyed all of mankind, as far as I can ascertain. The three of us are the only human beings on Earth. And when I go back to

1999, there will be only two of you. I hope you didn't think I'd bring you to a place and time where it would be possible for you to escape."

Fear gripped her. That Pope was using them was one thing; destroying them, condemning the two of them to solitary confinement in an uninhabited future was quite another. "You mean to leave us here, the two of us, *forever*?"

Pope had not really given it much thought. "No," he said, after giving it a little more, "I'm not cut out to be a warden. Sure, I'm using Franz here to build up a little stockpile of music. But once I have it, I'll be back to transport you to wherever and whenever you want. At the rate he writes music, it should only be a couple of months."

Schubert, who was vainly trying to follow the conversation, kept tugging at Pope's sleeve, asking him what they were saying. Pope told him that the woman, Philipa Dedeny, was one of his most devoted admirers and had importuned him to bring her to meet him and be his companion. The composer, hearing those reassuring words, took her hand, bent over, and kissed it tenderly. He looked at her with an expression of utter enchantment.

Philipa Dedeny felt her breathing quicken, a maidenly flush rising to her cheeks.

Justin Pope quietly left the room, and the fortieth century.

They did not notice.

Philipa Dedeny whistled while she worked. Dressed in jeans, with a shirt knotted around her waist, she swept out their bedroom with wild broom she had picked on a walk through the foothills. Then she prepared a lunch of canned and dehydrated food Pope had left on his last stop about a month before and longed for the snows to disappear so she could plant the vegetable and fruit seeds she had prevailed upon him to order from the Burpee catalog for spring 2000. But aside from fresh fruits and vegetables, she could not complain: Pope had brought them everything within reason they had asked for—even the solar cells and high-density storage batteries to replace the smelly, inefficient generator.

She was a contented woman. Contented and happy to be away from the noise and swirl of her office in the Time-Life Building. There was so much to do there with Franz that she scarcely ever gave a thought anymore to her life in New York twenty centuries earlier. When she thought about it at all, she wondered how she could have imagined that she was happy. *This* was happiness.

Her day was organized but unhurried. She got up late and had a leisurely cup of coffee with Franz, who had risen with the sun and had been busy composing in the next room until his morning break, when he awakened her with a kiss. She usually took a long walk in the hills with Ronnie at her heels until the sun was high, then prepared lunch. During that meal and later, while she worked on an oil portrait of him as he edited the music he had written that morning, they talked.

At first it had been mainly with signs, but not for long. Franz, thanks to his musical ear, was exceptionally adept at languages. Within a month he could make himself understood. Within two, he had mastered the basic English sentence and intonation patterns. By the end of the fourth month he had memorized all the American idioms she could recall, and by now his speech was fluent and almost without accent.

In the late afternoon they took a nap, together more often than not, and then parted again, each to work in his own area—their living quarters now comprised four comfortable rooms—Franz on his music, she practicing on the violin Pope had brought at her request, an instrument she had not touched since her college days. Dinner was leisurely, followed by reminiscences of their respective times and lands. Once in a while they would put on a disk of an old movie, but mainly they talked, or read, or walked in the green hills.

Being the last woman on Earth did not bother her at all. Since there were no wild animals or significant insect predators abroad, or robbers or rapists, she felt free to go anywhere any time the desire moved her. She could drink out of the rushing mountain freshets without fear of infection or pollution. Neither existed. Nor did disease. In the months she had been here, neither had suffered so much as a sniffle. As for stress, it was a word and concept that had disappeared from her consciousness. Here those ancient Swiss of the twentieth century had lived to be centenarians thanks to the tranquillity of the towering mountains and lush green valleys; that being the case, she and Franz should live to be a thousand.

Every month or so—she really did not keep track of time any longer—Justin Pope would suddenly appear in their midst, bringing their latest order. At first, she had eagerly awaited the latest copies of *Time*, the *Economist*, and a few other magazines as well as current popular literature. But as the months passed, she lost interest completely in the twentieth—now the twenty-first—century and turned to the Greek and Roman classics and works on philosophy and history.

Franz, by contrast, became an avid reader of books and magazines about the times she had left behind her, quizzed her incessantly on the habits and interests of the American people, developed an interest in American professional football, which he saw with increasing frequency on disk, and yearned to drive the car and fly the airplane Philipa had told him about. So many things to do! He wondered how she could be so content at having left so many fascinating things behind her.

On every trip, Pope brought some of those fascinating things which supplied Schubert with endless entertainment: kitchen gadgets, electronic instruments, computer games, a quartz watch—which Philipa surreptitiously threw in the river—beautifully hologrammed books of animals he could not quite believe had ever existed, a digital camera, running shoes, several cases of California wine, and a learned history of Vienna of the nineteenth century, in which he figured prominently and about which nearly everything was wrong. He took away only the digidisks of the music Schubert had composed during the interim, with each and every change and emendation recorded.

"Don't you ever miss your old life?" Schubert asked her one night for the hundredth time.

"Certainly not."

"But so many exciting things were happening—wars, and medical advances, and silly political events like the presidential conventions, and the Miss America contest, and Russia and America shaking hands with each other, and—"

"Fists, not hands. At, not with."

"Yes, shaking fists at," Schubert said, impressing the expression on his memory. "And here all you have is me and a sufficiency of boredom."

"Don't say that," she replied sharply. "I'm *not* bored. I'm happy."

"In spite of not having an office to go to, friends to talk with, shows to attend, trips to make."

"Hah!" she said. "The trips I made were mostly from Queens to Manhattan. You don't know what it's like having elbows thrust in your ribs and strangers' hands clutching at your backside and your feet trampled every day riding in to work and home again on the subway. It's awful."

"It sounds very *gemütlich*."

"No, it's awful." She walked out of the room to put on water for coffee. Over her shoulder she said, "You should try it sometime."

Franz Peter Schubert watched her go. "I intend to," he whispered.

9. *FUGIT*
16 MAY 2000

"POPE," SAID PRESIDENT HORATIO FRANCIS TURNBULL, his silver hair scintillating in the flash of a hundred bulbs as the three most famous men in the world posed for the cameras of the assembled press corps, "it is my pleasure and honor to present to you the *American* Pope."

The pontiff laughed dutifully and shook the hand of Justin Pope warmly. "The pleasure and honor are mine, Mr. President," Pope Hadrian VIII replied in an English faintly tinged with his native Portuguese but made fluent from seven years as a parish priest in New Bedford, Massachusetts, and three years at Catholic University in Washington. His elevation to the Papacy had been due to a deadlock in the College of Cardinals between the Italians and the French. Because of his pro-American sympathies, the cardinals from the United States, with the largest number of faithful in the Catholic world, had proposed him as a compromise candidate; his saintly demeanor, plus a little discreet pressure from the White House, had done the rest. The gesture, Turnbull shrewdly foresaw, would help sew up the Catholic vote in the presidential elections of 2000.

Since his investiture in 1997, Pope Hadrian VIII had never had the opportunity to visit what he considered a second home. But now, on the eve of the presidential campaign, he saw a means of paying his debt to Turnbull, delivering a little papal bull on the subject of homosexual priests, and, above all, attending the premiere of Justin Pope's Mass in F Minor, which Turnbull had prevailed upon Pope to compose and dedicate to His Holiness for the occasion. Such political stratagems came as naturally to Horatio Francis Turnbull as writing masterpieces came to Justin Pope.

Justin Pope, a non-Catholic, took a step toward His Holiness, who waited with outstretched hand. Instead of shaking it as expected, he went down on one knee, took the hand in his, and kissed the papal ring. By that act, he won the hearts of the 67 million American Catholics, including the few who until that meeting was televised internationally had never heard of Justin Pope.

Those few surely lived beyond the reach of electric power and the daily press, for in six short months Justin Pope had become the most famous man in America except for President Turnbull. In other countries, people who did not know Turnbull from a Brahma bull recognized the picture of the handsome, self-effacing American musical genius on sight. He was a throwback to the days of Paganini and Lizst, when women threw flowers—when they did not throw themselves—at the man whose works stirred in them the most elemental forms of human passion. His modesty and his obvious manliness had won him equal acclaim among male listeners. And his music, so melodic, so fresh, so inventive and original, swept away a generation of thumping, dismal, repetitious rock music and rekindled in the young the realization that music was made to be beautiful.

That night in the White House passed as a gossamer, silken dream to Justin Pope. He was courted by the great and would-be great at cocktails, was toasted by the Holy Father following a state dinner, and conversed with savants and artists, who clung to his every word as the symphony orchestra and choir assembled in the new West Wing auditorium for the performance of his latest work. Finally the audience fell silent as President Turnbull stood to present him.

"Your Holiness, distinguished envoys, ladies and gentlemen," said the President, "the birth of a masterwork is a rare and awesome occasion. Imagine what it was like to have been Pope Julius II as he gazed at the finished ceiling of the Sistine Chapel, or Cosima Wagner as she descended the stairs of her home on her birthday to hear the Siegfried Idyll, or Michelangelo himself as he lay down mallet and chisel to regard the just-completed *Pietà.*" President Turnbull glanced around his audience. Nobody had cracked a smile. His speech writer was right: Most of his guests had no more idea than he what he was talking about, but they were sure eating it up.

"Well, tonight you can experience the thrill of a Pope Julius, a Cosima Wagner, a Michelangelo, as you hear, for the first time ever performed, Justin Pope's magnificent Mass in F Minor, dedicated to His Holiness Pope Hadrian VIII. How can I say magnificent, you'll ask, if it's never been heard before? I so characterize it, distinguished guests, because Justin Pope is the greatest composer America has ever produced, a fountainhead of melody, a wine-dark sea of musical fantasy, an ocean of soul-stirring harmony. When it comes to music, Pope springs eternal."

Justin Pope rose, bowed to His Holiness, to the President and first lady, to the wildly applauding seven hundred-odd guests who packed the small auditorium, and strode to the stage, where a ninety-piece orchestra and a chorus of 140 waited. He closed the open score on the podium, glanced down at the concertmaster, and raised his baton.

Forty-eight minutes later he lowered it. For a few seconds, as the last strains of the mournful but hauntingly beautiful coda died away, there was the silence of the tomb. Then the crowd surged to its feet, roaring its acclaim. The pontiff himself walked to the stage, took Pope in his arms, and kissed both his cheeks. When the applause finally subsided, the Pope extended his left hand. A rotund monsignor hurried forward and handed him an open velvet box. The Holy Father took out the Grand Cross of the Most Holy Order of St. Paul and draped its mauve watered-silk ribbon around Pope's neck. Not to be outdone, President Turnbull added the Medal of Freedom to the cross Pope already bore.

Pope gazed out over the sea of adoring faces and smiled sadly. Well, this is what you wanted, Justin Pope, he said to himself, and it only took six months to get it. Now, where do you go from here?

Angelica Hunter asked him the same question the next day, when he returned to his penthouse apartment overlooking San Francisco Bay.

"I wish I could tell you, Angie," Pope said, scratching an unshaven jaw. "Where *do* you go when you've reached the top? Do you just stay there until the public gets sick of your face, or come down out of the clouds and try to live like other people?"

"You, living like other people?" She snickered. "You couldn't do it if you tried. And don't give me that bored celebrity bit, either. You love it—every single minute of it."

"Sure I do. At least I have up to now. But—"

"I know—where do you go from here? For a start, why don't you try putting down that damned cup of coffee and crawling into bed? And close that window—I'm cold."

Pope laughed mirthlessly. "*You* cold? Is that a fact?" It annoyed him to hear her talk that way. Why the hell, at this late date, did she still have to pretend? It had been clear from the first day he had met her that she was interested in him only for the money she could get out of him. And just when he was convinced of this obvious truth, she had to go and say or do something that awakened disquieting speculations.

The week after she had moved in, for instance, they had been sitting in the swing in the penthouse garden, talking about the future and looking out over the bay. As dusk came upon them, they grew silent, each with his own thoughts. A chill invaded the night air, she shivered, and he took off his jacket and draped it across her bare shoulders. His arm lingered a moment longer than he meant it to, and the next thing he remembered was that they were on the cold balcony tiles, making love as he had never imagined it.

The next day she had been all business, as though he had become something between acquaintance and stranger. She never alluded to the incident, and it was not repeated until, again almost by accident, three weeks later it happened that he stopped by her bedroom in mid-afternoon to ask about that night's concert. The door was ajar, and he walked right in. She was sitting at her dressing table, brushing her long black hair. She was bare to the waist. He saw her looking at him, her eyes deep in shadow gazing back at him in the mirror, her lips parted, her brush never missing a slow, sensuous stroke.

He drew up short, a word of apology stillborn on his lips. Then, impelled by a force he felt no desire to resist, he floated into the room. He stopped directly behind her, looking down at her in the mirror. His hands sought her hair, her shoulders, her breasts. She did not stir. Not then . . .

And that had been the way of things ever since. Never any words. Only when the meeting was unexpected did she respond. On all other occasions her only response was the sharp elbow or sharper rebuff. He had the usual male desires—perhaps more than usual, having suppressed them so long as he studied and stole round the clock to achieve musical fame while he was still young enough to enjoy it. Yet whenever he deliberately sought to express those desires, she buttoned up, as cold as a clam.

She was absent from the house on business—his business—as much as she was at home. She was gone for as much as a week at a time, flying to European capitals, to New York, to Tokyo, to Toronto, arranging for recitals or appearances as guest conductor with the world's leading symphony orchestras playing his works—or, rather, Schubert's, although of course she had no inkling of *that*. He supposed, from the fleeting physical contacts they had enjoyed, that she fulfilled the needs of her passionate nature with other men. Hell, he *knew* she did. There was simply no other explanation for their on-again, off-again relationship. He was nothing but a pinch hitter when the first string was not available. And the realization made him sick with frustration and jealousy, for although he never quite admitted it even to himself, he was hopelessly in love with Angelica Hunter.

Not that he would ever say so, to be sure. She had made it very clear that she had a hold on Justin Pope and intended to squeeze him for all he was worth. It was true that she occasionally did make provocative suggestions, such as that oblique invitation to crawl into bed with her. It had happened before, and as soon as he had crawled in, she would crawl out, her gentle laughter trailing behind her like a wisp of smoke. If it were not for her maddening knack for making him mistake her intentions every single time, he would have been a happy man.

He had every reason to be. He enjoyed the plaudits of the world. He had played in recital and published and recorded no fewer than eighteen major pieces in the months since Franz Peter Schubert had become his complaisant guest, including one violin and three piano sonatas, a sextet, an opera in one act, a symphony, a piano concerto, and the two concluding movements of the Eighth Symphony, which Pope dedicated "to that brilliant master, Franz Peter Schubert, in the spirit of his monumental Unfinished Symphony." His photograph adorned magazine covers around the world. Angelica Hunter had been forced to engage the services of full-time security men to protect him from his adoring public. Whenever either of them left the building, they had to engage in elaborate subterfuge to avoid being followed by newsmen eager to interview them. It was all very heady, but after six months the novelty had worn thin. After all, when you had been entertained and fulsomely praised by heads of state, groveling music publishers, and Nobel laureates and battled crowds of ecstatic young women dying to surrender their virtue, or a reasonable facsimile thereof, in return for your caresses, what more was there to wish for?

For Angelica Hunter's love, he guessed. He could think of nothing else he wanted now that he possessed everything he had always yearned for. But he resolutely put that thought out of his mind. Her love was one thing he was not going to get. He knew that when she had wrung him dry, that would be the last he would see of Angelica Hunter.

Meanwhile, the routine of the rich and famous engaged his energies. Everyone wondered where the energy came from. He had not had a single day off since the *Time* crew had first come to camp at his doorstep. Three concert or guest appearances or recording sessions a week were his norm; the other four days, informed speculation went, were spent in composition, though to produce as much fine work as he did argued that the man never slept. Unquestionably, Justin Pope was a prodigy such as had not graced the musical world since Mozart, who in a burst of creation had written three great symphonies in the six twilight weeks of his life.

Even more remarkable than Pope's titanic output was its extraordinarily high quality. The musical river within the composer seemed to grow wider and deeper with every new composition. It was as if he had compressed an entire musical career spanning decades into a few short months.

What only Pope himself knew was that those compositions reflected nearly two centuries of musical development, as he had promised they would the night he had premiered the Brig Variations, thanks to the careful rationing of new works to Franz Schubert on his weekly trips forward through time to the Brig of the future. His first trip, to 10 November 3919—25 November 1999 San Francisco time—had been followed by a visit on 16 December 3386—1 December 1999. The third came on 29 January 3387, which was only a week later San Francisco time—8 December 1999. To Schubert his visits were a month apart, during which time he had composed a formidable stack of music. But thanks to the Flier, they were seldom more than a week apart. During his brief visit to Brig, he would replenish the fresh-food supply and bring in a stack of new digidisks and whatever else Franz and Philipa had ordered. But more important to both Franz and Pope were the volumes of bound music and compact discs of Schubert's heirs to musical genius.

Pope had promised to recapitulate his musical heritage since the beginning of the nineteenth century and gradually lead his listening public into an appreciation of works like the *Malibu* Symphony, which were but an aesthetic extension to all that went before. New forms, new rhythms, new instrumentation were called for. They were all found in the music Pope brought each trip.

The first batch of printed music and discs contained major works by composers who were roughly Schubert's contemporaries. Of the music Pope brought, Franz had heard some but far from all. Masterpieces by Mendelssohn, Chopin, Rossini, and the youthful Schumann lent him inspiration when his own wellspring of melody went temporarily dry and sent him off on new tangents of creation. Several trips later, Pope brought him a bonanza from the next generation—compositions by Offenbach, Borodin, Bizet, Paganini, Liszt, and, above all, Berlioz and Wagner. If Schubert was overwhelmed by this flood of great music, he was drowned by the next batch, which included works by Grieg, Franck, Saint-Saëns, Dvořák, Brahms, Tchaikovsky, and Verdi. And on the most recent trip, bringing him up to current tastes, he had brought the gifts of Ravel, de Falla, Debussy, Puccini, and Rachmaninoff.

From each of those renowned composers Schubert borrowed elements of harmony, style, phrasing, and instrumentation, as writers of music have done ever since the first notes were committed to paper. He learned that the size of the orchestra had more than doubled since his day, and he wrote works correspondingly monumental. He exulted in the pyrotechnical complexities of Berlioz and Wagner, the rich orchestrations of Brahms and Rachmaninoff, the lyricism of Dvořák and Mendelssohn, the tonal adventurism of Ravel and Debussy, and fused them into a style all his own. The works he heard with such wonder and delight stoked the furnace of his invention, and the more he heard, the more fiercely burned the fires of creation.

But two years of unremitting effort had left him exhausted. Philipa saw that he was losing weight, slept fitfully, and became distant and preoccupied where he had been her warm, cheerful, and loving companion. He desperately needed a vacation from that life of constant labor, but where did people go for a vacation when there were only two of them left in the world?

Justin Pope had the same problem. Six months of celebrity honors, riches, and the frustration of trying to solve the insoluble problem of Angelica Hunter had just about burned him out.

"We've got to get away someplace for a while," he said one day in early May of the first year of the third millennium. "My fingers are beginning to feel like sticks of wood from practicing for and playing so many concerts, and if I sit any longer on a piano stool, I might as well have it grafted on."

"Suits me," Angelica said. "Where do you suggest?"

"To graft the piano stool, or go on vacation?"

"How about Alaska?"

"Where in Alaska?"

"Does it matter? We have enough money in our accounts to buy a couple hundred square miles, if you want to be alone. For all I know, we can afford the whole state."

"Doing pretty well, are we?"

Angelica Hunter laughed gently. "If I told you how

much we have salted away in banks around the country, you'd probably want to ship it all to Switzerland.''

Justin Pope looked at her sharply. ''What do you mean by that?''

She shrugged. ''That you're going to have to fork over a huge chunk to Uncle come tax time unless we can find some way to put it in a numbered account in Switzerland. What else would I mean?''

''Oh, nothing. I was just thinking that—''

The ring of the telephone from the security crew in the lobby interrupted him.

Angelica Hunter picked up the phone. ''Who? Never heard of him . . . Well, all right. Send him up.'' She hung up the phone and looked at Pope. ''That was the police. They want to talk to you. Have you been speeding again?''

Pope shook his head. ''Not guilty.''

''You'd better not be. Trouble is something we can do without.''

The doorbell rang. Angelica opened the door to admit a tall, neatly dressed man with mournful, basset-hound eyes.

''My name's Rivers, ma'am,'' he said. ''Detective Lieutenant Rivers.''

''Please come in, Lieutenant—'' Angelica Hunter smiled. ''—and tell me how I can help you.''

''You can't, Miss—ah—''

''Hunter.''

''You can't, Miss Hunter. It's Dr. Pope I want a word with.''

''As many as you like,'' Pope said hospitably, advancing from across the room with outstretched hand.

Rivers examined the world-famous composer. Pope had put on a little weight since he had last interviewed him a year ago about the disappearance of Dr. Thaddeus Klemper. Most of the weight was on his jawline. No doubt about it, success had been good to the young genius. The apartment was luxurious in a quiet, tasteful way. Pope was dressed in cashmere slacks and a shirt open at the collar with a silk foulard knotted loosely around his neck, his bare feet shod in beautifully worked doeskin sandals. And the woman—well, Rivers had seen a lot of them but few who were in Miss Angelica Hunter's league. She was a knockout. He had pulled her file, of course, but it was without blemish. She had never had any known contact with either Dr. Klemper or Philipa Dedeny. But Justin Pope had—with them both . . .

Rivers cleared his throat and chuckled. "I'm sorry, Dr. Pope, but I'm afraid I'm going to have to spring one of the oldest police clichés in history on you."

"Spring away."

"Right. Where were you on the night of 22 November 1999?"

Pope looked blank. He did not know. He did not have the foggiest idea. He said so.

"Let me refresh you. You drove your van to San Francisco International, boarded a Swissair plane for Geneva, and arrived there eleven hours later."

Justin Pope snapped his fingers. "Say—I believe you're right, at that. I *did* make such a trip—make them frequently, in fact. The clean mountain air clears my mind. But I never remember dates. That's what I employ Miss Hunter for."

"Sure . . . Did you ever meet a lady by the name of Philipa Dedeny? Worked as chief of the arts section of *Time* magazine?"

Pope massaged his chin. He shook his head. "I can't be sure. I meet a lot of the press, you know."

Lieutenant Rivers nodded. "Funny thing. She rented the apartment just below yours in the middle of last November, moved in with a bunch of reporters, wired up your apartment in hopes of getting material for a cover story—"

Angelica Hunter and Pope looked at each other, feigned shock turning to feigned outrage.

It was pretty well done, Rivers thought, but he had

been conned by professionals. "Yeah, well—to make a long story short, she disappeared abruptly the same night you went to Geneva. We *do* know she took a flight to New York, picked up the passport her secretary had waiting for her at the airport, and flew on directly to Geneva. After that, we've lost track of her."

"That's an interesting coincidence, all right."

"Not the only one. We've spent a lot of months, we and Interpol, piecing together what happened next." He paused, considering just how he would phrase the accusation so that, no matter how much clout Pope had at city hall—and a civic monument like him would have plenty—he could not get Rivers fired for harassment.

Pope nodded encouragement.

"It seems that she rented a car and disappeared. Of course, it wasn't hard to trace her to Geneva, to the rental car, and finally to Brig, where the car was abandoned. It was the next step which took time. We had to find somebody who had seen her after she parked the car. It wasn't until yesterday, after months of flashing her picture around every canton in Switzerland, that Interpol finally came up with a lead."

"Yes?" Pope felt the foulard tightening around his neck.

"Yes, sir. We found a little old village lady who recognized her. She'd been visiting her son in Brig. She recognized Miss Dedeny. You know how old village women are—they take note of everything so they'll have something to gossip about with their neighbors. She saw Miss Dedeny—she was certain it was Miss Dedeny she saw—climb out of her car and into a closed gray van which had pulled into the parking slot next to hers just half a minute before. She was the last person known to have seen Philipa Dedeny alive." He looked at Pope speculatively.

Pope frowned. "It sounds as if you're trying to tell me something, Lieutenant. I hope you aren't suggesting you found her body or something grisly like that?"

"You have a gray van, do you not, Mr. Pope?"

"Actually, I do."

"It would be a great service to us if you could bring it down to headquarters where our forensic crew can have a look at it."

"Are you accusing me of *murdering* Miss Dedeny?" Pope's indignation was real.

"No, no. We just want to clear up this detail."

Pope shrugged. "I guess I can do it, if you insist."

Angelica Hunter looked hard at Pope. "Better put on socks and shoes if you're going out."

Pope nodded and headed for his bedroom. Angelica Hunter excused herself and followed.

Closing the bedroom door behind her, she hissed at Pope: "You told me you weren't going to hurt that girl! You said you'd pay her off, keep her from snooping around. You said you promised her $500,000 to get lost for a year."

"Calm down, Angie," Pope said wearily. "It's all a mistake. I didn't touch a hair on that girl's head."

"Then what *did* you do with her?"

"It's a long story." He tied his shoes and stood up. "I'll tell you when I get back."

Her face was taut with strain. "Hurry back, will you? You know I'd die if anything happened to you."

"To me—or to my bank account?"

She looked at him incredulously. She slapped him, putting her shoulder behind it.

He shook his head free of cobwebs, then enveloped her fiercely in his arms and mashed her face flat with a kiss that went on longer than strictly necessary to get his point across. "I don't know how long this is going to take," he said, coming up for air, "but when I come back, I'll have two things to tell you."

"Yes?" Her heartbeat was strong, but her voice was faint.

"First, that I love you."

"I—I—"

"Second, right after I tell you I love you, we're going out and get married."

"*Now* you tell me."

"I don't know the way to headquarters, Lieutenant," Pope said in the lobby of the apartment house.

"That's all right, Mr. Pope. You can follow me. I'll wait for you at the garage entrance."

Five minutes later the steel door to the garage opened and the gray van nosed out into the street and took its place behind the black-and-white. Rivers drove slowly, keeping Pope in the mirror. He was not afraid he would try to get away, of course, but it would not do to allow an important person like that to go astray and have the commissioner come down on Rivers's head. He turned a corner. The gray van followed. When Rivers came to the next intersection, he looked back.

The van had vanished into thin air.

II
Impromptu

10. ABOUT FACE
1 MARCH 3919

THEY WERE BOTH ASLEEP WHEN JUSTIN POPE TRUDGED wearily into the cavern at the base of the Jungfrau, 1,919 years after he had hurriedly departed from San Francisco, although it seemed to him like yesterday. It had been a very busy time however one counted it.

He had been continuously on the move for most of the preceding twenty-four hours. When Rivers had turned that last corner on his way to police headquarters, Pope had flipped the time-transition units dial two notches back, to 16 May 1998, and hit the "Run" button. A tenth of a second later, to his horror, he found himself on a collision course with a young woman jaywalking not forty feet dead ahead down the two-lane street. It took but a split second for him to realize that there was no time to brake. Furthermore, if he swerved to the right, he would crash into the line of parked cars on the right, or if to the left, into the line of approaching traffic. Without conscious thought, he flipped the time-transition dial hard to the left, simultaneously hitting the "Run" button. He abruptly disappeared before the eyes of the terrified girl, who was frozen to the spot, and reappeared in the middle of a street brawl that, with his appearance, suddenly turned nasty.

As best he could reconstruct events later, he had materialized in the Tenderloin area. From the clothing the men wore, the ramshackle wooden buildings, and the sidewalks of warped planking, he judged he was back in the late 1860s. From the insults and curses that ricocheted from the walls of the unpainted frame houses on either side of the dust-clouded street, he concluded he had dropped smack in the middle of a dispute between a crowd of demobilized soldiers from the north and the south. His unexpected incarnation in their midst must have startled them as much as it did him, for before he could put the van in gear and depart in haste, bullets began to sing. One grazed his neck as he headed for the hills, and the van suffered half a dozen holes in the body, fortunately none of which even dented the thick steel housing of the time machine. Many a man who saw the strange, roaring wheeled vehicle, which moved faster than the fastest horse, became a teetotaler that day.

Once out of town and out of sight, he thought more carefully about which year he would next honor with his presence as he stanched the flow of blood from his neck with his handkerchief. The safest, he concluded, would be about 1997, the year he had bought the van. The near future—any time after the year 2000—would be perilous, for the police would still be looking for him. The past was filled with Indians, Civil War veterans with hair-trigger tempers, and other pugnacious types. Besides, he would need money and anonymity, and both had been available in Berkeley when he was working on the time machine.

Accordingly, he returned to the summer of 1997, withdrew $10,000 from the account that had been set up with his sale of Dr. Klemper's gold, went downtown to the passport office, squinted into the retinagram hood, then waited nervously the thirty seconds it took the machine to query the National Registry in Washington, D.C., and print the passport.

He drove toward the airport. The shuttle to Geneva was, mercifully, only a third full, and when it took off, his van was aboard in the cargo hold with half a dozen other vehicles. He stretched out on four empty seats and promptly went to sleep.

Rigor mortis had set in when he finally awakened, still emotionally exhausted, over France. He walked up and down the aisle a couple of times to loosen his muscles, did some deep-knee bends, drank half a gallon of water, and began to feel human again. In the bathroom he changed the dressing he had put over the wound back in California, shaved, and began to look more like he felt.

The road to Brig was familiar now, but night had fallen some hours before he arrived. He decided not to awaken Company F, as he fondly called the happy pair, Franz and Philipa, and instead wrapped himself in a blanket and lay down on the concrete floor to sleep, perhaps to dream . . .

It felt like rigor mortis had set in again when at last he awakened. He could not move his limbs. It felt as though his arms and legs were encased in concrete. He opened his eyes.

Silhouetted against the soft fluorescent ceiling light was Franz Peter Schubert, looking down at him contemplatively.

"Hi, there, Franz," Justin said sleepily. "God, what a night."

Schubert did not reply.

Justin Pope tried to shake some life into his arms and legs. They would not move. He struggled to sit up. When he at last succeeded, he saw that he was tied with clothesline, hand and foot. "Hey! What the hell's going on?"

"*We're* going on," Schubert replied. "To somewhere else. To some other time. We haven't decided where or when just yet."

"Come on, Franz," Pope said, trying to keep the desperation out of his voice. "You *know* you love it here—no distractions, the attentions of a woman who loves you, time to devote to your music, fresh air, quiet, none of the nasty aspects of life that make civilization such a pain in the ass."

"There must be *something* in it, for you want to keep going back."

"Habit, that's all," Pope said.

"We're going to help you break it."

Pope struggled, thrashing about on the concrete floor. "Come on, Franz! Quit horsing around."

Franz Peter Schubert, dressed in cords, plaid wool shirt, windbreaker, and porkpie hat, called over his shoulder: "Are you ready, Phil?"

Philipa Dedeny came into the room. She had shed the jeans and knotted shirt she customarily wore when Pope popped into their midst and was dressed in the same neat suit she had been wearing when she had followed him into Switzerland six months—twentieth-century time, two years her time—earlier. Unlike Schubert, who was bubbling with good humor, her face was clouded with concern. Justin Pope hoped it was for him.

"Philipa, how about trying to talk some sense into Franz. He doesn't know what he's getting into."

"I've tried. Believe me, Justin, I've tried. But it's the great unknown that's attracting him—the crowds, the applause, the meeting with heads of state, the life of affluence. He's never had any of these things. I guess you can't blame him for wanting to sample the life of the idolized genius."

"He won't get away with it," Pope warned. "All the music that I've taken away from here has my name on it—Justin Pope."

"Oh," Philipa Dedeny said airily, "that's the least of our problems: there's a lot more where that came from. She was silent for a long moment. "Still, what you've said *is* something to think about."

"You're damned right. Now, how about untying me?"

She shook her head. "Sorry. But if you work at it for an hour or two, you'll be able to get loose. Or, after we leave, you can inch your way to the kitchen, get the knife I've left on the floor there, and cut the ropes."

"You're not going to get away with this," Pope warned savagely. "You don't know how to operate the *Fugit*. And when I get loose, I'll—"

"You'll be able to sample all the comforts of home you've provided us with over the past two years. And don't worry, from time to time we'll come back to deposit some little goodies within easy walking distance of the cavern entrance. It'll give you something to do, going out each day to see if we've left something for you."

"Like I said," Pope growled, struggling with his bonds, "you won't be able to budge the Flier."

Philipa Dedeny laughed. "You're forgetting that I made a study of all the available information on Justin Pope before I made my trip to San Francisco. My researchers talked with your teachers, all the way back to grade school, just for one example."

"So?"

"So they discovered that although you showed musical aptitude, you wouldn't know a crescent wrench from a peasant wench. Mechanical aptitude is a talent one is born with. You weren't. Also, your knowledge of physics is what you learned watching television commercials for bran flakes. That means you didn't put the *Fugit* together."

"The hell I didn't," Pope said indignantly.

"Well, maybe you did. But you certainly didn't design it. And whoever did made it simple enough for a science illiterate like you to manipulate. If you can run it, so can I."

Pope licked his lips. As fast as he thought of an argument, he discarded it. He simply did not have time to come up with one that would convince them to abandon their plan; they had obviously discussed every alternative he could think of on the spur of the moment. "All right. How long do you intend to leave me here?"

Philipa Dedeny shook her beautiful head. "I don't know. I suspect probably about as long as you intended to leave *us* here." She bent over and tugged at the ropes, making sure they were still securely tied. She spotted the bandage on his neck. "What's that?"

"It's a long story," Pope said disgustedly.

"Well, your long story is still bleeding. Roll over on your side and I'll change the dressing."

"Don't bother. I won't bleed to death."

"That's not what I was thinking of." She left the room and returned a minute later with a first-aid kit. She peeled off the bloody dressing, dropped it into a plastic bag, and expertly put a clean gauze sponge on the wound.

"Ready, Franz?" she asked the composer, who had been standing to one side impatiently.

"Ready. See you around, stranger," he said to Pope with a smile.

Pope made one last attempt to make them see reason. "Remember me, Franz? I'm the guy who rescued you on your deathbed. I'm the guy who nursed you to health, provided you with every possible material comfort, brought you the woman who loves you."

Schubert looked at him sadly and nodded. "I won't forget."

And then they were gone.

Operating the *Fugit* was even easier than Philipa Dedeny had imagined. Within fifteen minutes of their leaving Justin Pope, they left the fortieth century A.D., too, winging back through time to the present she had left two years before, now only six months later, twentieth-century time.

As she drove slowly down the winding road to Brig, passing grazing cows with huge brass bells suspended from their necks, youngsters on bicycles, peasants trudging along the side of the paved road, cars whizzing past at what seemed to Schubert a phenomenal speed, she regarded him with amusement. "What do you think of it all, Franz?"

"It's beautiful, breathtaking! Look at this splendid road. As smooth as water. What is this black material covering it?"

"Asphalt."

Schubert frowned. "What is asphalt, pray tell?"

"Well, it's the heavier fraction of crude oil, as I recall my chemistry."

"And crude oil?"

"It comes out of the ground. Look," she said hurriedly, "there's a lot you'll have to take on faith. I'll explain it as best I can as we go along, but for God's sake don't ask questions like that when we're with anybody, or they'll lock you up as a madman."

"Very well. And since we're alone, where is that man going in such a hurry? And why isn't he dressed? Can't he afford clothing? I thought you told me everyone in the twentieth century in this country was well clothed. If that's—"

"He's a jogger," Philipa explained. "And he isn't going anywhere. He has clothing back home—probably whole closets full."

"Then why is he half-naked? Doesn't he have any sense of propriety?"

Philipa sighed. It was going to be a hard few weeks before Franz Peter Schubert lost his feelings of wonder at the gadgetry and conventions of civilization. "Listen, Franz," she said. "We'll be in Brig soon. Please don't stare at anybody or anything. Just follow my example, and everything will be all right."

"Very well. I'll follow your lead, of course. Where are we going first?"

"To the Brig public library."

Half an hour later a policeman directing traffic pointed it out to them. She parked the van in front of it, made sure both doors were locked, and went in, followed by Schubert, whose head seemed to be mounted on a swivel. "What are we doing here?" he whispered.

"You'll see."

She asked the reference librarian for *Time* magazine for the past ten years and was handed a compact disc and directed to the viewing room. Within ten minutes she found the article in the special section she had dimly recalled from an issue two or three years earlier. "This is what I was looking for," she whispered.

Schubert read the article without comprehension. He recognized most of the words, but some he had never seen before. He shrugged his puzzlement.

For an answer, Philipa Dedeny took from her handbag the plastic bag that contained the bloody bandage from Justin Pope's neck and held it up.

"You're out of your mind," an unbelieving Franz Peter Schubert said.

11. INCIDENT AT ARLES
18 MAY 2000

"IT'S A BEAUTIFUL IDEA, PHIL," SCHUBERT CONCEDED as he climbed between the sheets in their suite at Brig's most elegant hostelry, the Hotel Shireen Khairallah. "But not, I think, very practical. For one thing, there's the question of money."

"Money is no problem at all with the *Fugit* in our possession," Philipa assured him. "I've looked through the van and found that Justin has anticipated rainy days: he hid about $100,000 in golden eagles under the floorboards."

"Is that a lot of money?"

"Yes, but not nearly enough."

"Well, then?"

"Be patient, my darling Franz," Philipa said. "All things come to those who wait."

Schubert looked down at her. Her head was in the crook of his arm, her lithe body pressed tightly against his. "And I take it you're my lady-in-waiting?"

Philipa laughed throatily.

They spent five days at the Shireen Khairallah, giving Schubert an opportunity to become acclimated to the twentieth century. So far, she had not dared to let him out of her sight for fear that some anachronism of behavior would arouse police attention and questions she did not want to answer. But aside from his archaic German, which the good people of Brig assumed was an obscure Austrian dialect, he was soon managing quite well. He had learned to order a meal at a restaurant, shop in a supermarket, board a trolley, cope with the city's traffic, and identify Europe's main Cup contenders. Now, Philipa decided, it was time to go.

With new bags packed with newly purchased clothes, they set out one fine spring morning for Geneva, where they paused for a week to give Schubert the flavor of a truly cosmopolitan city. Philipa was not in a hurry. Time was her slave, ready to do her bidding. Besides, Schubert was a child with a new toy—the twentieth century—and it would have been a shame to deprive him of his exuberant enjoyment of it. He liked everything he saw: the crowds, the movie theaters, the concert halls, the beautiful, immaculate parks, the boats on Lac Leman, the stylishly dressed women, the imposing banks and their top-hatted, tailcoated doormen, and especially the airplanes he saw flying overhead, which he swore he would never get closer to than he was right now.

While Schubert scribbled music in a notebook in a garage waiting room, Philipa watched as mechanics gave the van a complete checkup. She was not quite sure yet just where they would be traveling, but it was somewhere in the past century, and if the machine broke down there, there would be no mechanics to fix it.

On the twenty-first of May, a day when chilling rains made a departure from Geneva a pleasure, they headed southwest toward Lyons and from there due south down the lovely Rhone valley, alive with blooming flowers and the scents of summer approaching down the road. At Nîmes they spent the night, and in the morning they drove southeast toward Arles. There they registered at an inn that claimed to have been in business since 1667. They rented a garage for the summer and, once the *Fugit* was parked inside, fastened its door with a substantial padlock.

The next morning they rose late as usual, had their breakfast, and retired to the garage with a suitcase containing clothing befitting a prosperous gentleman and his lady of the 1880s, made to their order—for a costume ball, they had told the tailor—during their stay in Geneva. Climbing into the front seat, with Franz beside her, Philipa Dedeny set the dial for 15 August 1888 and hit the "Run" button.

It was a handsome young couple that emerged from the garage, she with her long full skirt and white parasol raised against the simmering Provençal sun and he with starched collar, tailored waistcoat, tight trousers, straw hat, and cane. They strolled through the lovely medieval town, toured the Roman amphitheater and the remains of the city walls, and had a bountiful lunch at an inn—shared with clouds of flies, a bottle of good local wine, and, for the gentleman, a cigar with his cognac.

The lady's noble bearing no less than her beauty and fine dress attracted the attentions of the local gallants, one of whom soon found an excuse to introduce himself. The gentleman and his lady were obviously recently arrived to the area, he said, and therefore it was incumbent upon him, as the prefect of the district, and in the tradition of French hospitality, to offer his services in any way possible.

"As a matter of fact," the lady said, "we are much taken by the beauty of your town, and especially the surrounding countryside, and wish to see more of it. Perhaps you can advise us on the most picturesque sites to visit."

"With all my heart," he said. "But may I know from where madame comes, so that I may suggest the sort of panoramas which may be unfamiliar to you."

"From America, monsieur."

"C'est impossible!" the Frenchman murmured. "I am at a loss for words to discover that an American, and a lady, even one so ravishing as madame, could learn to speak our language so exquisitely."

Of course he *wasn't* at a loss for words—no Frenchman ever was. With a snap of the fingers he summoned his carriage, gently installed the lady and her husband therein, and took them on a tour of the countryside surrounding Arles that lasted the better part of the afternoon. Not until nearly the hour for Franz's afternoon nap did Philipa Dedeny's restless eye finally alight upon the figure she had come to Arles to meet.

"That man in the straw hat in the orchard there," she said, pointing. "How strange he looks!"

The prefect made a gesture of dismissal. "A madman. A dauber. A poor fellow who fancies himself an artist."

"And he isn't?"

The prefect shook his head. "He comes here nearly every summer, and his painting becomes wilder year by year. He drinks, he argues, he fights, he sinks into sullen despair, he splashes paint onto canvas, but he never sells. He is missing the upper part of one ear, cut off, I understand, by his own hand in a fit of drunkenness." He shuddered and turned their attention to a more pleasing vista, a ruined mill along the river.

"I would speak with him," Philipa said.

"But madame!" the prefect protested.

"I would speak with him," Philipa repeated. "In America I have worked," she went on, speaking nothing but the truth, "with many people of disturbed minds, feeble intellects, and twisted personalities, and I find that my words have a way of calming them." She instructed the coachman to stop. The prefect again remonstrated, but the lady put him off with a ravishing smile, stepped down, and, gathering her skirt in her arms, walked across the open field to where the madman was painting with bold slashing strokes.

He looked up at her approach, then returned to his work. Only when she stood beside him did he see her face, and his jaw dropped as he contemplated her exquisite features, her deep, intelligent, passionate eyes.

"Madame!" he said reverently, hastily pulling off his straw hat.

"Monsieur, I observed the scene you were painting and thought to see how closely your painting corresponds to it."

The painter shook his head sadly. "I fear you will be disappointed, my lady. My painting is not of the reality of the scene—nothing can comprehend the beauty of the reality of nature, even at its ugliest, if you follow me. What I put on canvas are the colors and forms which, at another time and place, will evoke the emotions I feel, the essence of the scene I see now with my eyes. I do not paint so that each detail will be shown. To me the scene we see is but nature's newborn lamb, which I shear to weave its wool into cloth, to cover the naked limbs of my soul and warm my heart."

Philipa said nothing. She looked at the ravaged face, the disfigured ear, and the tortured soul, committing them to memory.

The painter nodded gravely, as though she had spoken some great truth. "The prefect told you I am mad, did he not?" he said, gesturing toward the carriage. "Well, he's right, of course. No one but a madman would throw his whole life away painting pictures the world reviles. Only a madman would spend his life trying to sell what no one will buy."

"You have not had success in selling your paintings?" said Philipa, who knew what his answer would be.

"Oh, I sold one—once," he said bitterly. "For the princely sum of four hundred francs. I'll sell another someday, perhaps."

"Sooner than you think," Philipa said softly. She opened her bag, and took out a little leather pouch, and handed it to him.

In a daze, he opened it. It was full of gold louis, more money than he had ever seen. He could not speak.

Philipa could. "If you paint me a picture which incorporates every feature of your special style, those elements which set you apart from every other artist painting today, the gold is yours. You may take as long as you wish. The subject matter you may decide for yourself. My only requirement is that the picture be at least 150 centimeters by 250 centimeters, that is, of a size which will dominate the drawing room of my home. Pray do not be afraid to use your color with exuberance, and do not try to please me. Please only yourself. Will you do it?''

The painter nodded dumbly and grasped the leather pouch tightly.

''Good. When it is finished, bring it to me at the inn—L'Aiglon.''

''With the greatest pleasure,'' the painter said fervently.

''You may ask for Madame Labelle.''

''A felicitous name, madame. Mine is—''

''Yes, I know, monsieur.'' She gave him her hand.

He kissed it and watched her walk gracefully back across the field toward the carriage. He clutched the leather bag to assure himself that he had not had too much to drink and was dreaming.

To establish her pedigree as one who could come by such a work honestly, Philipa Dedeny fabricated a fictitious family tree that extended all the way back to Rosario, Argentina, where her ''grandfather had been heir to a latifundium of some two hundred square miles, or was it three hundred?'' Anyway, the family, once wealthy, had fallen onto evil times, and was now reduced to a single thirty-three story office building in Buenos Aires, apartments in London, Paris, and Rome, a shipping line, an investment bank, and ''of course this pied-â-terre'' on Avenue Foch in Paris.

The ''pied-â-terre,'' a seventeen-room mansion, tastefully done in Regency style, on the most fashionable street in Paris, which upon closer inquiry would have been revealed as rented furnished by the month, completely convinced the man from Sotheby's that he was dealing with aristocracy fallen on evil days, relatively speaking. Certainly Madame Madeleine Mathiot de la Bec was a lady whose upper-class lineage could not be doubted, especially when she took him into the dimly lit salon to show him the work on the easel that straitened circumstances were forcing her to sell.

She drew back the cloth from the picture and switched on the ceiling lights.

The man from Sotheby's gasped. He knew instantly he had discovered a masterpiece, a masterpiece, furthermore, of whose existence the world of art was unaware. He could not believe his eyes.

He did not. Only after a minute examination of every detail using every test that the authenticator of an artwork has at his disposal, including x-ray and ultraviolet analysis, as well as analysis of paint, canvas, brush strokes, even the amount and composition of dirt that would accumulate on a picture of a given age, did he pronounce himself satisfied that he had come upon a historic find: a genuine Vincent van Gogh. A van Gogh, moreover, which was superior in size, quality, style, and inspiration to any extant.

"Madame de la Bec," he said, trying to still the tremor in his voice, "do you have any conception of what this painting is worth?"

"Some," Philipa replied, offhandedly. "In early 1987, van Gogh's *Sunflowers* sold in London for precisely $39,921,750. In November of that same year, another van Gogh, *Irises*, a painting twenty-eight by thirty-two inches, was auctioned off by your firm for $49 million. No van Gogh has appeared on the market since then. Given the ten years that has passed since that date, and inflation, and the Japanese craze for fine art, and the uniqueness of this particular work—plus the fact that I wouldn't consider selling for one penny less—I should guess that it should bring at auction, after Sotheby's commission, at least $100 million."

As a guess, it was very close to the mark. When bidding ceased at the auction the following month, it had been knocked down to the Japanese corporation Hitachi for $137 million.

12. BLOOD WILL TELL
22 DECEMBER 2111

PHIL DEDENY HAD GIVEN THE COMING-OUT PARTY OF Franz Peter Schubert considerable thought and finally decided that Switzerland was probably the logical place for the operation.

Switzerland was stable. After all, it had not been invaded except briefly for more than five hundred years, and its immunity from foreign incursion would probably endure as long as the mountains stood as a barrier to the rest of the world and as long as it kept every able-bodied man, armed to the teeth, in ready reserve, able to inflict more damage on the invader than its craggy countryside was worth. Then there was the nation's immense wealth, not only in the form of bank deposits and bullion but in technical, scientific, and medical expertise, in libraries, in the free exchange of mechanisms and machinery, instruments, and ideas. And Bank Pictet, the Geneva institution where she had deposited the $116 million from the sale of *Summer's Dream*, was very likely destined to be around to transact her business in Switzerland for the next two hundred years if her business took that long.

Just in case it did, she bought a twelve-room chalet in the mountains above Vevey, even though the estate agent warned her that according to Swiss law, as a foreigner she would not be allowed to occupy the chalet more than six months each calendar year.

"If it weren't for that law," he explained apologetically, "our lovely country would be inundated with ex-dictators, decaying middle-European aristocracy, and criminals fleeing from the laws of their own country—

although I think it is obvious that you and Monsieur de la Bec fit none of those categories," he said with a ponderous attempt at wit.

"Six months will be entirely adequate," she assured him, handing him a check for the entire sum in exchange for the keys to the chalet and the massive stone garage that seemed to madame even more important than the luxurious appointments of the house itself.

He hurried away to cash the check, for something was not quite right about the young couple. He had his doubts about them. It did not seem logical that if they *really* had the money in the bank to cover the check for the house and spacious grounds, they would ride about in a mud-spattered American van.

The de la Bec bank account proved more than ample for the price of the chalet and the organ, piano, computer, and high-priced day staff of cook, housekeeper, maid, and gardener the American couple installed.

The neighbors found the young Americans amiable and outgoing, though they confined their hospitality to daylight hours. They entertained several times a week at lavish lunches for people of all sorts they contrived to meet—artists and engineers, businessmen and adventurers, scientists and bankers—and Mme. de la Bec especially took delight in drawing them out about their views on politics, society, and the arts and the details of their professions. M. de la Bec, presiding at the head of the table with a somewhat abstracted air, contributed little but bonhomie and an attentive ear. Sometimes he asked questions about the most commonplace things and drew startled looks from the assemblage. Yet there was no doubt that the man, in his own way, was exceedingly intelligent. He was a veritable mine of information about music in all its forms, which he was happy to illustrate at the keyboard, and his happy disposition lowered the eyebrow occasionally raised by his gaucheries.

At night, after everyone had left the grounds, the chalet had a different aspect. Mme. de la Bec herself locked the gates in the high chain-link fence surrounding the estate after the staff had departed, then returned to activate the electronic security system. Once it was engaged, even the scampering of a mouse on the lower two floors would set off alarms, light the flood lamps on the grounds, and summon the police from Vevey.

From beyond the fence, anyone who cared to notice would have observed that as soon as the lights were extinguished on the lower two floors, they would be lit on the third. But other than that, no activity could be discerned.

And yet, beyond the heavy drapes drawn over the windows, there was activity aplenty. In his soundproofed studio, Franz read manuscripts of other composers, wrote ever more ambitious compositions of his own, and occasionally relieved the strain of intense concentration by watching a television show or digidisk until the tedium of it all drove him relentlessly back to the keyboard, there to remain sometimes until dawn glittered off the lake at the bottom of the valley.

In another, larger room, Philipa Dedeny was quite as busy as the man she loved. Her computer was linked to the International All-data bank.

She had begun her researches in the middle of June 2000, shortly after *Summer's Dream* had been sold at a special Sotheby's auction in London, and they had quietly left their home on Avenue Victor Hugo in Paris to return to Switzerland. The first image she had called up on the screen of her computer was the page from *Time* magazine she had unearthed in the library at Brig. She had remembered it from an issue published shortly before she went to San Francisco to do the cover story on Justin Pope. Now she read it once, then again, and leaned back in her chair to decide what to do next.

The conservative thing to do—and as she was in Switzerland, it was quite natural to be conservative—was to go slowly but miss nothing along the way. Therefore, the first trip she took forward through time in the van parked in the stone garage was to November of the year 2010.

She had dressed for the occasion in the most casual but elegant ski togs she could buy. Even so, as she locked the garage door behind her and trudged down the ankle-deep snow into town, she was aware of glances directed her way from women whose own ski togs and boots seemed light and summery by comparison.

Vevey had changed remarkably little in a decade. The old buildings were older, the few new buildings scarcely altering the cityscape as she remembered it from the last time she had seen it, two or three days earlier.

Her first stop was at a clothing store, where she gave explicit orders for several dresses in the latest fashion, specifying hem length, color, material, and cut and asking when they could be delivered. The saleswoman shot her a look of surprise, laughed politely, then took her to the dressing room. She disrobed under the eyes of three television cameras. On the wall-mounted monitor the words appeared: "Madame's order will be ready in four minutes."

Simultaneously, her dress pattern was spewed from a printer in the workroom; the fabrics were cut, dyed, fixed with fast-acting mordants, heat-bonded into the finished product, and put on hangars. The saleswoman brought them into the dressing room, still warm to the touch. The process was repeated at the leather shop in the same block, where she ordered several bags and pairs of shoes.

Now inconspicuous except for her regal carriage and arresting features, she sought out the largest computer firm in the city and made her wants known. She explained that she had been out of the country for the past decade and that the firm's installation team must be prepared to renovate her computer room to state-of-the-art standards.

"Oh, yes, there's one other detail," she told the firm's manager, who, when he saw her, decided to handle this client personally, if she would only give him the opportunity.

"Your slightest desire is my command," the manager said, unctuously, allowing his voice to linger on the word "desire."

"My husband—" she began, then her voice faltered. When she regained control, she mentioned that, since she had last seen her husband ten years earlier, she could not bear the thought of anyone passing through the lower floors whose very dust she herself had, in reverence, not seen fit to disturb. "I use the back stairs, but they are too narrow for you to move your equipment, I am sure. Monsieur will be so kind, therefore, as to build a ramp to the third floor which will permit access to my computer room for the equipment I have ordered?"

Monsieur would be charmed, he declared. He would have been even more charmed had his elephantine overtures been taken seriously. But he had to be satisfied with a demure smile and a large check written on a bank in Geneva. And the hope of better luck next time.

There was no next time for him, but for Mme de la Bec there were several—eleven in all, each a decade apart. Each time she had to update her wardrobe and to account for the lapses in her knowledge of local conditions, modern appliances, means of transportation and communication, even the evolving French language itself, by pleading simple ignorance, for having been many years in a remote African land.

Each decade down the road she had to pause for a longer period to assimilate the culture of the day, and especially to review advances in the field that most interested her. And after each such sojourn into the future, she returned to the year 2000, telling the fascinated Franz everything and in return listening to the masterpiece or two he had tossed off in her absence.

In the year 2100 she knew she was getting very close to her goal. As after each journey she had spent three or four days at her upstairs computer room in the chalet reviewing the literature. But even that was a task that became progressively easier. By the year 2100 she was able to ignore the computer keyboard completely and address her questions orally in the language of her choice—translation was mechanical and automatic—and probe the limits of the new artificial intelligence. She could talk back to the machine, interrupt and demand detail, instruct the machine to look up applicable references, and dredge up from its enormous memory examples of the technology she was seeking, its pitfalls, its failures, its successes. By the year 2100 successes far outnumbered failures. She felt the time had come to act but, in keeping with her adopted Swiss conservatism, decided to tack on an extra decade for good measure. She revised even that figure, figuring that woman's intuition should count for another, making 2120 the year of decision.

"We're ready to go, Franz," Philipa told him one evening.

"Already?" Schubert was beginning to enjoy life in the Alps—the pleasant routine, the hearty meals, the long night stretches at the keyboard, their friendly if somewhat stiff and severe neighbors, even the appallingly white winter that had settled down over the chalet. On the other hand, it had been *his* idea to seek the plaudits of the world he had so long been denied, and it would be cruel at this late stage to deprive Phil of the joy she obviously felt in bringing it all about.

"Cold feet?" she mocked.

"Not if you say it can be done, my love."

"It can. Believe me."

"Yes, I believe you. I believe you the more because the issue will be much more pleasing to the eye."

She struck him on the chest with her balled fist, her dark eyes blooming with anger. "If you even *think* such a thing, I'll call it all off."

"Now, now, Phil," Schubert soothed her, holding her tight in his arms. "You know I don't mean it. You know how I love you. It's just that—well, my good fortune seems like one long, deliriously happy dream, from which I may awaken at any moment. And why a beautiful, intelligent, breathtakingly desirable woman like you should feel this way about poor old Franz Peter Schubert, who in his first incarnation was unable to feed and house even himself properly, let alone anyone else, is cause for bafflement. It's simply that I cannot quite believe my luck, you see."

"Well," she said, mollified, "just don't push it. Everything is going according to plan, and before you know it, it'll be a different life."

"I'd grown used to the one we have," he said wistfully.

"It's still your choice." Her voice was somber. "I won't try to influence you one way or the other. Decide."

He thought about it for a few minutes, but he really had no evidence on which to base a decision, and unless they went ahead, he never would. "We'll do it."

"I thought that would be your answer." She went to the computer room and brought back a suitcase in which were two winter outfits, one for her, one for him. "Get dressed."

The styles for the third decade of the twenty-second century had doubled back to the middle of the twenty-first, and they in turn closely resembled in many respects what had been fashionable for young women in the 1940s—short skirts, flat shoes, sweaters, and page-boy bobs. Men wore baggy trousers, but the necktie and lapel were gone forever—well, a few generations, at least—to be replaced by huge, bright-hued woolly sweaters. The outside wear was, of course, thermostatically controlled to produce the sensation of a mild spring day.

The town of Vevey had encroached almost up to their property line, pushed by the inexorable influx of foreigners seeking safe haven. Gone were motorcars, and in their place were two- and four-place electric vehicles, light, quiet, and fast, running on twin rails beside the main roadway, which was reserved for pedestrians and bicyclists. They picked one from the stand a few blocks from their villa and alighted at the Geneva Genetic Research Institute half an hour away, on the edge of the capital.

Dr. Tomaso Binda was waiting in his office when they arrived. He rose from behind his desk and greeted them with a warm but deferential handshake. After all, the client was a very important, very rich man, as he had to be to afford a treatment that cost so much—some SFr5.5 million, or $12 million in his patient's debased American currency—that so far no more than twenty-eight people, most of them women, had opted for the whole course.

"I wish to point out," the white-jacketed Dr. Binda began as he resumed his place behind the desk, "that while this procedure has been refined over the past forty years, some element of risk inevitably remains."

"Yes, I know," Mme. de la Bec said. "But it is my husband who must be reassured. Perhaps you would explain to him in more detail."

"By all means. You see, Monsieur de la Bec, we are simply going back to square one, as you Americans put it. As you know, every cell in your body carries the template, the genetic instructions, to produce the whole man, provided the nutrients, the temperatures, the matrices are all present. Bringing us to this state of medical science began more than a century ago, when man first cloned such living forms as strawberries, then single-cellular animals, the lower vertebrates, and only within the past twenty years the infinitely more complex task of cloning man. It is an incredibly complex process, requiring seventeen hours on the largest computer complex outside the United States merely to unravel and then unscramble the genetic code of each sample.

"A whole section of this institute, comprising more than 220 doctors, physicists, statisticians, mathematicians, nurses, and other personnel, works around the clock to effect a single complete transformation over a period of thirty-seven hours, although of course we very seldom are called upon to tackle such a formidable task. Most of our work consists in rejuvenating the sexual glands of nonagenarians, restoring the youthful breasts of women, restoring limbs to those unfortunates suffering amputation in accidents, regenerating eyes, livers, kidneys, and other age- or disease-impaired organs. These, as you must imagine, are much simpler processes, really everyday genetic routine. Would you like me to go into the process on the molecular level?"

"Not really," Schubert said. "I understand the broad outlines of the process." He was not sure what the molecular level really was, except that he was sure not to understand it.

"Very well, shall we get on with it?"

"Yes, I suppose so."

"Then we can start immediately." He tapped a buzzer, and a large, formidable Wagnerian-soprano type in starched whites entered. "This is Dr. Swann, Monsieur de la Bec. She will be your constant companion through the rather tedious but not particularly painful—we have methods of reducing the discomfort to a minimum—course of treatment. Dr. Swann, you may take Monsieur de la Bec and prepare him for surgery, which will begin in"—he consulted his watch—"in just about two hours."

"Yes, Doctor," Dr. Swann replied, taking Schubert gently by the hand and smiling reassuringly.

Schubert and Philipa Dedeny embraced, then the composer turned and left the room, not looking back. In thirty-seven hours he would be seeing his beloved again.

But Philipa Dedeny watched him go with misery wringing her heart. It would be the last time she would ever see him.

Dr. Binda cleared his throat.

Philipa Dedeny opened her bag, extracted a bank draft for the sum demanded, and handed it to Dr. Binda.

"There's just one other thing—"

"Yes, I know," she said, and brought out the plastic

bag containing the bloody bandage she had removed from the neck of Justin Pope.

The entire process, including time spent in intensive care, was closer to ninety-six hours than thirty-seven. Most of that time Philipa Dedeny spent in a hospital room, sleeping off and on and pestering nurses about the progress of her husband. Not until the beginning of the fifth day was he in condition to receive her.

"Well, Mme. de la Bec," Dr. Binda said, smiling and washing his dry hands, "I think it's time for the unveiling. Would you like to accompany me?"

Philipa Dedeny allowed him to take her arm and guide her down brightly lit corridors to the room where Franz Peter Schubert lay, swathed from head to foot in bandages.

"Shall we start with the head?" Dr. Binda asked, when he had cleared the room of all the staff.

Philipa Dedeny nodded.

Dr. Binda cut through the bandages, then unwound them layer by layer until a small heap of blood- and plasma-impregnated bandages lay at his feet. Only when he had the head completely exposed and Franz Peter Schubert had opened his eyes did Dr. Binda step back to view his handiwork. He gasped.

"But that's—that's—"

"Justin Pope?" Philipa Dedeny supplied.

"Yes, Justin Pope. But where did you get that blood sample? He disappeared more than a hundred years ago. It's impossible that you could have obtained a blood sample from a man who disappeared more than a century ago."

"Don't worry about that, Doctor," Philipa Dedeny said.

Dr. Binda was silent a moment, thinking fast. There lay the perfect replica of the greatest composer of his time, perhaps of *all* time. It would be a sensation—or would it? They could not possibly pass him off as the composer for the simple reason that *nobody* could compose masterpieces such as Justin Pope had written—and anyway, Justin Pope had been dead for at least a century. There must be some deeper motive. And whatever it was, its success depended on Mme. de la Bec keeping his identity secret until he got out of the hospital, at least. And if she wanted to keep a secret like that, she would obviously be willing to pay for it.

He stepped swiftly to the door and shot the bolt. He returned to the recumbent man's beside, took a roll of gauze from the dressing tray, and began to wrap up Schubert's face again.

"What are you doing, doctor?" Philipa inquired coldly.

"I'm doing you a great favor, Madame, and I may as well tell you, I expect your generosity to be my reward."

She put her hand on his. "Don't bother. And as for gratitude, you already have twelve million thank-you notes, printed in green."

"Do you know what this means?" Dr. Binda said menacingly.

"No, but I'm sure you'll explain it to me in language I can understand."

"It means that you are obviously going to try to trade on the false identity we have somehow, willy-nilly, created. Money can be your only possible motive, especially since Justin Pope's legacy from recordings royalties, compounded annually, must be enormous by now. And, so far as I recall, Pope died intestate. Therefore, money must be your motive. Indeed, money is the *best* possible motive, for anything. It is *my* motive in aiding you to succeed in your subterfuge. And if it is going to succeed, you will need my help."

"Thank you very much, but your help is not required."

"And if I expose you?"

"How would you do that, doctor?"

"It wouldn't be difficult, I can assure you. I would

have the police extract the late Justin Pope's fingerprints from the American FBI's files and show that this impostor's fingerprints are identical. Ergo, he must be a clone, not a look-alike descendant, no matter how much forged documentation you produce to prove otherwise."

Philipa Dedeny laughed. All doubts that Franz Peter Schubert could pass himself off as Justin Pope had now been resolved by the good, the greedy, the foolish Dr. Binda.

13. A FINE PUZZLEMENT
16 MAY 2000

PHILIPA DEDENY WAS NOT VERY GOOD AT DATES. SHE was even worse at arithmetic. Still, despite the changes in time zones she had experienced before Franz Peter Schubert was finally in shape to travel back to the year 2000, she was able to compute how long she had been missing from San Francisco of the year 2000.

When they had taken over the *Fugit*, she had had the good sense to consult the log that automatically recorded the hour, day, and year that was the destination of each journey through time. They had begun their stay in Brig on 18 May 2000, the same day Justin Pope had come calling for the last time and made the mistake of falling asleep when he should have been on the qui vive. She had arrived in Switzerland on 24 November 1999. That meant she had been missing for very nearly six months. That was true even though she and Franz had been in the cavern above Brig for something like two years, judging by the passage of the seasons.

It had been two years since she had seen her parents, three brothers, and baby sister, all of whom she loved dearly. They, on the other hand, would have missed her for only six months, provided she returned to the time when Pope had left for Switzerland. Better yet, she could return to 17 November 1999, when she had followed Pope to Switzerland, and they would not miss her at all. But that was only the half of it.

If she returned to 17 November, she would of course have to bring Franz with her—couldn't leave the innocent lamb wandering around in limbo—and since Pope had maintained his headquarters in San Francisco until he too disappeared, on 18 May 2000, San Francisco would be treated to the spectacle of Justin Pope bumping into Justin Pope. Couldn't have that.

Since Pope had appeared in Brig on 18 May 2000, presumably having left home the same day, in order not to arouse suspicion he should reappear in San Francisco very close to that date, preferably 19 May. To be sure, the problem remained of breaking the news of her survival to her bereaved family, compounding the shock to those who doubtless thought her dead. Yet there did not seem to be any other way. Nor could she bring Justin with her—*that* would bring the media wolf pack howling at their heels—nor could she perform the bittersweet task by telephone. No, this was something she had to do—wanted to do—in person.

The dilemma kept her awake the entire flight from Geneva to San Francisco. Meanwhile Franz, who suffered Philipa to drape his face in fake mustache and beard to keep Pope's fans at bay, snored at her side. He had ingested the better part of a bottle of cognac to still the demon inside that told him that no metallic contrivance as enormous as the 747 could possibly stagger into the air and stay there—and would doubtless crash trying. He slept like the dead, which was appropriate, since everyone thought he had been for 172 years.

As she and a hungover Schubert passed through immigration in San Francisco, using her own passport and Justin's, which she had thoughtfully extracted from its owner's pocket while bidding him adieu, she decided that the plan she had formulated was the very best possible under the circumstances. The van was off-loaded, and they drove it to the apartment building Justin Pope had left on the previous day. It was dusk when she arrived at the front entrance, told the doorman to keep an eye on the van until her return, and entered on Schubert's arm.

It had been six months since she had been in the apartment building, but the concierge recognized her immediately. "Why, Miss Dedeny," he said with delight, "how nice to see you again. And a very good evening to *you*, Maestro," he added deferentially, bowing at the waist to Schubert. "I thought you had gone back east, Miss Dedeny," he added.

"As a matter of fact, I did," she replied, but thought it unnecessary to tell him how *far* east. "Tell me, is Miss Hunter in at the moment?" If she were, that would require the use of Option Two, which was to have Schubert summon her by telephone to some other place, preferably distant. As it was, Angelica was out, so Option One would work very well. She nudged Schubert with her elbow.

Franz came out of his reverie and smiled. "I have a great deal of work piled up," he said, reciting the words Philipa had rehearsed with him, "and I am going to need an uninterrupted period of time to get through it. Until I finish, and so notify you, I do not wish to be disturbed."

"I understand, Maestro."

"By *anyone*—except, of course, Miss Dedeny."

"I understand, Maestro," he repeated, and this time he really *did* understand. In fact, the composer's wishes were eminently understandable. Miss Angelica Hunter was certainly one of the most lovely creatures ever to grace his marbled, chandeliered domain. And yet this black-haired woman was equally beautiful, though of a totally different type. As the French said, "*Vive la différence!*" For certainly a genius like Justin Pope could be forgiven for wishing to change his luck.

"I shall require all meals to be sent up to me. Miss Dedeny will make arrangements," Schubert continued, reciting his speech. "The trolley will be left outside my door, and you shall ring me when the waiter who delivers my meals leaves the building. Otherwise, I am to receive no telephone calls. There will be no exceptions—except, of course, for those from Miss Dedeny."

"Naturally, Maestro. It shall be done precisely as you order. You can depend on me."

"I will." Schubert laid an envelope on the mahogany desk, smiled, and withdrew to the elevators with Philipa.

"Do you think we gave him enough?" Schubert asked.

"More than enough. He'll see that the security staff doesn't sleep, you can count on it."

"I see no security staff."

"It's that kind of apartment house. If you could see them, it wouldn't be. Now, then, do you have everything straight?"

"Of course, darling Philipa. I'll only be doing what comes naturally."

For the three or four days Philipa would be absent in New York, he would be working up the cello sonata that had been running through his mind the previous week. He would see no one and speak to no one, and when she returned, she would take care of the one loose end that stood in the way of his imposture—Angelica Hunter. It would be a simple matter. She would tell Miss Hunter that she had been replaced in his affections by Philipa Dedeny, and Schubert would back her up. Miss Hunter would have no recourse but to leave with what grace she could muster, aided by a generous gift that Schubert would bestow for services rendered. Then the world would be his and Philipa's.

"Godspeed, and hurry back to the man who loves you," Schubert said, kissing her hand reverently.

"I will, Franz—*Justin*," she whispered, looking up into his eyes but seeing Schubert behind them.

His physical transformation left her vaguely uncomfortable. She conceded that Justin Pope was more favored by nature. He had none of the baby fat that had begun to settle around Franz's middle and smooth out his jawline. His hair was neatly combed, not wild and disheveled. His teeth were white and regular. He was tall, trim, and athletic. None of those adjectives applied to Franz Peter Schubert. Pope dressed elegantly, and breaking a trouser's crease was to him as unthinkable as breaking wind. On Franz, by contrast, even the best-tailored clothes seemed to slump and wrinkle. And yet despite all these shortcomings she loved him, and maybe because of them she loved him more.

"I won't be long. And I'll phone you every day."

She strode swiftly to the entrance, mentally reviewing the situation. Franz had already taken the elevator to the penthouse. She would personally put the van in its parking place in the garage, lock it, and take a taxi to the airport. She would be in New York five hours later and at her parents' home on Central Park West in time to have breakfast with them tomorrow morning. They would be full of questions to which she had no answers as yet, but she was confident that on the flight east she would think of a good story. It should be no trouble to concoct a plausible yarn to put her parents' curiosity to rest. It might take a little time to think of it, but what the hell—she *owned* time.

Angelica Hunter had gone to police headquarters for the second time that day in the late afternoon. She had been asked to come by Detective Lieutenant Rivers, who questioned her about possible places a figure as well known as Justin Pope could hide. Angelica Hunter could offer the lieutenant no enlightenment. For five hours he quizzed her, sure she was holding something back.

She was: her temper. She wanted to know how Justin had disappeared and where he had gone, and she was furious because Rivers refused to take her denials seriously and, instead of grilling her, get on to the job of finding Justin. She was certain something had happened to him, since he seemed to have vanished into the San Francisco fog.

The police had put out an APB on the van within five minutes of its disappearance. Since they had not found a trace of it, they assumed that Justin Pope must still be in possession of the van, so Rivers refrained from putting out an APB on him as well. It would not look good for the department to have the media laughing at him for letting Pope get away—if Pope was a criminal—or being harassed by the police if Pope proved not to be. He decided to give the search until the morning and then let the press have it.

At nine o'clock that night Rivers finally told her she could go. She went. Paying off the cab, she proceeded to the desk, where she asked the concierge if there had been any messages.

"No, Miss Hunter," he said, his voice tense from the thought of the coming confrontation. "I'm sorry."

"That's all right." She walked dejectedly to the elevator. At the bronze doors, a security man blocked the way. "Kindly get out of my way," she said.

"Sorry, ma'am. No visitors to the penthouse."

"I'm not a visitor," she blazed. "I live here. Get the hell out of the way."

"Orders, Miss Hunter," the security man said. "I'm really sorry."

"*Orders?* Whose orders?"

"Mr. Pope's."

"Is that right?" she said, her lip curling.

"Yes, ma'am."

"And when did Mr. Pope give these 'orders'?"

"About an hour and a half ago."

Hope flashed in her eyes. "Do you mean he's *here*?"

"Yes, ma'am."

"And he said he didn't want to see anybody?"

"That's right."

"But of *course* he'd say that. He didn't want to see anybody except *me*."

"Anybody. We've even had instructions to keep his staff away, to send his meals up and make sure that the waiter left the building before being notified that his meal had arrived."

"We *are*, I presume, speaking about the same Justin Pope?"

"Yes, ma'am."

"You saw him?"

"I saw him. I see him practically every day. It's Mr. Pope, all right."

"And you won't let me into my apartment?"

The security man shrugged apologetically.

Angelica Hunter marched to the concierge's desk and asked to be connected with the penthouse.

The concierge shook his head miserably. "I'm afraid I cannot, Miss Hunter. No incoming calls. Orders."

"I see," she said quietly. "Very well." She turned, went out the revolving doors, and hailed a cab.

Twenty minutes later a police car rolled up to the apartment-house entrance and Angelica Hunter, followed by Lieutenant Rivers, got out. Behind them, four uniformed police emerged from a second patrol car and took up posts at the door and in the lobby.

Rivers conferred briefly with the men who remained outside. Two walked off toward the back of the building. Rivers strode into the building with Angelica Hunter in his wake.

At the elevator, the same security guard said, "No visitors, sir," but without conviction.

"Get the elevator, and get it now," Rivers growled.

The security man did as he was ordered.

Thirty seconds later, the elevator reached the fourteenth-floor entrance and Angelica opened the locked door with her key.

Across the salon was Justin Pope. He was sitting barechested in his underpants at the grand piano, his pen poised over a score resting on the music rack. He looked at her as though she were a total stranger. He looked at Rivers as though he had never set eyes on him, either. "Yes?" he inquired politely.

"Get your clothes on, Mr. Pope," Rivers said harshly. "You're coming with me."

"I am? Where?"

Rivers laughed nastily. "Three guesses."

"I am not very good at guessing games, sir," Schubert said. "Perhaps you will be good enough to tell me what you want."

Angelica was suddenly alert. Something was wrong. In fact, several somethings were wrong. The pen in his hand was the first thing that jarred her: Justin always used a pencil and wore out erasers on his manuscript. But this musical notation was swift and sure, and only two measures on the two pages visible had been crossed out. Also, the musical notation was different. Then there was his dress: Justin never worked in his underwear. Citing the example of Haydn, who always dressed as though he were receiving visitors and wore a powdered wig and white gloves before sitting down to compose his music, Justin invariably wore a pair of comfortable slacks, silk shirt, foulard, and loafers. And looking closer, she noticed that the scar was missing, the jagged scar below his right knee from a compound fracture he had received in a game of sandlot football when he was eleven. He called Rivers "sir." That was not like her Justin Pope. And he did not seem to recognize her, the woman to whom he had sworn his eternal love only the day before.

And yet he could be nobody else. Nobody could impersonate him so perfectly. Nobody but Justin Pope himself could write the music that was on that rack, that had been resounding through the closed door as they emerged from the elevator. She felt a little dizzy.

"Get dressed," Rivers repeated. "Get dressed now or I'll have my officers drag you down to the police station the way you are. Which way you go is up to you."

Comprehension dawned, to be replaced by unease. "You are the police?"

"No, I'm the mayor's welcoming committee. Are you coming along quietly?"

Schubert hesitated. Philipa's instructions had been very

clear, but apparently she had not thought of everything. She had not mentioned the possibility of an official greeting ceremony. "Of course I shall come. I am honored, indeed, to be welcomed by the mayor," Schubert said straight-faced, rising.

"The fewer the wisecracks, the better it will go for you, Mr. Pope," Rivers growled. He started to follow him to the bedroom, but Angelica Hunter put her hand on his arm and instead went herself, closing the door behind her.

Schubert was picking clothing out of the closet, matching a plaid shirt with flannel trousers and a checked sport jacket. That did it. Whoever he was, he was not Justin Pope.

"Who the hell *are* you?" she said in a stage whisper.

"Justin Pope, of course," he said carefully. "And you are Angelica Hunter."

"Well, you're half-right. Where is Justin? *What have you done with my Justin?*"

Schubert did not answer. He thought he had gone quite far enough to accommodate these people. He would merely refuse to answer any further questions, say not a single word, except to the mayor, and to him he would limit himself to a terse expression of gratitude.

He was terrified into silence when he realized that he had misunderstood Rivers, that he was being put in *jail*. Knowing not what else to do, he maintained his silence through the two hours of questioning by Rivers that night and was then committed to a cell. He refused the services of an attorney, knowing them to be more untrustworthy than even police officers. The next morning they brought him before the judge for arraignment. The charge was conspiracy with intent to commit murder, an extraditable offense for which he would be tried in Switzerland.

"*Murder?*" said a shocked, incredulous Schubert. "*Whose* murder?"

"The murder of Philipa Dedeny," the prosecutor said.

From the back of the courtroom came an amused and sardonic voice. ''What absolute rubbish!'' Philipa Dedeny said.

14. VICIOUS CIRCLE
18 MAY 2000

"YOU'RE NOT GOING TO GET AWAY WITH THIS," ANGELica Hunter said evenly.

"Of course not, dear Angelica," Philipa Dedeny said with a patronizing smile. "But just think of the fun we're going to have trying."

"I want to know what you did with Justin Pope."

"You're worried?"

"Of course I'm worried. If I thought you touched a hair on his head, I'd tear you to pieces with my bare hands."

"How delighted he'll be to hear of your concern, dear Angelica."

"So he *is* alive? And quit calling me 'dear Angelica.' "

"Oh, he's alive, all right. I hope you didn't take me for a murderer. The only thing I've ever been guilty of murdering is the king's English."

"Then where is he? Are you holding him prisoner?"

"You might say that."

"I see." Angelica Hunter was sandwiched between the Angelica and Schubert in the back of her—*her*—Rolls-Royce, which the damned *Time* reporter had had the gall to whistle up when the judge had handed down a stern warning against Detective Lieutenant Rivers about bringing false charges against the eminent Justin Pope and dismissed Schubert with profuse apologies. She turned to Schubert. "And where did she dig *you* up?"

Schubert, whom Philipa had told to hold his tongue,

held his tongue. But it did not stop him from favoring Angelica with a sickly, apologetic smile.

"You don't *know*?" Philipa said incredulously.

Angelica stiffened. "If I knew, would I have asked?"

Philipa Dedeny looked at her narrowly and decided she was telling the truth. But on second thought, how *could* she know? If she had any brains at all—and she had enough to have engineered Philipa Dedeny's departure for Switzerland and subsequent disappearance—Angelica Hunter would have known that Justin Pope was stealing "his" masterpieces from somewhere. And if Franz Peter Schubert, whose portraits were very lifelike, had suddenly appeared, she would undoubtedly have put one and one together and arrived at the truth. But Schubert no longer looked like Schubert, so the second part of the equation was missing. For all Angelica Hunter could know, he had to be a ringer, someone off the street who happened to look exactly like Justin Pope. That opened up a number of interesting possibilities.

For one thing, Angelica Hunter probably did not know of the existence of the *Fugit*, a circumstance that could prove very useful. For another, she would doubtless attempt to prove the ringer an out-and-out fraud who, with the assistance of Philipa Dedeny, intended to milk Pope's considerable bank account and escape in the night. Those conclusions must have seemed obvious to Angelica Hunter. However, it would stretch Angelica's imagination to the breaking point to conceive that this man, who was a perfect ringer for Justin, was also a virtuoso pianist and could compose great music as well.

Philipa Dedeny loved Schubert with all her heart and was thankful for the circumstance that had brought them together. But that did not excuse Angelica Hunter, who undoubtedly had put Justin Pope up to getting rid of her. She owed Philipa a debt, and Philipa was now in a position to collect.

How? By simply doing nothing.

Convinced that "Justin Pope" was a fake and that he

and Philipa Dedeny were conspiring to raid his bank accounts at the earliest convenient opportunity, she would strike back with energy and imagination. Well, let her. Philipa and Schubert had nothing to fear. Still, it would be well to keep an eye on her.

"Where are you staying, my dear?" Philipa inquired sweetly.

"In my home, of course."

"You mean the penthouse?"

"I do, indeed."

"You don't think it will be a trifle crowded?"

"Not at all. It has always been ample for the two of us."

"But now there are three."

"We have the servants' quarters."

"That will be matey," Philipa said. "I hope you find them comfortable."

"That wasn't what I had in mind."

"Yes, I know. You expected to share the master bedroom. But I believe it would be the civilized thing for the master himself to choose his bedmate."

Both women turned to Schubert.

He was gaping at several couples strolling down the street, their arms entwined about each other.

Even to Angelica Hunter the shock on his face at seeing man embracing man was so genuine that she knew Philipa Dedeny had recruited him from some area so remote—the hills of southeast Ohio, perhaps—that he did not realize that such behavior was not only commonplace but actually the norm for San Francisco. Such a naive man could not possibly know or understand classical music. Then a thought occurred to her: what about that fountain pen poised above the music stand when she and Lieutenant Rivers had burst in on him? On the heels of the question came the answer: he had been coached in his part. Hearing the key in the lock of the door, he had rushed to the piano bench, picked up a pen, and pretended to be interrupted in the throes of composition. Philipa Dedeny had thought of everything.

How long would the imposter and Philipa need to clear out his local bank accounts? A day at least. If they succeeded, of course, they would get away with millions. But provided she was with him every minute during banking hours, he would be thwarted if he tried to abstract money from their joint accounts. On the other hand, if she *were* with him, then *he* would be able to keep *her* from transferring their assets to an account in her name. A Mexican standoff, but it would last only for one day, because by tomorrow evening she would prove to the world that the man who pretended to be Justin Pope was nothing but an impersonator.

"The maid's quarters will do nicely," Angelica Hunter said finally, between her teeth.

She was up at sunrise. It would be a day of watching, but what she watched was an empty salon until, just before eleven o'clock, Philipa strolled through dressed in a long quilted housecoat, greeted her, and headed for the dining room, where the day staff had as usual put breakfast on the sideboard. She helped herself to scrambled eggs and crisp bacon, toast, and two cups of coffee. She read the morning paper with exceptional interest, for six months from the years 1999 and 2000 were total blanks. She had not had time to read a word on the plane east two nights earlier, for she had been sleeping off her jet lag. On the return flight three hours later, after the concierge had finally telephoned her at home and told her that the police had taken Maestro Pope away, she had had five hours to kill, but worry had kept her turning pages without comprehending a word she read.

Schubert arose at one in the afternoon. For the next three hours, until the banks were safely closed, Angelica Hunter kept him engaged in conversation that merely cemented her conviction that he was an utter fraud, and a very strange one at that. He did not seem to know anything useful about Washington politics, or fast food, or the San Francisco Forty-Niners, or current movie stars, or Las Vegas, or Nob Hill. When she asked what he thought of Carnegie Hall, he looked her straight in the eye and said he had not had the pleasure of meeting the gentleman. She did not know where he came from, but it must have been somewhere deep in the hills. But on second thought, not southern Ohio—more like the Hindu Kush.

At three-thirty she told Schubert and Philipa that she had a few errands to do and would be back in an hour or two. She actually returned at six-thirty, by design.

He and Philipa were sitting in the swing on the veranda, watching the fiery sun being quenched in the blue Pacific.

Angelica Hunter pretended surprise and shock. "Aren't you dressed yet?"

"Dressed?" Philipa replied. "Why should he dress?"

"Well, I hope dear Justin isn't going out on the stage at Opera Hall in his cords, plaid shirt, and running shoes." She was looking intently at Schubert for signs of panic. Instead, he looked at Philipa for a cue. "I mean," she went on, "you don't want to disappoint your public, do you? After all, if you don't play and aren't sick or out of town, people are going to suspect something is wrong, won't they?"

Philipa licked her lips. "There's a concert tonight?"

"You bet your little ruffled culottes there is, sweetie," Angelica Hunter said. "It's been scheduled for three months and sold out the first day. And if your hayseed friend here doesn't show up, *I* will, to explain just why he didn't. And what do you think of *those* onions?"

Philipa Dedeny's eyes were those of a trapped animal. She bit her knuckle, massaged her earlobe, tapped her foot. "You'll go," she said to Schubert. "Go get dressed."

"But I—" Schubert began.

"Just go. And don't worry—I'll think of something."

"Such as?" Angelica goaded.

Philipa took a deep breath. "Well, there are several things we could do, I guess, but I think the safest would be for him to trip over a music stand coming on stage, 'bruising' his arm, then make a handsome apology and get the hell out of there."

"It won't work, you know."

"Maybe I'll think of something better before we get to the opera house. I always do, you know."

The applause when Schubert, resplendent in tails, walked onto the stage was "rapturous," "frantic," "thunderous," "deafening," or "tonitruous," depending on which critic one read the next day. Angelica Hunter added hers to the rest, calculating that the louder the applause, the more stunning the silence that would greet him when and if he actually attempted to play. It was an all-Pope program. He was to perform his Concerto in E Flat Major and his *Golden Gate* Sonatina and conclude with his Mass in C Minor. He would conduct the ninety-two-piece orchestra in the concerto from his piano bench and, after the intermission, the orchestra and 140-voice chorus from the organ in the one-hour-and-five-minute mass. Of course, he would—could—not go through with it.

He flipped his tails neatly out of the way and sat down on the quilted-leather piano bench. The audience grew still. He fiddled with the knobs, first raising the bench, then lowering it a fraction of an inch. Angelica Hunter held her breath in spite of herself. He could not get away with it much longer. Two or three more seconds and he would have to swoon away in a dead faint or grab his shirtfront as though he were having a heart attack.

He did neither. He raised his hand, the kettle drums rolled, the cymbals clashed, the clarinet section warbled the opening motif, and Schubert's hands came crashing down on the keyboard in the magnificent opening bars of the great E Flat Concerto. He was well into the first movement when Angelica Hunter finally managed to get control of her jaw, which seemed to have become temporarily unhinged. She glanced at Philipa Dedeny, sitting placidly next to her, drinking in every sound as if it were nectar of the gods.

Well, she had to admit, it *was*. The real Justin Pope was a virtuoso pianist, but this imposter played like an angel, with an expression, emotion, and conviction that made the concerto, of which she knew every note from Justin's practice sessions, an entirely new and infinitely more wondrous work of art. She sat mesmerized. The solo *Golden Gate* Sonatina was cut of the same bolt from the blue. Intermission came after a dozen curtain calls. Angelica, as immobile as a poleaxed heifer, remained in her seat, allowing the beauty of the music she had just heard to soak into her inner consciousness. When the stage again filled, Schubert raised his baton. In a dream she listened to the Mass in C Minor, listened as though she had never heard it before, listened with tears rolling down her cheeks. She was not alone. No applause greeted the conclusion of the work. For some long seconds the hall was utterly without sound. Then came a sigh from a thousand throats, and the crowd was on its feet, joining the orchestra and chorus in rapturous, thunderous, and tonitruous applause. From all sides came the cries "*Bis, bis!*" and "Encore, encore!" even though everyone knew that Justin Pope never consented to play encores.

For ten minutes the crowd roared, and for ten minutes Schubert walked from the wings to take his place beside the organ, bow and shake the hand of the concertmaster, and walk back to the wings. He walked the better part of a mile that evening.

Finally, to still the clamor, he raised his hand for quiet. A hush settled upon the hall. "The musical director has just informed me that we are honored tonight by the presence of the eminent Nobel laureate, Dr. William O'Hara Babbage." He looked down at the audience, followed the eyes of the people in the first few rows to a distinguished old gentleman with the rosette of a commander of the

Legion of Honor in his buttonhole, and bowed. "Sir, since the audience seems to want more and I am happy to oblige, I would like to dedicate to you and your services to humanity a musical offering, a theme and variations which I will improvise for the occasion on the notes B-A-B-B-A-G-E."

Before the crowd could react, he sat down at the organ and played the seven notes, with a full rest between, in slow succession. He paused so long, his hands poised above the keyboard, that someone in the rear of the hall, thinking his inspiration had suddenly run dry, sniggered. At that moment his hands fell, and a cascade of pure invention inundated the packed auditorium. The theme was elemental, as catchy as a nursery tune. But then the embroidery began, and he wove the notes into a veritable Bayeux tapestry of sound. His hands coaxed music from the instrument that even he had not known was in it, while his feet stroked the pedals with the grace of a ballet dancer. No sooner had he reached a climax, and everyone knew he could not possibly wring another single idea from those seven notes, than he switched to the piano. From this instrument he provoked a new musical tempest, then crossed to the harpsichord and embarked on another odyssey of musical discovery, which finally drew into port, after how many minutes or hours no one could later truly say, on the seven-stranded thread of those same unadorned notes.

The audience applauded once more, but only half-heartedly. They did not rise to their feet but sat subdued, emotionally exhausted. Somewhere a man was heard to sob.

Angelica Hunter did not sleep that night. She tossed, she turned, she stared at the ceiling, mottled with reflections from the streetlights. Her own reflections were still more jumbled. Who *was* this man, this *super*man? Where did he come from? How had he come there? Now that Philipa Dedeny was on the scene, what was going to happen to Angelica Hunter? Most of all she wondered what had happened to the real Justin Pope, what would become of him now that the imposter had shown himself to be a genius several orders of magnitude greater than Pope himself. At dawn she slept.

When she arose at ten, she knew that the imposter had no intention of grabbing the cash and running. Why should he, when he could command any sum a worshiping public could bestow?

Both Schubert and Philipa had still not made an appearance when Angelica dressed and left the apartment. In a pay telephone booth on the street she looked up a name and called a number. An hour later she was ushered into an office of unpretentious elegance and invited to tell her story.

For the next five days she avoided both Schubert and Philipa, saying she did not know what the hell was going on, but whatever it was, she could not take it anymore and had decided to seek other accommodations. Every day she visited the office downtown and came out no wiser than she had gone in. On the sixth day she was greeted with a smile.

"Good news," said a portly, middle-aged gentleman dressed in a gray suit. "I think we have something you'd be interested in hearing. Would you like the whole sandwich or just the meat?"

"Only as much as I need to hear."

"Very well." The man pushed the button on the tape recorder on his desk. He let the tape run for thirty seconds, then switched it to play.

"—if you think that's wise," the impostor was saying.

Then came Philipa Dedeny's voice. "Wise or not wise, I'd better do it. I just can't leave him there, hanging in limbo."

"Why not?"

"Because—because—well, what if it were *you* instead of him?"

Silence. Then, "I suppose you're right. When are you planning to go?"

"As soon as possible. The flight that brings me into Geneva at six-ten in the morning would be the most convenient. It leaves in four hours."

"And what if Angelica asks where you've gone?"

"Stall her. I'll be back on the next plane. Tell her my mother became ill and I went to New York for a couple of days. And see that you keep your hands off her while I'm gone."

"Of course, Philipa," the man said soothingly. "You know me."

"I do. And that's what I'm worrying about."

Angelica Hunter held up her hand, then produced a checkbook from her bag. She wrote a check, handed it to the gentleman in the gray suit, thanked him for his efficiency, and hurried from the office.

Angelica Hunter hung back in her rented car as she followed the van along the north shore of Lac Leman, always keeping two or three cars between them. Her eyes were beginning to smart from fatigue when the van finally pulled into Brig. Philipa Dedeny climbed down from the van and disappeared into a shop with women's wear displayed in the window. She was gone a very long time, so long that once or twice Angelica felt herself nodding off. That would never do. If she slept now, she would lose Philipa on the maze of roads leading out of town. She got out of the car, stretched, squinted through the plate-glass window, and saw that Philipa was still trying and buying, as though a cold winter were coming.

Angelica glanced at the van with its solid sides and opaque glass. The rear doors were unlocked. Maybe there was a place inside where she could hide until Philipa led her to Justin Pope. She opened the door cautiously and saw in the dim light a large metal container of some sort, just big enough to hide behind. She climbed in, eased the door shut, and squeezed behind the big metal box in a semirecumbent position. In ten seconds, exhausted by the long day of travel, she was asleep.

When she awakened, the town of Brig had disappeared. So had Philipa Dedeny. Craning her neck around the metal container, Angelica saw that the driver's compartment was empty. Outside, on the passenger side of the van, was a verdant meadow, ablaze with wildflowers. On the other was a forbidding concrete wall in which two huge ferroconcrete doors opened into the side of a mountain. In the entrance was a stack of cardboard boxes. She listened for signs of life, heard none, and quietly opened the passenger door. She walked around the van. No sign of Philipa. The valley spread before her, full of vegetation, empty of other life. She glanced past the doors and down the tunnel into the mountain. Adjusting her eyes to the darkness within, she saw a string of light bulbs on the ceiling leading into the interior. She took a tentative step in the direction of the lights, paused, then realized that had to be where Justin was held prisoner. She walked rapidly into the cavern, not looking back.

Had she done so, she would have observed Philipa Dedeny emerging from behind the door and walking quickly to the van. The van door closed with a metallic thud. A moment later, the van had disappeared.

III

Ragtime

15. OUTCASTS 25 SEPTEMBER 1928

FROM THE HILLS OVERLOOKING LAS CHIPAS, IT SEEMED a pleasant enough village: a church spire, a water tower, clumps of trees, the inevitable spider thread of railroad line, and rows of neat houses silhouetted against the sun. But it was farther away than he thought.

When Skardon at last reached the sprawling farm on its outskirts, the sun had almost set and he was dusty and thirsty. Up ahead, a farmer hoeing a row of irrigated lettuce observed his approach, paused, leaned on his hoe, and looked him over narrowly. He spit.

"Good afternoon," Skardon said as he approached the farmer.

The farmer grunted. His eyes were hostile.

"Is this Las Chipas?"

The farmer nodded once and returned to his hoeing.

"Could you spare a little water for a thirsty traveler?"

The farmer did not appear to hear the question.

"Is there a rooming house in town?"

The farmer snorted by way of reply.

"How about a bus?"

The farmer turned his back and began hoeing in the direction Skardon had come.

"Thanks very much," Skardon said evenly. "I'll do my best to remember all this valuable information." He trudged on toward town.

What passed for the village restaurant was called the Empire Café. By the time Skardon swung onto a seat at the counter, the regulars had already come and gone and a wan, tired, sour-faced woman, the café's only occupant, was piling chairs on tables to liberate floor space for her mop to redistribute the dirt.

"What's yours, mister?" the woman said, coming around the counter and wiping her damp hands on her apron. She was broad-hipped and narrow-lipped, with straggly gray hair that matched the mop.

"Do you have a menu?"

"You won't be needing any menu. All we've got left is corned beef hash."

"I'll have the corned beef hash." He was hungry enough to devour beef on the hoof.

After two forkfuls of the indefinable gelatinous mess on the plate, he pushed it back and reached for the coffee, another miscalculation. "When's the next bus through here?" he asked the woman, who had given up on the mop and was picking her teeth with a match as she kept her eye on the cash register.

"Day after tomorrow."

"Train?"

"Milk train comes through at four-thirty."

"Good."

"It don't stop at Las Chipas."

He silently commended the train conductor's good judgment. "Is there a rooming house?"

The woman laughed nastily. "Well," she drawled, "they's a *house*, if that's what you mean. Number 122 Main, down the street and across the tracks."

"I see." He put a silver dollar on the counter. At 1928 prices, it should have bought a seven-course meal.

The woman scooped it up, put it in the pocket of her apron, and looked hard at Skardon, daring him to ask for change.

He did not. He picked up his toolbox and walked out into the street, where dusk had fallen.

The town apparently believed in street signs to the same degree it did in grace and hospitality, so he accosted two townsmen who were walking toward him on the wooden sidewalk, engaged in grave conversation.

They were undoubtedly of the village aristocracy: middle-aged men in shiny serge suits with ponderous bellies anchored by gold watch chains, shiny black derbies, ebony walking sticks, and expressions that left no doubt that they bore the burdens of the world.

"Excuse me, gentlemen," Skardon said, "but can you tell me how to get to Main Street?"

The men paused. For a moment Skardon thought they would ignore him and walk on. "This is Main Street," one of the men said finally. "Whom are you looking for?"

"I don't know the name, only the number: 122."

"Yes, of course." The man who had replied looked at his companion. They exchanged amused glances.

"I was told it was a rooming house. Was I misinformed?"

"Oh, dear, no." The other man laughed. He looked at the man before him, in his workingman's clothes and toolbox, up and down. "I'm sure it's just what you're looking for. Keep going straight, across the tracks. It's the—ah—establishment on the right a hundred yards beyond, with the gravel path and the front garden full of withered turnips."

The two men passed on, chuckling.

As he walked down Main Street, Skardon guessed that Las Chipas was a village of three or four hundred dwellings, but even at that early evening hour it appeared all but deserted. The business establishments—two general stores, a bank, a filling station, a café, a dismal railroad station on the line that bisected the town—were all dark.

As far as the railroad line, most of the houses lining the main street were snug and substantial, middle-class houses with ordered lawns and hedges and here and there a hitching post at the gate of dwellings of those who apparently believed the automobile was only a passing fancy. Behind those darkened windows the local burghers would be sleeping, snug and secure. Even at that hour they would probably respond to an unexpected knock at the door by a stranger by summoning the dogs or the law, if any. Beyond the tracks the houses were smaller, decrepit, unkempt. He crossed the tracks.

Ahead on the right he saw the glimmer of light seeping around the edges of drawn curtains in a house that seemed rather neater than most. Instead of weeds in the tiny front yard, rows of vegetables grew. A gravel path led to the door. Skardon walked to the door, mounted the three steps, and knocked.

From inside there was the sounds of a chair scraping on a wooden floor, and steps approaching, then a light switched on above the porch and the door opened. Skardon was momentarily at a loss. He had half expected a black maid in a handkerchief-sized white apron. After more years in prison than he cared to think about, his thoughts, since he had heard the suggestive sniggers of the two burghers, had begun to proceed along predictable channels. But the woman who faced him was not at all what he had expected.

"Good evening," she said. She emerged from the darkened vestibule into the light of the porch. She was about thirty, plainly dressed, with her dark brown hair gathered in a schoolmarm bun. No makeup, no flirtatious smile relieved the fatigue on her face.

"I'm very sorry to disturb you, madam," Skardon began, truly sorry. "But I have just arrived in Las Chipas a few minutes ago, on foot, and have nowhere to spend the night. I was told you could accommodate me—that is," he added hurriedly, "that you might have a room to let to a traveler."

"Yes," she said dryly, "I can imagine what you were told. Your car broke down?"

"Well, yes. I was looking for a hotel, but they said that—"

The woman smiled wanly. "I can imagine. No, there's no hotel. But I do take in an occasional paying guest."

"You have room?"

"If you have two dollars, I have a room. Of course, that includes breakfast."

"Fine."

The woman held the door for him and showed him to a clean, rather bare upstairs room with a hard four-poster bed and, on the table beside it, a porcelain basin and a jug. "I'm sure you're hungry after your walk. I have some stew left over from dinner," she volunteered.

"I don't wish to put you out any more than I already have, Mrs.—"

"Miss Ferguson. You won't be putting me out. It'll be ready in twenty minutes."

Skardon watched her walk down the stairs. It was the walk of a woman twice her age, though her body, outlined by the light at the bottom of the stairs, was lithe and smooth-limbed. Her face could have been very pretty, too, had the fatigue and despair not been so obvious.

Half an hour later Skardon joined her in the dining room. On the table were brown bread, a glass of milk, and a steaming bowl of stew, rather light on the meat but tasty and welcome.

While he ate, she excused herself to take her place at a sewing machine in the corner of the room, illuminated by an unshaded light bulb, sewing sleeves for women's dresses. She worked silently, swiftly, and expertly. She did not seem to be aware of his presence but worked steadily and without pause at the pile of precut pieces.

"Aren't you working rather late?" Skardon asked.

"Yes," she said, "but I must. There's always so much to do. I have to send this batch to San Francisco by tomorrow noon." She sighed. "Anyway, I only have another eighteen or twenty to do."

Skardon consulted his watch. It said seven-thirty. "What time *is* it, by the way? My watch seems to have stopped."

She glanced at the tin clock on the mantel above the fake fireplace. "Nine-five."

Skardon finished up his repast and thanked her for taking the trouble. She did not reply. He added conversationally, "Nice quiet little town, Las Chipas. Kind of place I'd like to live in. I envy you."

Her hands froze.

"I'm sorry," Skardon said, puzzled. "Did I say something wrong, Miss Ferguson?"

She sat transfixed, her hands clenched, her eyes staring blindly out into space.

Skardon did not know what to do.

Suddenly the women swept the table clear of the pile of cloth, banged on the table with both fists in exploding rage, then buried her face in her hands, sobbing uncontrollably.

Skardon went to her, lifted her gently from her chair, and held her close, her face wet on his shoulder. He smoothed her hair and made comforting noises. It had been a long time since he had held a woman in his arms. Her warm body hard against his and the unaccustomed scent of female flesh revived the feelings he had so long repressed in prison. His hand slipped from her shoulder to her waist.

"No, no!" she protested, pushing against him with both hands. "You don't understand." In her voice there was no trace of coquetry.

Skardon did not let her go. He kissed her on the cheek, softly, then on the lips, hard. She held her lips firmly closed. Suddenly her lips parted, and she responded with a fervor that surprised him. Then she tore herself loose, holding him at arm's length. "Please don't," she whispered, her body shaking as with fever. "You don't know anything about me."

"I'll learn," Skardon said, picking her up in his arms and walking to the stairs.

Emily Ferguson was a bastard, she told him the next morning, when the sunlight came streaming through the window. A bastard and a wanton woman, she said bitterly. And evil. Had she not been evil, she would not have done what she did.

"What the hell are you talking about?" Skardon growled sleepily.

"Well," she said, avoiding his embrace, "maybe not completely evil. That's why I made you—go to the bathroom, each time. They say if you take the proper precautions afterward, things won't happen."

"Sounds like you're afraid you might get me pregnant." Skardon laughed.

She sat up in bed, letting the bedclothes fall away from her full, ripe breasts. "Don't joke. It's no laughing matter. You see, I have syphilis. I'm dying from it."

"Syphilis?" Skardon said numbly.

"I know it was selfish, and it was rotten of me to allow it, and I'm sorry, and I know you won't forgive me, and I don't blame you."

"You're sure of this?" Skardon said.

"Certain."

"How long have you had it?"

"I've known about it for one year, eight months, and eight days. It's in the secondary stage, the doctor said. When it reaches the tertiary stage, my brain will go, and all sorts of other horrible things will happen. I'm sorry—God knows I'm sorry."

Skardon took her hand. "Okay, you have syphilis. Now tell me about the bastard part."

"What is there to tell? I was born out of wedlock. My mother became pregnant when she was seventeen, and I never knew who my father was. She moved to a town in southern California from Pennsylvania, got a job at the local store, scratched out a living for a couple of years, moved a couple of times, then disappeared. I was taken in by the owner of the general store here as sort of a live-in servant. On my eleventh birthday, he gave me a gift." Her lips became hard. "Himself."

She had run away. The police had found her in San Fernando and returned her to Las Chipas and the storekeeper. She had told him, very quietly, that she would stay and work for him. But if he ever touched her again she would kill him, and she showed him the ice pick she would do it with. After that, he left her alone. The store-keeper's wife was wonderful. She never knew anything about her husband's attack. She was protective, treated her as her own daughter—she was childless—saw her through high school, and taught her to keep the store's books and to sew. When the storekeeper died, she stayed on to help in the store. When the storekeeper's wife died two years later, she left Emily the house, with a clear title. But the new store owner let her go, and she began to take in sewing to support herself.

From there on it was the old story of men and promises, ardent love, midnight assignations, and betrayals. She had slept with a fellow she knew in high school, but discovering she was not a virgin, he had beaten her up and left. She had slept with him just that once, and only after he had insisted that he would not marry her unless she did. It took her nine years to get over that. From then until she met the second, no man's hand had touched her. The other man was kinder: he made love to her half a dozen times over a period of weeks, then left her for another woman. He said that she was loose and that she could not expect him to marry "spoiled goods." At least she had the consolation that, when she died, he would have preceeded her to the grave, since he had given her the fatal infection.

"Let me get this straight," Skardon said when she finished her doleful tale. "Being raped as a minor and sleeping with two men over the past ten years or so makes you a wanton woman?"

Emily Ferguson nodded miserably.

"How much money did you take?"

She hit him on the face with her doubled fist. "That's a filthy thing to say!"

He chuckled and grabbed her arms before she could strike again. "You know, you're a damned good-looking female, Emily. You've got spirit. A shame you've got to die."

She stared at him, speechless.

"Are you absolutely *sure* you're going to die?" he went on.

She nodded slowly. "I deserve that. I risked your life. I didn't tell you the truth. And now you want to hurt me. I guess I deserve it. But you don't know what it's been like for me these past twenty months."

"Tell me."

"I've been ostracized. Nobody in town will talk to me. No one. Ace Karras saw to that. You're the first person who has spoken to me—*looked* at me, into my eyes, in nearly two years. Even children have been warned not to speak to the 'scarlet woman.' When I buy things at the store—the same store I worked at for nine years—I have to pick out what I want myself and leave the money on the counter. The only man that talks to me is the station-master, when I send my consignment of finished dresses to the contractor in San Francisco the fifth of every month. I won't tell you the filthy suggestions he makes to me. The local doctor won't treat me: I've got to take the Greyhound to the city each month, and I'm sure the doctor there charges me more than other patients. Why do you think I work every day until midnight? And now, after more than a year of treatment, he tells me I'm going to die."

"Ah, what the hell do doctors know?"

Emily Ferguson's eyes, which had blazed with anger, now grew clouded with tears. "I don't want to die."

Skardon put his arms around her. "Don't worry, Emily. You're not going to die, not for a very long time. And as for people not talking to you, I'm here. I'll talk to you."

"That's what Ace Karras told me."

"You don't believe me."

"Why should I? Three men have hurt me. I'll never trust another man as long as I live."

Skardon rolled out of bed and stretched, the sunlight glinting off his smooth powerful torso, the product of hundreds of hours pumping iron in the Las Chipas Maximum Security Facility weight room. He patted his hard flat abdomen. ''Get your lovely butt down to the kitchen and make me that breakfast you promised me last night. I've got work to do. When I get through, I'm going to buy Las Chipas and throw everybody out in the street. How do you like them onions?''

Emily Ferguson shook her head. Boy, could she ever pick them.

16. WHAT GOES UP . . .
28 SEPTEMBER 1928

JOHN K. SKARDON KNEW PERFECTLY WELL WHY HE WAS hanging around. He had been railroaded unjustly into prison six years earlier for a crime he had not commited, and within an hour after he had contrived once again to become a free man, the man upon whom he had bestowed the gift of time, Justin Pope, had imprisoned him in the past. He knew all about the bitterness of suffering an unjust fate. If he could somehow manage it, he would return to the year 1999 and take his revenge. It was too late to have the pleasure of killing Professor Doktor Doktor Thaddeus Klemper with his bare hands, but Justin Pope would be the next best thing.

But for now that delicious thought was but a dream. He was back in 1929 and had to make the best of it. He had things to do but, fortunately, plenty of time to do them. Meanwhile, a perfect target for his pent-up hatred and frustration lay ready to hand: he would wreak vicarious vengeance on the mean-spirited bigots of Las Chipas who had given so much pain to Emily Ferguson, who had given him so much pleasure.

The next morning, he waited until the town was well awake and the street outside well peopled and made his exit. He walked slowly down the street, trading equanimity for cold stares. The more hostility, the easier it was going to be. When he came to the bank, he entered and asked to speak with the manager.

The clerk to whom he addressed his request was a prim, thin-lipped cashier who viewed the middle-aged but powerful-looking man with unconcealed distaste. Whatever he was, dressed in an open-throated denim shirt, blue jeans, and workman's boots, he certainly was not the type of man the manager would care to see.

Seeing refusal forming on her features, Skardon said with an authority she could not fail to recognize, "Get him, and be quick about it."

When the manager finally appeared after an interval meant to show his visitor he had better things to do with his time, Skardon took an instant dislike to him. He was a large self-important man of about forty with the flushed face of a secret drinker and an ample belly across which a gold watch chain was draped.

"I am Mr. Virgil Wheaton. Did you want to see me?" the manager said, favoring Skardon with a fishy eye and a look of contempt when he observed the cloth bag the stranger carried. Obviously a farmer with the pennies and nickels he had laboriously collected over the months.

"I wish to open an account."

"Miss Baines will accommodate you, providing you have the proper credentials and a minimum of ten dollars."

Skardon smiled thinly and upended the bag of coins on the counter. They poured out in a golden stream, some falling to the floor and clattering across the room. When Skardon made no move to collect them, Miss Baines scurried from behind the teller's cage and started to pick them up.

"These are my credentials," Skardon said. "Approximately five thousand dollars worth. Needless to say, this is only an initial deposit, to which I will add really important sums once you can assure me that my account will be in good hands."

For the next half hour Mr. Virgil Wheaton purred assurances, over coffee and cigars in his office, that his client, Mr. John J. Jones, had made the right choice in entrusting his account to the First National Bank of Las Chipas. He dilated on the bank's sound, conservative investment policies, which his father had passed down to him, and the dividends that had been paid on the nailhead every quarter for the past thirty-three years. "Your money couldn't be in safer hands."

"I'm sure I'll be satisfied," Mr. Jones said. "Meanwhile, there is a service you can perform for me."

"You have merely to name it, Mr. Jones."

"I would like to have a telephone installed this afternoon, so I can be in daily contact with my broker in San Francisco."

"Certainly, sir," a beaming Virgil Wheaton said. "I shall take care of it personally. I presume you have bought the Olsen house? It is the only one in town really befitting a man of your station."

"I'm staying with Miss Emily Ferguson."

"With—with—*who*?"

"With *whom*? With Miss Emily Ferguson, at whose residence I would be pleased to see a new Pierce-Arrow drawn up at the front door, its tank filled and its title in my name, by three o'clock this afternoon. I hope I can rely on you for this favor."

Virgil Wheaton's mouth opened and closed like that of a fish in shallow water. He finally managed to choke out an assurance that everything would be done as Mr. Jones had ordered.

Mr. Jones nodded, managed not to notice the manager's proffered hand, and walked out onto the street. He stopped to gaze into several dust-streaked store windows, with their pathetic displays of ready-made clothes, musical instruments, chinaware, and bottles of liniment, giving the news a chance to spread. Five minutes after he left the bank, he entered the store where Emily had worked for nine years and placed an order for enough food to feed a platoon. "I'd like to charge this to my account, if I may," Skardon said offhandedly.

"By all means, Mr. Jones," replied the unctuous store owner, a man who had more hair sprouting from his nostrils than from his head.

"And send it along as soon as you find it convenient."

"Yes, sir," the owner said without having to inquire where the order should be sent, the village grapevine having already told him all he needed to know.

That afternoon, after a home-cooked meal such as he had not enjoyed in years, John J. Jones retired to his room for an hour, took a nap, and awoke to find a gleaming black Pierce-Arrow awaiting him in the front of the house, Virgil Wheaton standing beside it shooing away the local kids who ventured too close. Jones went out to inspect it, expressed his regret, and apologized for not having informed Mr. Wheaton that he had neglected to specify that he wanted a *white* Pierce-Arrow—black was so *depressing*, wasn't it?—but since it was so late in the day, tomorrow morning at eight sharp would do.

"Of course, of course," Wheaton stammered. "Happy to oblige." He would oblige, all right, he said to himself, and tack another hundred onto the commission he had already demanded from the Pierce-Arrow dealer in Sacramento thirty-five miles to the north.

Jones started up the short path to the house and then, as an afterthought, turned back and remarked casually, "And while you're at it, bring along a Buick—no, make that a Cadillac—runabout for Miss Ferguson. Let it also be white, so it won't be mistaken for all the other Cadillac runabouts around here."

That night lights burned late at Las Chipas, and more visits were exchanged than in the whole previous month. Who was this rich, mysterious John J. Jones? Where had he come from? What was his connection with Emily Ferguson? His ordering one of the most expensive automobiles on the market for her argued a close relationship, but what could it be? He was not her husband, clearly—he called her "Miss Ferguson"—and he was too young to be her father. And with the name Jones he could not be her brother. Questions were many, answers few, and caution indicated. A man like John J. Jones in their midst meant that golden crumbs from the rich man's table would drop in their laps. He had to be treated with care and deference, and that required that Emily Ferguson also be treated with civility and, in time, warmth, doled out in unobtrusive but ever-increasing measure.

Many eyes observed Jones's departure the next morning at nine. He wore the same clothes as the previous day, a faded blue denim shirt and trousers. The townspeople of Las Chipas thought it an amusing eccentricity, unforgivable dress for the street in any ordinary, respectable citizen but entirely appropriate for a millionaire, if that was what he wanted.

The white Cadillac sat outside the house the entire day. Emily Ferguson did not make an appearance, not even when the dusty Pierce-Arrow drove up late in the afternoon and John J. Jones got out with an armload of gaily wrapped boxes.

The next day he and Emily were seen to leave the house at midmorning. She was so transformed that if she had not come out of Emily Ferguson's house, few would have recognized her. She wore a smart short-skirted yellow silk dress, a broad-brimmed hat, silk stockings, and high-heeled pumps, all bought to her order during Jones's visit to San Francisco the day before. She had let down her hair so that it cascaded about her shoulders, applied lip rouge, and darkened her eyebrows. But even more remarkable was her bearing: rather than the foot-dragging, slump-shouldered downcast woman they had known for months past, she held her head high, walked with a spring in her step, and radiated a joy that had never been seen on her face before. She was not only beautiful, she was breathtaking.

Jones held the door for her as she took her place behind the wheel for her first driving lesson.

It was not the success Jones had hoped, but by the end of the day—and dented fenders on four townspeople's cars, a wooden fence knocked flat, and a crushed cat—she had mastered the fundamentals of making the car go more or less in the direction she aimed it. Jones deferred tuition in the reverse gear for the present, cheerfully paid damages without disputing the inflated demands, and left orders with a persistent young man who had attached himself to Jones to have the Cadillac repaired and repainted and at the front door on the morrow.

"It's all a dream," Emily Ferguson said, slipping out of her dress and caressing its silken softness before hanging it carefully on a wooden hanger. "I know I must wake up sometime, but please—not just yet."

Jones sat in the bedroom's only chair, his eyes caressing her silken softness. "Come here," he said quietly.

She walked over to him, took his head in her hands, and pressed it against her breasts. Each had things to say to the other, but somehow they never got said that night.

But the following morning Emily confronted him. "I think it's time we had a talk, John. I don't know anything about you, and you don't really know anything about me. I don't know why you're here, how long you're going to stay, where you're going when you leave me, but—"

"What makes you think I'm going to leave you?"

She sighed. "I'm the kind of woman men leave. That's what always happens to me, and there's no use fighting it. Anyway, you don't have to lie to me, whatever you do. Even if it was only for two days, you've made me happier than I ever hoped to be. I've had people who wouldn't even spit on me before you came into my life bringing around fresh-baked pies, and inviting me to the church social, and smiling like the hypocrites they are, and believe me, that alone will make me die happy. But—"

"What's this about dying?" said Jones, who seemed to have forgotten the affliction that would kill her.

"I told you. You can't have forgotten *that*."

"No, I haven't forgotten. Actually, I meant to break the news to you last night, but somehow we got distracted, and it slipped my mind."

"News? What news?"

Telling her to wait, Jones went to his room, where he brought down the metal toolbox Pope had given him from the closet shelf. From it he took a thick reference book and reread a passage in it twice. Then he took out a small glass vial from the compact but comprehensive medical kit Pope had thoughtfully included in his gift and picked up the package he had purchased the day before at a pharmaceutical supply house in San Francisco.

"Now look, Emily," he said, unwrapping the box to reveal a package of cotton, alcohol, and a dozen glass syringes and needles, "what I'm going to do is something you must never reveal."

She looked blankly at the needles.

"You've got to trust me, Emily." He held up the small glass vial. "This liquid will cure your syphilis."

"What are you?" she asked, drawing back. "Are you a doctor?"

"Yes, I am, although not a medical doctor. It's a long story, and I'll tell you one day, but meanwhile you must trust me."

He swabbed off the rubber cap of the vial with an alcohol sponge, drew back the plunger carefully, and inserted the needle. He emptied the syringe of its two milliliters of air and drew in two milliliters of the clear liquid. "Bare that beautiful butt of yours, Emily. It won't hurt much."

She stood before him indecisively. She did not know a damned thing about the man, except that he was a mysterious stranger who had given her two nights of ecstasy such as she had not known existed, was very rich, and now proposed to shoot an unknown liquid into her buttock. How could she know he was not some kind of lunatic? How could she know he would not inject her with poison, watch her die in agony, and leave as unobtrusively as he had come?

Jones watched her. It did not take a genius to guess what she was thinking. He held the needle in his right hand, the alcohol-impregnated swab in his left, waiting.

"All right," she said finally, and pulled up her dress. She felt a sensation of cold, then a sharp stab, then the cold again. "What was it?"

"Thank you for asking me after, not before," Jones said, putting his arms around her. "It's an antibiotic called floccacillin, and it'll cure your syphilis in forty-eight hours."

She looked at him gravely. "Can you tell me why I believe you—and what's an 'antibiotic'?"

"Never mind. Just trust me."

And she did. Every day he spent with her, she trusted him more. Her trust was complete when, on one of his frequent trips to San Francisco, eighty miles to the west, he took her to an eminent gynecologist for a complete examination. Three days later she received his report in the mail, to the effect that she was in excellent health, with no diseases or abnormalities.

Meanwhile, Jones had been busy. At first he had been obliged to go to San Francisco to establish his credit with a stockbroker there with the deposit of the other $5,000 in gold Justin Pope had given him. But that was his single visit to the broker; thenceforth his affairs dealing with stocks were handled entirely by telephone.

On the afternoon of the second of November, his broker, Mr. Oliver Sneed, telephoned to inform him that his flier in futures of Western Fir and Spruce, Inc., had, as a result of the huge forest fire in central Washington state, taken off "like a Fourth of July rocket," and what were his instructions?

"Sell," Jones said.

"But sir," Sneed protested, "are you not passing up a marvelous opportunity? I think that if you bought in, the price will steadily increase, and—"

"Sell," Jones repeated, "and take a short position for the $18,000-odd you realize on the stock."

"You want me to sell *short*?"

"That's what I want. I will be in touch with you about when to cover."

Four days later he told the dumbfounded Mr. Sneed that he should cover by the close of business that day to take advantage of the offer by Finnish newsprint producers, nervous because of a suspected imminent Russian push across Karelia, to American printing interests to undersell any American paper manufacturer for the next three months. Apparently the Finnish government was encouraging all exporters to obtain all liquidity possible as a hedge against expected Russian economic pressure.

Jones's first market coup netted him $87,000 in the first week.

He began to decentralize his operations. Dividing his profits regionally, he opened accounts with brokers in New Orleans, St. Louis, Chicago, and New York in addition to that with Mr. Sneed's firm. He transferred funds to banks in each of those cities and carefully kept all operations separate, under different names, so that no one would suspect the extent of his investments or their phenomenal profitability. Every time his profits with a single broker exceeded the $100,000 mark, he divided them, amoebalike, and began to nurture new entities in other cities. Before four months had passed, Jones was a millionaire many times over, and he had to be careful to lose once in a while to divert suspicion.

At the beginning of October he sent Emily Ferguson off on a trip to Europe, engaging a multilingual French female companion and a chauffeured automobile that met them in Le Havre to take them on a grand tour of the European capitals. She had been reluctant to go, insisting that she wanted nothing more than to be with Jones. Jones obtained her assent only by gently telling her that her expanded intellectual and social horizons would be of benefit to him in his work, although he had never explained exactly what his work was.

Whatever it was, he spent a good deal of time at it, mostly over the telephone in brief long-distance conversations, which he conducted from his bedroom and cut off the moment she opened the door to bring coffee. He also got a great deal of mail, which swelled as time passed to exceed that received by all of Las Chipas's townspeople combined. It did not take long for the word to spread that the mailbag of letters to Mr. John J. Jones was from an accommodation address in San Francisco, but more than that no one could discover.

After the first shock of discovery of the strange habits of the rich man in their midst and the discovery that he was a very hard man to know, the townspeople of Las Chipas substituted speculation for fact. He remained immured at Emily Ferguson's home the whole of every other day because he had a rare blood disease that required total bed rest or, according to another theory, because he was engaged in sexual orgies with the woman. On the days he was absent in San Francisco, it was because he was receiving transfusions for his disease or to replenish a blood supply depleted by his libidinous appetites. The latter theory gained currency upon Emily Ferguson's departure in October for Europe.

The day after she left, a caravan of trucks descended upon the town, and the residents of the block on which she lived began to load their possessions into the trucks and move to other cities or vacant dwellings in Las Chipas. They confided gleefully to the friends they left behind that their properties had been bought out at prices from two to three—and in the case of the school principal, who was reluctant to leave his position, nearly *four*—times their market value, and the offers were too attractive to refuse. Each family was as surprised as everyone else to discover that their neighbors had received the same irresistible offer, but it did not slow their exodus.

On the fourth of October yet another caravan entered Las Chipas. This invasion was of skilled carpenters, masons, plumbers, electricians, and other construction specialists. They proceeded to raze the entire block to the ground and, working days and into the night under floodlights, build a peculiar low-slung mansion of sixteen rooms and six baths, designed by some fellow from Arizona named Frank Lloyd Wright. While they were still working feverishly on the dwelling, landscape engineers enclosed the property in a small forest of trees and ornamental plants and shrubs and even constructed a small artificial waterfall backlit at night.

During this period, John J. Jones was nowhere to be seen. Rumor had it that he was traveling throughout the United States on his far-flung businesses, and for once, rumor was correct. He finally found the place he was looking for in Oregon, within seven miles of the Kotawanee Dam on a tributary of the Columbia River. He was back in Las Chipas the day before Emily Ferguson returned from Europe.

She was pleasantly surprised to find the beautiful new mansion but overjoyed to find Jones waiting for her. She had had a miserable time in Europe, fearing that Jones would disappear during her absence.

"Well, now you've seen what *I* did while you were gone," Jones said as he concluded a guided tour of their new home. "What did *you* do?"

"I hated every minute of it. I don't think I need tell you why."

"That's all right," Jones said easily. "Next year we'll *both* go, and you can relax. Meanwhile, did you learn any French?"

"Plusieurs mots, pas beaucoup."

"That's plenty. All you need is a vocabulary of five words, spoken with confidence, to knock over these yokels."

"Why should I want to do that?"

"Have you forgotten already what they've done to you all these years? We're going to make those sons of bitches sorry they ever looked cross-eyed in your direction."

"Oh, I see—you expect them to die laughing at my French. Well, it's a possibility, at that."

"Nothing of the sort, my love. I expect you to play

the grand *hostesse*, dine the perspiring proletariat of Las Chipas, wine them with the best bootleg hooch money can buy, and generally make yourself lovable.''

''And what is all this in aid of, may I ask?''

''Isn't it obvious? We're going to make friends and influence people. And when we've done so,'' Jones continued, his smile suddenly becoming as menacing as that of a grazing mako shark, ''we're going to confound them, smite them hip and thigh. And when we've had our fun, we're going to break them, every single goddamn one of them, and plow up the town and sow it with salt.''

17. CHRISTMAS PRESENT 24 DECEMBER 1928

NO BOOTLEG WHISKEY WAS SERVED AT THE PARTY GIVEN on Christmas Eve 1928 by John J. Jones and Emily Ferguson to the townspeople of Las Chipas: the guests drank only the best smuggled scotch whiskey and French wines and cognac, served by a professional staff of forty-eight brought from San Francisco for the occasion. Yet the 460-odd guests who had eagerly accepted Jones's hospitality, however happy to soak up all the alcoholic beverages in sight, would have been equally content to drink tap water merely in order to view, finally, the inside of the mansion and the terraced gardens.

The buffet was similarly sumptuous. A veritable menagerie of wild fowl, venison, stuffed turkey, and huge Smithfield hams, arrayed on long linen-draped tables on both sides of the parquet-floored sitting room, covered with precious oriental carpets, fell prey to the appetites of the ravenous horde. And when, hunger refreshed by dancing to the music of the twelve-piece band, they returned to the board, the good people of Las Chipas always found waiters in tuxedos waiting to fill their glasses with liquors they hastened to knock back, for surely they would never have the opportunity to drink such booze again.

Long before midnight, most of the townspeople were comfortably swacked, laughing uproariously at each other's supposed witticisms and exuding a bonhomie that included all the world. As they recalled it later, John J. Jones was drunker than anybody, reeling about the room, good-naturedly banging the men on the back, kissing the ladies' hands, singing songs rather too ribald for the tastes of the church crowd—although like good Christians they forgave him when they discovered the quality of his liquor—and buttonholing community leaders to express his confidence in the American way and the blessings it had brought to him on this Christmas Eve.

"The American way—let's drink to it," he said, his arm around the shoulders of Myron Parsley, a deacon of the local Methodist church. He hoisted his glass.

"To our beloved commonwealth," a tipsy Parsley assented, raising his own.

"Commonwealth," Jones said. "Mr. Parsley, you just said a mouthful."

"Uh, how do you mean?"

"Common wealth is the American way, tha's what. Wealth for the common man, tha's what the Founding Fathers had in mind. Tha's what this country is all about. Why—looka me!"

Parsley looked, his eyes alternately trying to focus on one of the two identical figures wavering before him.

"Looka me," Jones repeated. "If it weren't for the American way, what would I be now?"

Parsley thought the question quite reasonable, but no answer came.

"Nothing, tha's what," Jones supplied.

"Wha's what?" Parsley said, having already lost the thread of the discussion.

"Exactly what I been saying. 'Fit hadn't been for good old-fashioned American free enterprise, could I have bought Black Star when it was selling at twenty-one cents a share? 'Course not. Could I have built this house if the stock hadn't zoomed to $7.45 a share after a three-for-one split? Sure not. But that's the American way."

A zone of silence radiated from the corner of the room where Jones was holding forth. Brains too deadened by alcohol to remember the middle name of their wife's mother now had ineradicably engraved upon them the words "Black Star," "twenty-one cents a share," and

"$7.45 a share after a three-for-one split." None of the listeners was particularly gifted in mathematics, but all instantly computed that a dollar invested in Black Star, whatever Black Star was, had increased in value by something like ten thousand percent. The revelation did not precisely dampen the proceedings, but it certainly shortened them as men who had overheard the secret of Jones's sudden, spectacular riches decided that the best Christmas present they could have was a good night's sleep and an early rise and a clear head on the morrow, when they would find out where to lay hands on some Black Star stock. Within minutes, the fifteen-odd men who had picked up the scent of easy money were saying their farewells and dragging their protesting wives away from the best party they would ever attend.

It took another hour or so of such slurred, stage-whispered indiscretions by Jones to reveal to those who remained that they too could make a killing on Wall Street. The trickle of couples making for the door after a hasty good night became a flood. Well before midnight, when Jones had let it be known that he would have gifts for everyone, the stragglers left, fearful that should they drink any more, they might inadvertently share their priceless secret with a neighbor. That would never do. Besides, nothing that Jones could bestow on them could compare with the fortunes they were about to possess.

"Do you think you're being quite fair?" Emily Ferguson asked, brushing her long brown hair as Jones peeled off his dinner jacket in their bedroom.

"Very fair, indeed," Jones assured her. He popped a bicarb tablet to counteract the gallons of tea he had consumed during the evening. "The Black Star mining stock *did* increase in value something like ten thousand percent over the past two months, and during the next ten will continue to soar. And so will the other stocks I mentioned."

"But how can you be sure?"

"Very simple. These unlisted stocks are being traded, as our fellow townspeople will soon learn, by certain brokerage firms. They are firms which I own, and in which my firms alone make the market. I will offer inducements for Las Chipas stockholders to remain with those firms."

"But what if they don't? What if they go to another firm and learn that those stocks are worthless?"

"They'll go back to my captive brokers, of course, and threaten them with the law. Whereupon my brokers will offer to buy the so-called fraudulent stock back at a handsome profit. The natural conclusion of the owners of the stock will be that, for some reason, its true value is unknown to the other brokers, and thenceforth they'll keep the secret of its worth strictly to themselves."

"Of course," she persisted, "they could also conclude that their brokers are pretty dumb, offering good money for worthless stock."

"In which case they will reason that they're smarter than the brokers, a common—and not always foolish—assumption."

"Yes, but what if they then take the brokers up on their offer to buy the stock back?"

"They will be very wise. Do you wish to wager how many will do so? My own guess is that the suspicions of each and every one of them will be laid to rest and that they'll go into hock to buy even more stock. When you stake wisdom against greed, greed wins every time."

Emily removed her lipstick thoughtfully. "I hope you know what you're getting into. You'll have to pour out millions to keep those dummy companies afloat. Worse yet, you'll have to pay enormous dividends to keep them coming back for more."

"That's exactly the idea, my pet. Once they've bought and seen their dividends roll in, they'll plow them back into more of this over-the-counter stock. I won't need to manufacture any more ten-thousand-percent bonanzas from now on: just doubling the price of the stock every quarter will be more than enough to keep the suckers coming."

"And then?"

Jones smiled. "More fun and games."

Since he first had occupied the extra bedroom at Emily Ferguson's old house, John K. Skardon had kept the metal toolbox locked and on the top closet shelf. It was only one of the many secrets he kept from Emily Ferguson, who since he had cured her of the syphilis that had afflicted her accepted everything he did or said on blind faith. Her confidence in him was so complete that if he had told her to climb to the top of the Las Chipas water tower, spread her arms, and fly away, she would have tried. Well, almost . . . And his confidence in her was nearly of the same order—almost, for he always kept the box securely locked when he himself was not in his study alone, the door locked behind him.

On New Year's morning 1929, John K. Skardon sat at his desk in his book-lined study. Nobody else, not even a cleaning woman, not even Emily, was allowed inside. The reference books, which constituted nearly half the sizable collection, were all on physics, engineering materials, magnetism, and electrical generation. The rest of the shelf space was occupied by catalogs of suppliers of scientific equipment, mainly switches and vacuum tubes, exotic alloys, and generators. Every afternoon Skardon spent several hours drawing up plans and laboriously making calculations with paper and pencil, wishing that Justin Pope had had the foresight to include among the box's contents a pocket calculator.

The other contents of the box nearly made up for the omission, however, though a calculator *would* have been welcome to compute the regular and enormous profits Skardon had made thanks to other items in the toolbox: a magnifying glass and four rolls of microfilm from *The New York Times* for the years 1928 and 1929. Knowing the stock market quotations a week or even a day in advance allowed Skardon to play the market without risk, provided he threw in enough losers to keep his brokers from suspecting that he had inside information, which might trigger an unwanted investigation. His only worry was to make sure that he spread his business so thin that his presence in the market as the biggest speculator of all time was never revealed. Part of his strategy was to keep shifting in and out of stocks, some winners and some losers, but always at the end of a week or so showing great profits, which were distributed among accounts in more than three hundred banks under so many names that by September merely keeping track of his money was taking three hours a day.

Skardon, though a cynic, was not so utterly ruthless as he imagined himself to be. During September he made a point of having his stable of tame brokers call each of the citizens in Las Chipas who had an account and warn them that what went up ultimately came down. The brokers reminded their customers that good business practice suggested that, having pyramided their investments many times over, they at least retire the debts with the banks and the mortgages they had floated to finance their investments in the first place. Even then, their profits would be spectacular. Even then, every single speculator would be wealthy enough to retire on a comfortable income for the rest of his life, with enough left over to excite the cupidity of his heirs. During the month that followed, only a dozen-odd investors took this excellent advice; three of them, observing the continued rise of the market as September gave way to October, recanted their decision and again put everything they owned and could borrow into the stocks they had overheard Jones recommend.

As that fateful year of 1929 unfolded and the stock quotations each day quickened men's pulses as they saw themselves transformed from clerks and schoolteachers and grape farmers to men of substance, their attitude toward John J. Jones also underwent a subtle change. They still greeted him cordially enough, for after all, he was still by far the richest among them, but they no longer had time for small talk with the man whose simple greeting on the street had a few months previously been a small social triumph. They needed their spare moments to study the market and to speak self-importantly among themselves of their sagacity in seizing the golden bird on the wing. As for their wives, few had returned Emily Ferguson's hospitality, and then only to show off their new acquisitions rather than out of a spirit of gratitude. Even so, they managed to convey the impression that she was being received as a mark of grace on the part of her social superiors.

On October 6, 1929, John J. Jones began to issue a long-planned series of orders to his captive brokers. They were to begin quietly to sell off his huge investments. Jones's holdings under his myriad names were so enormous that even his carefully timed sales caused the market to tremble. By Tuesday the fifteenth, all his stock had been sold and the proceeds deposited in his hundreds of bank accounts. On Monday the twenty-eighth, he gave orders for his brokers to take short positions in the stock of more than 180 different major companies. If the stock had then gone up, his immense fortune would have been wiped out overnight. But when word of the orders hit Wall Street, the market, already nervous, panicked.

Most of Jones's sell orders had been concentrated on Monday afternoon, being executed just before the closing bell. When the stock exchange opened Tuesday morning, pandemonium broke out as brokers attempted to rally their frightened clients, then led the attempt to sell off their stocks as they began the long plunge downward. The day before the last despairing and bankrupt broker leapt out of a Wall Street office window and the market finally bottomed out, Jones covered his short sales, and the injection of cash led the feeble rally that signaled the end of the market crash of 1929.

Jones's investment of the $5,000 in gold coins Justin

Pope had given him, with the help of *The New York Times* microfilms, had ballooned with the bull market to more than $600 million in slightly more than a year. By selectively selling short, he had multiplied this sum within days to close to $2 billion, and so diligently had he spread his operations around that no one, not even Emily Ferguson, suspected that next to the Rockefeller and Mellon families, John J. Jones was the richest man in America. And even Jones himself did not realize that far from having anticipated the market crash, he had caused it.

Jones's good fortune was matched by the reversal of those of the citizens of Las Chipas, with the exception of the few who had taken to heart their brokers' advice. The banks called in their loans and, when no money was forthcoming, seized their assets and auctioned them off to the highest bidder at approximately ten cents to the dollar.

John J. Jones knew too much about human nature to hang around Las Chipas. He knew that sooner or later word would get out how he had had them for lunch before they had him for dinner. They would remember the uncharacteristically expansive manner at his Christmas party of the usually reticent stranger. They would contrast his present wealth with their newfound poverty. They would remember his loquacity about the Black Star gold mine stock and the others that had made them rich—temporarily—and poor—permanently. Some public-spirited citizen would bring a rope and toss it over a high limb, and the good people of Las Chipas would string up John J. Jones to it. That was not exactly the punch line he had planned for his little joke on the people of Las Chipas, who had treated so abominably the woman he did not know he loved.

Two days before the first sheriff's auction, John J. Jones locked up his mansion and disappeared with his wife, Emily, from Las Chipas forever.

18. ROGUE RIVER 30 MARCH 1930

ROGUE RIVER CITY WAS AN 1890S GOLD PROSPECTOR'S bad joke. A collection of eight or nine sagging, abandoned frame buildings, the "city" was to a village the size of Las Chipas what Las Chipas was to Chicago. That suited John K. Skardon just fine, because it huddled in a depression in the mountains of western Oregon, far from any present habitation but only twelve miles from a new hydroelectric plant on the Rogue River itself.

In mid-1929 Skardon's agents had found the site, bought up eighteen sections, erected a chain-link fence around the property, and built a comfortable log cabin on a bluff with a view toward the Pacific Ocean, fifty miles away. It also overlooked a man-made plateau, perfectly flat, some two hundred yards on a side, where the trees had been cut and the ground leveled and paved with concrete. The site was linked with Crescent City, California, on the main coastal highway south, by an all-weather road built on Skardon's orders. The ramshackle buildings that gave the settlement its name were put in habitable condition, and the construction crew departed, wondering what the mysterious project portended.

The following week another crew, from the local utility company, erected the last of a series of pylons winding its way through the mountains from the hydroelectric dam on the Rogue and strung high-tension cables to a transformer station newly built at the edge of the bare concrete slab. They too left, no wiser than the crew that had preceded them.

The site remained empty except for security guards on

patrol along the chain-link fence, shotguns cradled in the crooks of their arms, until the first week of November. First to arrive were John K. Skardon and Emily Ferguson, who took up residence in the cabin on the bluff. A few days later men began to occupy the refinished houses of Rogue River City itself. By the end of the week, trucks bearing large wooden crates and others loaded with I beams and huge spools of cable had arrived at the site.

For the next two months Emily Ferguson scarcely saw Skardon except at mealtimes, and the quiet smile that was always on his lips when he looked at her had disappeared. The work, whatever it was, was obviously going badly. She had never dared to ask about it, though she was sure that what John did was somehow not what other people did. Nor did she really want to know, for fear that the knowledge might come between them. Knowledge would compromise his privacy, the compartmentalization of his life into the personal aspects, in which she participated, and his business affairs, from which she was rigorously excluded. She feared that the intimacy of confidences, added to the confidences of intimacy, might prove too large a commitment for Skardon to accept, and he would feel morally obliged to marry her. Although there was nothing more in the world she desired, she was too proud to put the man she loved into a position he so obviously did not desire.

And all the while, the weird structure rose on the vast gray plain below the bluff. Day by day, through binoculars, she watched Skardon hurrying from one work party to another, verifying transit sights of the steel columns and beams connecting them that rose like a gigantic spider's web over the field, directing others in the assembly of what could have been black light bulbs into huge flat arrays, strung together with electrical wire, welding, cutting, fastening, encapsulating, discarding, and, above all, changing things from morning until long after dark, when the floodlights cast a ghostly glow over the huge project, which resembled nothing so much as one of those Rube Goldberg inventions in the Sunday cartoons.

The second week in June the workers packed up and left. No one remained on the property but Skardon and Emily Ferguson. Even the security guards who patrolled outside the perimeter on horseback had their own line camps and did not venture inside the fence. But if anything, Skardon worked harder than ever. He was up well before dawn and usually worked until after dark, taking sandwiches to lunch on at the site. He was looking positively cadaverous, she reflected, from three months of unremitting labor, without having taken a single day off. His eyes were bloodshot and feverish and glowed with religious fervor, as if he were about to receive a vision.

And then, on the third day of July, he finished . . . whatever it was he was working on. At eleven in the morning, he climbed into his Pierce-Arrow, no longer lustrous but caked with mud, and drove up the long winding road from the work site to their cabin.

Emily Ferguson, standing on the edge of the bluff, looked down through the perpetual Oregon mist upon the man-made plateau and the monstrous, sprawling structure standing upon it and shook her head. It would not keep water out. It would not keep one warm in winter or offer shade from the summer's sun. It was not utilitarian. And it certainly was not beautiful.

She heard him come up behind her and felt strong, reassuring hands encircle her waist.

"You know, Emily," he whispered, "you are a most peculiar woman. If I didn't know from firsthand experience, I might guess you're not a woman at all."

"Oh? And why not?"

"Because you lack that most conspicuous of all female traits—curiosity."

She gave a little brittle laugh. "Is that what you think?"

"Of course—what else? You haven't expressed the

slightest interest in what I've been working my butt off at ever since we arrived here three months ago.''

''It was none of my business. If you wanted me to know, you'd have said something.''

''What absolute nonsense! I would have told you anything you wanted to know, but I was afraid I'd bore you. After all, this is pretty esoteric stuff.''

''No excuses—go ahead: bore me.''

''Well,'' Skardon said, leading her out of the mist-become-rain into the cabin and throwing a log on the fire, ''don't say I didn't warn you.'' He sat down in the leather easy chair, and she curled up on the couch opposite. He thought about where best to begin. ''Very well,'' Skardon said finally, ''I'm from the future. The year 1999, just seventy years from now, to be precise. Before I came back to the year 1929 I was condemned to life imprisonment in the maximum-security facility at Las Chipas for first-degree murder. And before that I was a professor of physics at the University of California at Berkeley, specializing in magnetic molecular resonance.''

Emily Ferguson was stunned. Except for the wild look in his eyes, he seemed normal enough. But she had heard that when people worked too hard, their brains could suddenly snap. ''Listen, John,'' she said soothingly, ''why don't you lie down and take a nap while I make dinner, or relax and listen to *Amos 'n' Andy*?''

''Listen, sugarplum,'' Skardon growled, ''you asked me to explain, and an explanation is what you're going to get. Now, sit down.''

Emily sat.

''I guess I'd better start at the beginning, back in graduate school when I first detected thermomagnetic time-lapse phenomena and wrote it up for old Herr Professor Doktor Doktor Thaddeus Klemper. The Atomic Energy Commission awarded me a grant based on the paper's promise, and—''

"Atomic Energy Commission?"

"It's a—well, you never heard of the atomic bomb, of course, so—"

"Atomic bomb?"

"Yes. The smallest of them, about big enough to fit into a Boy Scout knapsack—it's actually called a knapsack bomb—has the explosive power of 55,000 tons of TNT."

Emily felt an icy finger on her neck. "Fifty-five thousand tons of TNT," she echoed in a faint voice.

"Of course, a hydrogen bomb is many times as powerful, but I don't want to get sidetracked . . . Now, after I had spent about eleven years working on the problem at UC, I was joined by a very smart female crystallographer, and we became rather matey, and . . ." Skardon hesitated, not seeing the point of going into detail about Fortuna Fonteneau. "And so old Klemper killed her and blamed me for it." He smiled weakly.

Emily Ferguson, who felt like crying, smiled gamely back.

"They condemned me, of course, but thanks to a lady chief justice of the California Supreme Court who doesn't believe in capital punishment, my sentence was commuted to life, to be spent at Las Chipas Penitentiary."

"I see. Las Chipas Penitentiary." The town's prison, she recalled, consisted of a bare, unbarred room in town hall where the occasional drunk was put overnight to sleep it off. And a *female* chief justice of the supreme court, when even women *lawyers* were a novelty!

"Exactly. But you see, somehow Klemper managed to build a machine from my notes, took it for a test run, and got speared by some Indian back in the year 1011 B.C." He laughed.

Emily laughed, her heart beating wildly.

"After that, you can guess what happened."

"I'm sure, but why don't you tell me—it would be more fun to hear it from your own lips."

"Well, this music major—a *music* major, imagine!—

fell asleep and went along for the ride and somehow wound old *Tempus Fugit* back to the year 1999. He ran me down in prison and, on my instructions, rigged up a miniaturized *Tempus Fugit* in a van. He took it back to the last century, parked it in the yard, and I, being a trusty, was able to climb in and make a getaway. But as you have no doubt guessed, this creep double-crossed me and dumped me back in 1928, figuring I'd never catch up with him.''

''But you will, won't you, John?'' Stark raving mad. She had heard about cases like this: too much work, and suddenly everything fell apart.

''You bet your sweet little tootsies I will,'' Skardon replied, his eyes blazing. ''Just wait. I'll—''

''Never mind about *him*, darling. Why don't you just tell me what happened next.''

Skardon looked at her strangely. ''Well, hell, you *know* what happened next. I walked into Las Chipas that night, and knocked at your door, and—''

''Oh, of course. I remember. You were carrying that cute little overnight bag.''

''I was carrying a machinist's toolbox. One thing you can say about that boy Pope—''

Good God! He was off again, talking about a boy pope. And for a moment there, she thought he had gotten his mind back on track.

''—including that floccacillin that cured your syphilis, along with a pharmaceutical reference book, a little gun with crowd-control gas, and, best of all, ten thousand bucks in golden eagles and a magnifying glass and a microfilm of *The New York Times*.''

''Microfilm?''

''Sure, you know—oh, of course you *don't* know. It's a transparent photographic film in miniature, which reduces a whole page of newsprint to the size of a thumbnail.''

''Very useful, especially for midgets with the runs.''

''Well, that, too,'' Skardon said, laughing. ''For a minute there, I didn't think you believed me.''

''What a thing to say! But tell me more about the midgets.''

''Yeah,'' Skardon assented, ''my boy Pope really came up with something cute. He had put the complete file of the *Times* for the years 1928 and 1929 in that box, and it was all I needed, along with the golden eagles, to beat hell out of the market.''

''The stock market, you mean.''

''What else? You see, once I had set up brokerage accounts all over the country, I could make money on the bulls *or* the bears, since in 1929 there were no restrictions on short sales. Since I knew what the market would be tomorrow, or six months from now, I couldn't lose. It was only a matter of keeping a low profile and raking in as much money as I wanted.''

''And you made a lot, I bet.''

''Well, if you want to know to the closest million,'' Skardon said with a smug smile, ''I can't tell you. Must be somewhere around one billion nine hundred million.''

''Dollars.''

''Dollars.''

Emily Ferguson nodded. ''In the bank.''

''Hell, no!'' Skardon exploded. ''Nobody with any sense would put money in a bank these days. After all, President Roosevelt is going to close them all in 1933.''

''Who?''

''President Roosevelt—the guy who's going to succeed Herbert Hoover.''

Poor John. Overwork had *really* scrambled his brains. Roosevelt had been president way back at the turn of the century, succeeding the assassinated President, William McKinley. It was a hopeless case. All she could do was humor the poor dear and hope he did not become violent before she could get him to a good doctor. ''Well, where did you put all those millions if not in the bank, John?''

''Why—under our house back in Las Chipas.''

"Funny, I never saw it. One billion nine hundred million dollars must take up a lot of room."

"Aha, my dear. You forget that the house was built during your absence in Europe. Beneath the basement is a storeroom constructed of reinforced concrete. Access is through a false wall in the bird's-eye-maple-paneled basement bathroom. If you open the medicine cabinet and flip up the empty upper shelf, a vertical panel slides back, just like in the Fu Manchu movies."

"And?"

"Open shelves stacked with bearer bonds, shares in companies like IBM—worth about five thousand times more today, or rather, in 1999, than they were when I bought them—stacks of gold coins, rare stamps, impressionist masters such as Renoir, Gauguin, and Cezanne, a portfolio of original Dürer drawings, some—."

"I get the idea," Emily said dryly.

"The bottom line is that what I've invested will be worth twenty times that amount when we get back to 1999."

"Oh, we're going back to 1999, are we?"

"That's right. We—"

"Darling," Emily Ferguson said, rising, "I've had all the travel I can take for one day. Do you mind if we put off our trip to 1999 until tomorrow?"

"Not at all, my love. A day more or less can't possibly make any difference," Skardon responded graciously if inaccurately.

19. TARADIDDLE
30 MARCH 1930

IT TOOK EMILY FERGUSON FIVE AND A HALF HOURS TO drive the 155 miles south along the inland highway from Rogue River to Sacramento and another three-quarters of an hour to Las Chipas. She arrived at nearly two in the morning, when the town where she had grown up was fast asleep, as was the man she loved and had left behind.

Now, as she drove up the semicircular driveway to her darkened home, she began to question the wisdom of coming back. Maybe she was being as irrational as John's stories of immense riches and time machines and a prison past and a professorship at UC. When John had flopped into bed, still in his sweaty work clothes, and gone immediately to sleep, she had sat some time staring into the fireplace, trying to make some sense of the wild ramblings that kept reverberating through her mind.

It was not that she had not tried to pin him down to some verifiable falsehood, so that she could show him by visible evidence that his mind was overtired and that what he took for fact was an exhaustion-induced delusion. But he had a ready, if entirely improbable, explanation for everything. She had heard that schizophrenics followed the logic of their own dementia and within that framework were often most convincing.

That imaginary $2 billion for instance—why had she never heard of it before? Because, he said, he had wanted to keep it as a surprise until they retrieved it in 1999. Very well, then: he had mentioned possessing a huge hoard of stocks and paintings and gold coins and bullion, but why had he never mentioned bank notes, which would be much more easily negotiable? Negotiable now, he agreed, but once the United States went off the gold standard when Roosevelt came to power in 1933—there was Roosevelt again—the gold certificates would be worthless. And when she suggested he offer some proof that he could actually predict the market by producing those mysterious "microfilms," he airily replied that, being for the years 1928 and 1929, now history, he had destroyed them. Then how about that medical reference book that had advised him of the dosage of that magic injection of floccacillin to give her? The title page would have the date of publication, sometime in the 1990s, wouldn't it? It would, he replied, and did. But since, on the morrow, they would be moving ahead sixty-nine years to 1999 A.D., where even more up-to-date books were available, he had tossed it in the fire.

She had tried another tack.

He had told her that, from prison, he had given instructions to a young music student on how to build a time-transporter small enough to fit in a small van.

"I had to," Skardon said. "He was the only person who knew the secret besides me."

"Granting that—and you'll correct me if I seem stupid—but what exactly is a 'van' in the year 1999?"

"Fair question. More or less what it is now: a small enclosed truck."

"A small truck," she mused. "Yet you have required an area the size of several football fields to construct your present 'time-transporter.' "

"Oh, I see what you're getting at. The explanation is really very simple, Emily. In 1999—actually as early as the 1960s the device was fairly well developed—we had what is called the transistor. A device no larger than a pinhead, it could do the work of the glass vacuum tube such as we use in our radios. Within twenty years, though, somebody had invented the integrated circuit, the microchip, a device the size of a postage stamp which did the work of hundreds of transistors, thousands of vacuum tubes.''

Emily sighed.

John Skardon did not hear it. ''So with microminiaturized circuitry, and the power of a small generator, I could do what it has taken tens of thousands of vacuum tubes such as fill those modules down there.''

''And the dam?''

''Oh, well—naturally it takes an application of power commensurate with the number of tubes which must be heated to provide the electromagnetic impulse needed to propel a body from one time phase to another. With microcircuitry, a medium-sized portable generator is sufficient. With old technology like vacuum tubes, you need the output of a fair-sized dam.''

Emily Ferguson's head was beginning to ache. She saw she was getting no place with the inquisition. He possessed the devilish ingenuity of the psychotic, and when his answers were patently absurd, he covered them with scientific jargon that she could not have comprehended even if it was true.

''Let's go to bed, honey,'' she said wearily. ''We'll have plenty of time to talk about it tomorrow.''

Skardon shook his head. ''Tomorrow we leave for 1999.''

She would have willingly gone with him anywhere, including ''1999.'' God only knew what he intended to do with that weird junkyard of electrical gear, but whatever it was, she had to stop him. She had somehow to convince him that he needed medical care before he went down to the forest of high-tension wires and started pulling switches and electrocuting them both.

If only his manner had been less rational. If only he had raved like the madman his words branded him, it would have been so much easier to come to terms with the situation in which she found herself. But she had to admit that the whole bizarre story had some sort of inner consistency. If she could only accept his premises, she could accept everything.

The sole fact she could hang on to was his cure of her syphilis. There was no question she had been infected, and when he had come into her life was well along the road of no return. There was no question that she was now cured. But had his injection of the "floccacillin" cured her? She had heard of sicknesses even more deadly than syphilis suddenly going into unexplained remission. She had heard of the miracle cures at Lourdes, in France. Faith healers had on numerous occasions filled tents with townspeople at Las Chipas, and she knew for a fact that little Teddy Skillings, prayed over and feeling the touch of healing hands, had been cured of his warts, and old Mrs. Dorman of her lumbago, and Emerson Jenks of his migraines.

God knew she had faith in John J. Jones. She was ready to do anything for, believe anything of, the man who had appeared miraculously when she most needed succor and been her support and salvation. His strength had claimed her confidence and trust from the moment he had enveloped her in his arms, assuring her that for the first time in her life she had nothing to fear. Was it not possible, then, the magic "floccacillin" had been ordinary tap water, and her faith her cure? She had no way of knowing, but this was certain: either everything he had told her this night was true, or it was a brutal lie.

Either his "time travel," his term in a prison which did not exist, his wonder-working drug, his professorship at the university were facts, or they were the products of a disordered mind. She could not prove them one way or the other.

Either his trips to San Francisco had been to engage in the stock market manipulations he claimed or to commit crimes that would account for his sudden affluence: so much money in so little time could have been amassed in no other way. That, at least, she could prove.

He claimed that he had constructed an immense secret

vault beneath their home in Las Chipas. It was the only fact she could confirm or refute. If it was the truth, that would mean that *everything*, however preposterous, was the truth. If it was a lie, then *everything* he had told her, including his protestations of love, was a lie. For her, the knowledge would change nothing. She would follow him wherever he led. But at least she would *know*.

The house was dark as she drove up the driveway to the front door. She switched off the lights of the Cadillac and walked across the gravel and up the steps. By the light of the full moon, she unlocked the door. Inside, the house was filled with the dim shadows of furniture draped in dustcovers. She knew the house was untenanted, had not echoed to a footfall since they had left more than three months earlier. And yet she had a premonition that she was not alone. She was being silly, she told herself, but there was no reason to tarry.

She walked swiftly through the spacious hall, down the corridor to the kitchen, and pulled open the basement door. Out of habit, she flicked on the light switch. When nothing happened, she pointed the beam of her flashlight down the wooden stairs. It was at that moment that she heard sounds of movement on the second floor, then the creak of footsteps on the stairs.

"Is that you, Emily?" came the mocking voice of Ace Karras. "Sure it is. It's our little Emily Ferguson, coming home to roost." The footsteps came slowly, deliberately, down the stairs. She was frozen to the spot, too frightened to cry out.

"Don't be afraid, Emily," said the voice, now closer. "It's only me—Ace Karras."

"And me—Hal Minthe," came a voice from the other side, between her and the back door.

"Don't be afraid, Emily," Karras said. He was now at the foot of the stairs and moving leisurely toward her. "We just want to talk to you."

Her hands felt as if they were carved of wood as she reached around the edge of the door and removed the key. It rattled as she inserted it into the lock on her side and slammed the door shut. Too late the men on the other side grabbed at the handle and found the door locked.

Ace Karras chuckled. "Come on out, Emily," he coaxed. "There's no way out of that cellar, and you know it. Anyway, we're not going to hurt you. We just want to talk to you about your Mr. John J. Jones and what he did with all the money he stole from us with that phony gold mine stock."

Emily breathed as shallowly as she could, as if her silence would somehow convince them she was not there, after all.

"Come on—open up!" came Minthe's voice, suddenly hard. "Open up or we'll kick the door down, and when we do—"

"Don't pay any attention to Hal," Karras broke in. "You know how he is—impulsive, like . . . Come on, let's have some action, or when we get this door open, we may have to find out if you're still as good in bed as you used to be." He began to thump on the door.

Emily looked around like a caged animal.

Suddenly an ax split the doorjamb.

Emily turned and ran blindly down the stairs in the darkness, so terrified that she did not think to switch on the flashlight and stumbled and fell the last three steps. She picked herself up and flashed the light around her as ax blows methodically splintered the door. There was no exit from the basement, that she knew. She was trapped.

Then she remembered the bathroom. It had only a hasp on the inside of the door, but it was better than staying where she was. She ran inside, fastened the door behind her, and waited for the inevitable.

It came a moment later when she heard Karras's tread on the stairs. Once again he descended the steps with slow deliberation, allowing her to savor the full flavor of her dread. Tears coursed down her cheeks. She knew she could not delay the moment any longer. Now, at last, she would have to confront the truth. She was afraid of Ace

Karras. She was afraid of Hal Minthe. But she was even more afraid that she was about to learn that John was indeed a madman.

She turned, opened the medicine cabinet, mentally crossed herself, and pushed up against the top wooden shelf. Nothing happened, except that it felt as though her heart had stopped beating. She banged her fists against the bird's-eye-maple paneling. She felt a featherlike breath of air as the panel slid slowly up.

She stepped through the aperture, groped for the light switch on the wall, and found it. She pressed it. The panel, backed with steel plate, slid back into place with a muffled thud as overhead lights flashed on.

Down a long tunnel half the length of a football field were row upon row of steel shelves bearing bars of gold, shelves of stock certificates, and odd-sized rectangular wooden boxes that could have been crated old masters. On a shelf within arm's reach was a metal box that, when she lifted back the lid, revealed a full gallon of uncut gems.

She breathed a sigh of relief. Whatever he was, John was not a lunatic.

But maybe *she* was, to have trapped herself in the treasure room, a room with no way out. Ace and Hal knew she was down there someplace. Presumably they had set up camp in the house, confident that sooner or later either she or John Jones would put in an appearance, whereupon they would do what they had to do to regain their lost investments. Any moment now they would discover the secret of the basement storeroom. It might be minutes or it might be hours, but find a way in they surely would, even if they had to hack through the foot-thick concrete walls. They had waited three months. Another day or two would not matter to them.

She walked the length of the corridor, seeking another way out. She knew there had to be one. Skardon had said that he had been bringing treasure to the room for many months, and she knew he could not have used the entrance through the kitchen. Another secret entrance, perhaps giving onto the service road behind the house, was the logical way out. She began a methodical search, foot by foot, of the walls and central passageway. She found nothing. Meanwhile, the thudding of the sledgehammer on the steel bathroom wall never ceased. The two men knew she was behind it, for the hasp on the bathroom door had been fastened before they had pried it open, and there was nowhere else she could have gone. It might take a while, but they would break through.

She had sunk listlessly to the floor, awaiting the inevitable, exhausted from her fruitless search, when the pounding abruptly ceased. They must have found the trick shelf that opened the panel. She closed her eyes.

A minute later the steel panel slid up. A figure stepped into the light. It was John J. Jones. He walked down the corridor and gently pulled Emily Ferguson's hands down from her face. "I guess I'm not very convincing," he said, lifting her up and pressing her against him.

"I'm a fool," she whispered, holding him tight.

"Hell, I threw too much at you all at once. You'd have been a fool to *believe*."

"How did you know where to find me?"

"That was the easy part. When I woke up and didn't find you, I thought back over what we'd been talking about. This was the only thing you could really check up on."

"And the time travel—that's true, too?"

He smiled cryptically. He gestured toward the unconscious figures on the floor. "Why don't you ask Charley and Burt?"

"You mean *they've* traveled through time?"

"Not yet."

20. THE SOLID-GOLD RUNWAY 31 MARCH 1930

SKARDON SET THE DIAL FOR DECEMBER 1942, WHEN America's blooding at Guadalcanal was still fresh in everyone's mind. He had not been born yet, but he remembered his father saying how relentless in corralling draft dodgers and shoving them into uniform the draft boards had been at that particular moment in American history.

When he kicked them off the time platform, Ace Karras and Hal Minthe would make tracks for Las Chipas, little suspecting that a war was raging and that they would be wanted men, adult males who had not registered for the draft. Sooner rather than later, being of sound mind and body, they would be challenged. Hauled before the draft board, they would naturally protest ignorance of the war. That would mark them as men trying to escape conscription by feigning mental illness. Psychiatrists would be called in. Questions would follow. They would protest that they not only knew nothing of the war but had been kidnapped, trussed like Christmas turkeys, and transported to a far place. Those hairy-armed innocents could remember nothing more until springing full-grown from the womb of a passing decade. The psychiatrists would marvel at the inventiveness of their subjects and summon either the gendarmes, who would lead them off to prison for draft evasion, or the military police, who would set them on that long dark road that would lead, with luck, to the sands of Iwo Jima.

He pulled the switch.

An immense violet cloud appeared overhead, alive with the flashing of silent lightning. The earth shook with the force of an earthquake, and the air was filled with the acrid scent of ozone.

When the dust settled, the scenery around them looked much the same as before. A careful observer would have noticed that the forest had considerably thinned out, the cloud cover was perhaps more dense, and the lilt of song birds had diminished, but Karras and Minthe, being blindfolded as well as bound, observed nothing. Skardon untied them and allowed them to get a good view of the installation. It meant nothing to them—now—but they would remember later on.

Karras was a rangy, muscular man at least ten years Skardon's junior, but soft from too much food and too many hours working on his varicose veins behind the counter of the Las Chipas Haberdashery. Minthe had a short trunk and long, powerful arms from tossing sacks of grain at the local feed store. Between them they should have been the match of any ordinary man. Skardon stood before them, arms akimbo, a soft smile on his lips, as they measured him with their eyes.

"Well, are you or aren't you?" he said cheerfully. "If you care to resume the discussion, I will be only too happy to oblige. But you'll have to make up your minds, because I don't have all day."

The men looked at him uneasily, remembering the feline swiftness with which he had struck them down in the cellar of his home back in Las Chipas and the pain in their still-aching cheekbones, and conveniently recalled what was the better part of valor.

"No?" Skardon taunted. "Too bad. You'll never know whether—not being taken by surprise—you might have been able to beat the hell out of me, take my woman and that nice new Pierce-Arrow over there, not to mention more millions of dollars than you could believe, which I have socked away in my cellar back home."

Karras licked his lips, glanced out of the corner of his eye at Minthe, and swung from his knees. The punch grazed Skardon's jaw and was followed by a kick at the crotch. Unfortunately, he had telegraphed the blow.

Skardon took one step back, swept his arm up under Karras's leg at its maximum extension, and spilled him flat on his back with a mighty thump, deflating him like a punctured tire.

Then Minthe was upon him, raining blows without art or craft, but painful enough when they landed. Skardon weathered them, deflecting them with upthrust arms, allowing Minthe to weary himself with the onslaught. When he finally dropped his arms for a moment's rest, Skardon measured the distance with a practiced eye and launched a right jab flush on the other man's nose. The blow drenched him with Minthe's blood as Minthe's nose split with a crack of smashed bone. He let out an anguished howl and clamped both hands to his face, leaving his body vulnerable to whatever damage Skardon cared to inflict. Skardon cocked his arm, paused to sight in on Minthe's short ribs, then dropped it. There was not much fun in beating up a man who gave up so easily.

"Get in the car," he ordered. "And be careful of the upholstery. You spill a drop of blood on it, I'll rip off your scalp to soak it up."

Skardon waited until they got sullenly in the back seat, then took his place behind the wheel. He leaned out the window and said to Emily, "Back in ten minutes." He drove to the edge of the concrete platform, eased the long white car down on the dirt road leading to the main highway, and shifted into high gear.

Twenty minutes later he was back. He shifted into low, bounced back onto the platform, and set the hand brake. "Well, my dear," he said with a grin, "I think we've solved the Karras-Minthe problem."

"Where are we?"

"December 1942."

"Why 1942?"

He explained.

She thought the punishment fit the crime. "And now?"

"Well, that's entirely up to you. With one proviso: Wherever we go, it's going to have to be forward in time, where materials technology will have progressed to the point where I can build something a little less roomy than this time machine."

"And what's wrong with this?"

"Think. We aren't going to spend the rest of our lives here in the Oregon mountains, are we? So what happens when we go into the city and somebody stumbles onto this thing? There'll be no end of questions, investigations, newspaper stories. Environmentalist will take one look at this ugly contraption and demand that the state bulldoze it. If I, as owner, show up to protest, the law will come down on me for building without a permit. And if I don't, I'll have to start all over somewhere else if we decide we want to move on—or back. Only this time I won't have those blessed microfilms of *The New York Times* to build up my fortune again."

"Yes, that's another thing I wanted to ask. Why did—"

Skardon seized her wrist, his suddenly vigilant expression startling her into silence.

"A truck's coming this way. We've got to leave. Where do you want to go? Decide!"

She gestured helplessly. "I don't know," she said. "I've never been anywhere but here. *You* decide."

"Very well." Skardon twisted the dial to 10 August 2002 and pulled the knife switch. He knew everything there was to know about Emily Ferguson. He knew she would leave this decision, as she did them all, to him. All along, he had intended to time-transport them from the 1930s into the year 2002.

The decision had been the fruit of some deliberation. It made no sense to go back to an era through which he had already lived, a time of no surprises, of repetitious experiences. On the other hand, a time far in the future had little appeal. He would be in a milieu in which everything would be novel—new but not necessarily improved. It would have all the charm of breaking in a new pair of shoes. He would have to learn a whole new set of clichés merely to be understood, a completely new bestiary of political animals, how to operate the latest generation of useless gadgets, the fashionable new thoughts, the accepted new tastes in music and art, the great new historical truths based on the wisdom of hindsight. The mere thought of it drove him back to a more comfortable age.

Not the year of 1999, however. Too many people would still remember him. Wanted posters would still adorn post office bulletin boards. The FBI list of most-wanted criminals would surely be top-heavy with the name of the notorious John K. Skardon, murderer of the unfortunate Fortuna Fonteneau. But allow three years or so for the heat to dissipate and avoid the campus of the University of California at Berkeley, and he would probably be safe enough. The year 2002 had a pleasant ring to it, and a diamond ring of elephant-choking dimensions with which to adorn the fourth finger, left hand, of his lady was going to be his first purchase.

When the violet cloud dissipated, Emily Ferguson and John K. Skardon found themselves in quite a different landscape. The forest that had surrounded them was clear-cut, the stumps jutting out of the wasted earth like tombstones. The unprotected mountainsides, shorn of their verdant cloak, had been able to resist the ravages of nature no more than those of man: the rains had dissolved the topsoil and sent it in rivulets that turned into rivers roaring down to the sea. What fertility remained nourished scrub neither beautiful nor useful in place of the soaring firs that had been sawed and chopped into chips and pressed into board to make paperboard houses for new generations of destroyers of the defenseless world. For a moment Skardon considered going back to a simpler time. But only for a moment: the problems of the future would be no worse than those of the past, only different.

Skardon had no fear that the time platform would be observed by curious eyes in this wasteland. But its forelorn aspect made him impatient to leave, to look upon sights more pleasing to the eye. He made a round of the explosive charges, set the fuses for seven minutes, and turned to Emily.

"Shall we?" he said, extending his arm toward the car.

Emily Ferguson got into the car. Skardon closed the door behind her and climbed behind the wheel. He put the car in gear and drove off down the road, which was still dirt-surfaced, not looking back. They were three miles away when the mountains seemed to erupt with sound that echoed long after the time platform had been sent eons back into time, transformed into the atoms from which it ultimately had come.

"Where are we going?" she asked, finally.

"Back to Las Chipas."

"For the money, of course."

"Yes."

"But why? Why didn't we just take what we need? What need do we have for two billion dollars? I've lived with you long enough to know that luxury doesn't mean anything to you. You have no expensive tastes—or do you?"

"Actually, I do." And he explained.

During those years in the maximum-security facility at Las Chipas, he had reflected on why he had been unjustly imprisoned. It was not for want of competent counsel: his case had been presented fairly, but Prof. Klemper's fabricated evidence had been too convincing for even a clever lawyer to argue away. But what if he had been a rich man, a great figure in the community? His fate would have been very different. Apologists would spring up from every side. The police would manufacture evidence to order. The press would suppress any facts pointing to his guilt, as it had some years back when what's-his-name—

the name eluded him, though he well remembered the pasty, beefy face—had cravenly panicked and allowed a young woman to drown rather than save her life at the expense of his totally undistinguished political career.

He had decided then that if he ever got out of prison, he would so arrange affairs as to be able to buy anything, *anybody*, that he needed in order to protect himself. Money would confer immunity, vaccinating him against not only poverty but unwonted public annoyance. He would simply buy up the offending television station or newspaper and fire everybody. Ill health—he would buy out a whole hospital to treat his ailments if he so wished; an uncongenial climate—he could move anywhere, anytime, and drag the seasons along with him; and above all, the vicissitudes of stupid, small-minded politicians and administrators, who strewed the paths of virtuous people who asked only to be left alone with niggling laws and regulations, which money would give him the power to ignore.

Money was power. Until he was penned up like an animal behind bars, Skardon had never developed an appetite for power. But he craved it now. Never again, now that he had a basement full of what most men valued even above life itself, would he be beholden to another man.

"Besides," he added, "I have a promise to myself to keep: I am going to find Justin Pope. And when I do . . ."

"Will money really help?" Emily asked.

"Certainly. With the enormous power the time machine confers, Pope will have had more than three years to accumulate as much in the way of riches as anyone could want. Like every man who has enormous riches to protect, he will have enveloped himself in layer after layer of security, and it will take commensurate wealth to penetrate that cordon. The mere fact of my wealth will enable me to move in the rarefied circles he frequents—with suitable chin whiskers and false nose, to be sure. And when I have him alone . . ." He smiled. To Emily it suggested the smile of a piranha dropped into a goldfish bowl.

"Have you forgotten that this is the year 2002 and that we left Las Chipas over seventy years ago?"

"No, I haven't forgotten. I presume you're worried that our home may have been sold for taxes or demolished to make room for a shopping mall."

"A shopping maul?" She did not understand. A maul was used to drive fence posts.

"A shopping mall is a particularly pernicious innovation of the late twentieth century. It crowds a large number of stores selling stuff nobody really wants or needs into a cramped, noisy paved area and covers everything with a roof, keeping out every atom of sunshine and fresh air and keeping in and recirculating the rude exhalations of the unwashed masses, thus providing a steady supply of customers with upper respiratory ailments for greedy, thick-thumbed barbers and plumbers masquerading as physicians."

"Is that a sentence?" Emily Ferguson inquired innocently.

"It is—a sentence of death for twenty-first-century man."

"I can believe it," Emily said fervently. "But you haven't told me what you'll do if there *is* a shopping mall on the site of our home."

"As I will do with anything else which stands in our way, I shall buy and dispose of it. I take it you haven't looked in the trunk lately."

"No."

"Or noticed a distinct sagging of the rear of the car?"

"Oh."

"Quite so. I brought along with us, when we moved to Rogue River, approximately two hundred pounds of gold coins, which at $1,200 the ounce will buy any number of rustic shopping centers. After all, my dear Emily, Las Chipas is so far off the beaten track that I doubt if the population would have even doubled by now. The land is flat and barren, the resources mainly salt flats and scrub. A million dollars will buy back our abandoned house, never fear."

"I don't know, John," Emily said doubtfully. "Things change."

"Let them," Skardon replied. "I've thought of that, too. Among the other treasures I have also stowed in our capacious trunk are six ridiculous paintings, bought in 1930 for the equally ridiculous price of $300 for the lot. They are daubs—mere ugly daubs—the sort of thing you'd expect of a demented orangutan, but I must confess that my generation has been taken in by them, hook, line, and sinker. Today they sell for millions."

"Do I know the artist?"

"I hope not. Fellow by the name of Picasso."

Five hours after they left Rogue River, Skardon approached the familiar environs of Las Chipas. The road had been a two-lane dirt road when, seventy-two years before—or three, depending on how one looked at it—he had been deposited on it by Justin Pope. Now it was a well-paved four-lane highway with a median strip and sodium-vapor lights. He felt a twinge of apprehension.

He drove on. Houses had sprouted on every side, miles from the place where their old home had been. Maybe he would need those Picassos, after all.

In his headlights, he observed with relief that the houses again thinned out, that there did not seem to be any buildings at all in the far distance. However, just ahead he saw the light of a guard kiosk, and across the road a high chain-link fence. As he drove up to it, a uniformed figure stepped out of the kiosk and held up a gloved hand. From his shoulder was slung an automatic rifle. Skardon stopped.

"Your pass, sir?" the young soldier said.

"Pass?"

"Yes, sir. This is a government installation, you know, off bounds to all unauthorized personnel."

Skardon's heart sank.

The young man saw his expression. "Stranger around here, aren't you, sir?" he said sympathetically.

"Yes—yes, I am."

"Lost?"

"Well, I seem to be," Skardon faltered. "I thought I was near Las Chipas."

"Then you're not lost. This is it," the soldier said, pointing his thumb over his shoulder. "Or rather, it *was* it until a couple of years ago. The government bought up the whole area as a testing ground for the new Mach-24 hypersonic airplane. Hell, I thought *everybody* knew that. Anyway, they bulldozed the town, and all that's behind the fence now are hangars, workshops, and six miles of concrete runway about five feet thick."

IV
Quadrille

21. *GEMÜTLICHKEIT*
12 SEPTEMBER 2002

JOHN J. SKARDON WAS BACK WHERE HE BELONGED, ON the leading edge of the twenty-first century. The morning of the eleventh of August, he discovered that Justin Pope was still among them and in fact had apparently never left. Had the *Fugit* broken down? Or had he found life in other eras so little rewarding that, like Skardon himself, he had decided that he preferred the familiar to the unknown? Whichever the case, Pope was not going anywhere: except for concert appearances with the most celebrated of the world's orchestras (Pope had doubtless engineered the invitations by bribes to the orchestras' general managers in order to achieve a celebrity his meager talents would not sustain), Pope had remained in San Francisco. In fact, he had lived for three years in the penthouse of the Santorini of Nob Hill, five blocks from the more modest apartment Skardon had rented after he had learned that his treasures were buried forever beneath five feet of concrete at Las Chipas.

Forever?

Well, not necessarily. He could have retrieved his fortune with relatively little effort and in fact intended to do so in good time. He calculated that he could build a new model of the Flier in six weeks. With the improvements that had undoubtedly occurred in the fields of electronics and electromagnetism, he would probably be able to miniaturize the circuitry and power supply so that it would fit comfortably in the baggage compartment of a two-place jet VTOL aircraft, with plenty of room left over for long-range tanks. Thus equipped, he could venture not only to any time on Earth but also to any place. It was a heady thought.

Thus equipped, he would have two choices. He could go forward in time, to the thirtieth century or so, when the concrete runway of the hypersonic airplane base had finally crumbled and the underground treasure house beneath the site of his former home in Las Chipas would again be accessible. But by then the paper stocks and oil paintings might well have mildewed, crumbled and rotted away, though of course the gold bullion would not have been affected. Better to go back to, say, 1950, while the town he and Emily had lived in was still intact, along with his home.

But he could decide that later. Right now there was a more pressing matter: fixing the clock of the man who had stolen the treasure of time.

Whatever form it took, it would require careful spadework. Like the competent scientist he was, he would have to do the requisite research. Meanwhile, domestic issues intervened.

Emily Ferguson was his first consideration. He had promised to marry her, *wanted* to marry her, and marry her he would. To avoid the awkward inquiries that might have resulted from putting his name on the public register in California, he flew with his bride to be to an obscure, sleepy little town, Oxford, Ohio, chosen at random by sticking a pin in a map of the United States. They then proceeded for their brief honeymoon to England, Paris, Lisbon, and Vienna. In the latter city, which he remembered fondly from his doctoral and postdoctoral years at the laboratory of thermoelectrodynamics of the University of Vienna, he revisited his old rooming house, took his bride for sacher torte at the venerable Sacher Hotel coffee shop, and went across the street through the driving rain to a performance of *Don Giovanni* at the magnificent Statsoper.

It was there, as the Mozartian classic unfolded on the immense stage before them, that he conceived the plan by which he would gain admission to the presence of the closely guarded Justin Pope, alone, and then . . . well, like all great artists, then he would improvise.

They spent a week in Vienna, during which time Skardon engaged the services of an unusual multinational firm, Interpen, about which he had heard while in prison. The firm specialized in the procurement of fake passports, identity cards, and other documentation, the fabrication of bogus backgrounds, and very discreet inquiries. For considerably higher fees, blackmail could be arranged, the plans for a jewelry store robbery delivered, or a throat cut, but Skardon had no need of such commerce.

On their return to San Francisco, while Emily Skardon recovered from the culture shock of twenty-first-century Europe and, even more, that of the United States, her husband got down to business.

Comfortably well off with the sale of $300,000 worth of gold coins and a broom closet full of Picassos, which he refused to put on his walls as much from aesthetic considerations as for security, he was able to hire one of the best acting coaches in Hollywood. This gentleman, a Hungarian Jew who was fluent in no fewer than seventeen languages, specialized in coaching actors in English parts as spoken by foreigners of most European dialects. His assignment was to reconstruct Skardon's accent so that the Viennese background dialect showed through. Skardon was a quick study, and within ten days he was speaking his usual excellent English with the intonation, stress patterns, and vowel and consonantal realizations of one born within the Ring.

The Hungarian was succeeded by a Viennese character actor turned coach. Ten days later, Skardon's walk, gestures, posture, and expressions had absorbed the authentic atmosphere of the Austrian capital. With the clothing he had bought in Vienna and the aid of an expert makeup man who provided him with a spade beard and Kaiser

Bill mustache, a convincing network of fake wrinkles and sagging eye pouches, plus an artful collection of liver spots on the backs of his hands, John K. Skardon had aged twenty years, gained a dignified limp, eyes bleared with very dilute vinegar and the slight tremor of the hands signaling approaching parkinsonism.

His disguise was complete. Better yet, it was *good*. It *had* to be good to get past a most difficult hurdle, Justin Pope's private security staff.

Skardon was not sure just how he did it, but Pope was a very wealthy and yet revered international figure. Skardon had read music reviews from the past three years, which asserted without reservation that the compositions of Justin Pope were the culmination of the musical art. He combined all the best features of Bach, Mozart, Beethoven, Brahms, and Berloiz. His early music was eerily reminiscent of Schubert. And his personal character was fully as sympathetic as that of his music. He was fun-loving, adventurous—to the horror of his fans, he was an ardent windsurfer and as skillful in aerobatic displays in his vintage biplane as he was in improvisation on the keyboard—a man in whose presence women were known to faint, a connoisseur of fine wines—mostly Californian—and the last one to leave a good party, where he customarily played brilliant jazz until the early morning hours. He was regarded as a national treasure and was a harder man to interview than the President of the United States.

Skardon made his appearance at the security office on the first floor of the Santorini of Nob Hill at ten o'clock on the morning of 12 September 2002. The old man walked with slow deliberation and limped slightly but held his shoulders erect. He had a vague smile that included all the world in his geriatric benevolence. A gentle man.

Appearances were not enough for Bill Grace, the chief of security.

"Do you have an appointment with Dr. Pope?"

''No,'' Skardon confessed, ''but I have hope. Maestro Pope is the idol of the readers of my column in *Die Wiener*,'' he continued in excellent English indelibly tinged with a *mitteleuropäer* accent, ''and I have come to America in the hope that the maestro will bestow upon them a few words of special greeting.''

''You should have written for an appointment.''

''My written English is even worse than my spoken English. I feared that you would take me for an illiterate and refuse my request.''

''Such a request would have been,'' Grace said. ''Dr. Pope very rarely grants interviews, especially if he is to be asked questions about his personal life.'' Although Grace was unaware of it, that was because Franz Peter Schubert knew precious little about Justin Pope's personal life and found his celebrity a convenient excuse not to talk about it.

''Yes, I understand,'' Skardon said. ''Still, I have come far and ask for very little—merely a few words to convey to the music lovers of Vienna.''

Grace went through that sort of thing all day, every day. Always, he politely but indiscriminately regretted that Justin Pope would be unable to receive the cabinet ministers, archbishops, savants, sensation seekers, cranks, occasional paranoiacs intent upon achieving fleeting notoriety by assassinating a world figure, and the press—the latter usually without preamble or excuse. He had been gentle with this visitor only because of his age and the distance he had come. ''Well, I'll tell you what I'll do, sir: I'll notify Dr. Pope's personal secretary that you have come to see him, and if he sees fit to inform Dr. Pope himself, and Dr. Pope agrees—which I warn you I very much doubt—you can have an appointment, perhaps even this week, depending on his schedule.''

''That would be wonderful, wonderful,'' Skardon said, removing his glasses to wipe them clean of the mist of imaginary tears of gratitude.

"Of course, I would have to take the usual security measures. I'm sure you understand that."

"Well, I don't know exactly what you mean by 'security measures,' but I'll do whatever you require if it means having the honor of meeting the great Dr. Pope."

"First of all, sir, would you mind giving us your full name?"

"Not at all. Professor Hans Otto Graf." He spelled it. "My address in Vienna is—"

"Angeligasse 11/2."

"How on Earth did you know that?"

Grace smiled and pointed to the VDU screen on his desk. "When you came in, you gave me your last name and that of your magazine. Everything said here is being monitored by one of my assistants. He had a make on you within ten seconds."

"Then your 'security measures' have been fulfilled?"

"Not quite. Would you kindly step onto that low platform."

Skardon ascended the half step to the platform. Bill Grace, his eyes on his VDU, nodded. The man had no weapons. But was he indeed Hans Otto Graf?

"Have you worked long for the *Die Wiener*?"

"Twenty-two years."

"Who was your editor in 1991?"

Skardon feigned thought. "That would have been Willie Bonhein."

Grace nodded. "And the name of your wife's school in Innsbruck?"

"The *Frauenberufsschule*. It's not in Innsbruck, by the way, but Klagenfurt."

Grace lifted his eyes from the monitor. "Would you kindly empty your pockets on the desk?"

Skardon methodically emptied one pocket after another. Grace inspected each article. He unfolded the two linen handkerchiefs, one from each of Skardon's back pockets, and carefully refolded them again. He opened the worn wallet and removed and studied an unused Vienna-

Salsburg train ticket, an unpaid bill from a haberdasher, a press card, a complimentary ticket to a performance of *Die Fledermaus* in the Rudentensaal the coming Friday, several hundred schillings in bank notes, a worn color photo, slightly out of focus, of a handsome woman in her fifties, a grocery shopping list in German with all items checked off but *Baurenbrot* and *Speck*, a half dozen credit cards, an Austrian driver's license, a ticket for next week's drawing of the Austrian state lottery, and a physician's prescription in his name for Bronoton, a European remedy for migraine headaches. From his other pockets Skardon produced several Austrian and American coins, a flat metal box labeled Bronoton, a worn leather-backed notebook with half a dozen pages of scribbling in German, two not very sharp pencils, a key ring with four keys, including that for a BMW, a comb, and the business cards of Bookstore Deutsch, Hattlage and Die Wienerversicherung, all of Vienna.

Grace inspected each item in detail, then reached for the telephone on his desk. "Conrad," he said after a moment, "we have here a gentleman, a music critic from Vienna, who would like an appointment sometime this week, if possible . . . Yes, I explained all that to him, but he said he made the trip especially to see Dr. Pope, and he hopes to be able to tell his readers . . . It's *Die Wiener* . . . I see . . . Yes, I'll tell him."

He hung up and turned to the visitor. "It's what I expected, sir," Grace said apologetically. "Dr. Pope rarely gives interviews for any reason. However, if you will leave your name and a local address where you can be reached, I can assure you that a personal communication will be sent you from Dr. Pope's office sometime this week."

"Personal from Dr. Pope, you mean?"

"Signed by Conrad Karpiosky personally, on behalf of Dr. Pope."

Skardon grimaced. "Well, I thank you very much for your trouble, although I wish it could have resulted in a face-to-face meeting. It would have been the high point of my life, like meeting the great Johann Sebastian himself."

"I know, sir. You understand that even *I* have only seen him three or four times, aside from television broadcasts of his local concerts. He almost always leaves by the garage entrance, in a limousine with opaque windows, and a police escort." He pushed Skardon's belongings across the desk.

Skardon was not dismayed. He had scouted the lobby thoroughly and observed the routine of the desk men, the disposition of the security men at the stairs and elevator, the revolving doors with glass that was thick enough to be bulletproof. He had learned how visitors came and went and knew that uniformed police were their escort. Even while he was talking with Grace, he had formulated the bare bones of two or three schemes that would result in his coming into contact with Justin Pope for the few seconds it would take to make him regret forever that he had double-crossed John K. Skardon.

Skardon was putting his effects back in his pockets when the telephone on Grace's desk rang. The security chief picked up the receiver. He listened for a moment, then replaced the receiver in its cradle. "Dr. Pope wants to see you," he said incredulously.

"When?"

"Right now."

Five minutes later Skardon was ushered into the great man's presence. He had passed three checkpoints manned by unsmiling men who looked capable of sudden violence.

As he entered the studio, with a gleaming concert grand in one corner and banks of recording equipment along the adjacent walls, Justin Pope rose from the piano bench and waved away a tall thin man, presumably his secretary, who had been hovering at his elbow. The tall thin man left the room, closing the door behind him.

Justin Pope crossed the room, his hand extended.

This was going to be a good deal easier than he had imagined, John K. Skardon thought, shaking the other's hand. He had two weapons with him, both supplied by Interpen of Vienna, either of which was as effective as it was undetectable by cursory inspection, such as Grace had subjected them to. The eraser of the pencil, rubbed against anything Pope might touch—a cup handle, a sheet of music, the piano bench—would cause the thin film covering it to rupture. An invisible streak of a metallic salt that would then be deposited on Pope's skin would result in a slow but progressive irritation against which there was no known antidote or palliative. He would suffer a permanent case of hives, not disabling but making it almost impossible to snatch more than a few minutes of sleep at a time, and an itching that no amount of scratching would relieve.

An alternative weapon was a capsule from the metal box labeled Bronoton. A single capsule, placed surreptitiously in the piano among the strings, would slowly react with the air, in two or three weeks producing an airborne toxin that would cause a condition indistinguishable from emphysema in anyone who breathed it over a period of weeks. There was no known cure.

"I am honored meeting the man which his music has given me so much happiness," Skardon said in his carefully cultivated Viennese accent.

To his astonishment, the man who had taken his hand replied in what Skardon recognized immediately as an archaic form of Viennese German. "*Ich schätze Ihre Aufmerksamkeit, mich mit Ihrer Anwesenheit zu überraschen. Es ist schon lange her, seitdem ich das Glück hatte, ein echtes Wienerisch zu hören.* I do so miss the language," he went on in English. "Its parks, its splendid buildings, its lovely women. And now you bring me a taste of it. Please do sit down and tell me what you'd like to drink. Some *Wienerkaffee* with thick cream, perhaps?" His eyes sparkled.

"Yes, Dr. Pope," Skardon murmured numbly. "That

would be fine.'' He was shaken. Something very funny was going on. He had dealt enough with Justin Pope, had probed enough into his background to be sure of his reliability before he made the young man his partner, to know that he had never studied German. Nor could he have learned such flawless German—*Austrian* German, *archaic* Austrian German—in the short concert engagements he had spent in Vienna. Even if he had spent the entire three years since Skardon had last seen him studying night and day, he would not have learned to speak *Wienerisch* like that. It would have been like a Viennese of today speaking the language of the Boston of John Adams after having visited Cambridge four or five times.

''Tell me what's happening, what they're talking about in the cafés these days,'' Schubert said, still in his peculiar German.

''Actually, it's very much as it's always been, I estimate—the politics, the music, the women—''

''In German, *please*! I get so homesick for the language.''

''I wasn't aware that you knew German so perfectly, that you were so much at home in the language,'' Skardon said in German.

Schubert laughed, embarrassed. ''As a matter of fact, I don't mention it, but when I was very young I had a nurse from Vienna, and German was actually my first language.''

Now, *that* was an out-and-out lie. Pope himself had mentioned to Skardon that owning a van was a pleasant change from walking to school, as his family's modest circumstances had forced him to do since the first grade. Americans whose children had to walk to school could not afford to employ nurses from Vienna. Any real American could not but know that.

''I didn't realize that, Dr. Pope,'' Skardon said. ''And that's a coincidence, by the way—your having a Viennese who taught you German. I myself had an *American* nurse who taught me *English*. Her name was,'' he said, carefully enunciating the name, ''Jeanne K. Skardon.''

The smiling man opposite him did not bat an eye.

Skardon knew for certain now. Whoever the guy was, he sure as hell was not Justin Pope. And if he was not Justin Pope, who the devil *was* he?

22. RIVERS
11 AUGUST 2002

WITH THE SUSPICION OF A MAN WHO KNEW FROM PERsonal acquaintances in prison how easy it was to knock them over, John K. Skardon had a deep distrust of banks. Prison had also taught him that it was bad business to put all one's savings in any one bank. They were all too prone to succumb to the attentions of box men and amateurs in ski masks—if the bank president did not beat them to the punch by cleaning out the vaults and decamping to Brazil.

Accordingly, on arrival in San Francisco he had converted all his bullion but a single bar—getaway money—in various banks and deposited the proceeds in four other banks, each account under a different name. It was his misfortune that one of the banks was the Golden Gate Savings and Trust.

The security chief of Golden Gate was Percival C. Candy, a bright young man with no police experience but a considerable background in computer technology. He was ambitious and hoped to use experience gained at Golden Gate to launch his own security firm. Meanwhile, he generously used the resources of Golden Gate to put together a security system that he boasted made the bank impregnable. He had been empowered to bring in outside accountants for surprise audits to nip any defalcations in the bud. He had installed cameras that covered not only the counters and cashiers' cages but other areas as well. He reasoned that while robbers, knowing their faces would be recorded, would more likely than not don ski masks as they approached the tellers' windows, they would rip them off again as they dashed outside to prevent a hue and cry being immediately raised on the street. Therefore, he had planted cameras among the potted plants on each side of the front doors, which recorded on videodisk the faces of each person leaving the building. The disk was kept for a year before erasure.

Among his other devices, and the one of which he was most proud, was the palm-fax. No one but Candy and the chairman of the board knew of its existence. He had modified the device from similar instruments in use at high-security facilities and installed it himself over a weekend. To the naked eye it appeared to be nothing more than two oversized vertical lucite door handles with the unusual feature of emiting a gentle glow, which everyone assumed was for aesthetic reasons. The size of the handles forced anyone opening a door to grasp it firmly, transmitting a handprint instantly to Candy's data bank. To be sure, not all customers' handprints were thus scanned: those who wore gloves were immune from the surreptitious identification procedure, but then, how many people in San Francisco wore gloves?

Candy was on professionally good terms with the local FBI office, having volunteered to provide an instantaneous identification of every Golden Gate customer, some of whom would inevitably have prison records or be wanted for questioning. Software provided by the FBI allowed Candy's shop to encode every handprint within microseconds and relay the string of binary digits in which it was converted to FBI headquarters in Washington in real time. There it was compared electronically with the 95 million-odd fingerprints in the FBI's files, which spit out the names of anyone who, as the British put it, was sought to assist the FBI in their inquiries. The whole process took considerably less than half a second.

It was thus that, even while John K. Skardon was making his initial deposit at the Golden Gate Savings and Trust, an urgent message had flashed to the police headquarters, San Francisco, that an escaped murderer, one

John K. Skardon, was at that moment in the Golden Gate bank. He was probably armed and must be considered dangerous. A plainclothes car with four policemen was dispatched to the scene. En route, they studied the copy of the photograph of Skardon radioed from Washington. As they pulled up at the curb, unlimbered their pistols, and fastened their eyes on the main door, John K. Skardon limped out.

They paid no attention to the old man and consequently lay in wait for the half an hour it took the unsuspecting John K. Skardon to walk home. When they realized they had missed their quarry, they reviewed the photographs of the customers that day, supplied by Candy. But they were of little help: if all the customers who could have been Skardon in disguise were tracked down, it might take weeks. Similarly futile was an inspection of records of new deposits. Although they quickly identified, by comparing handwriting samples, Skardon's initial deposit for $60,000, the name and address were both fakes.

The trail, temporarily cold, was passed on to Detective Lieutenant R. B. Rivers, a man with a reputation for breathing new life into lost causes. The chief wanted quick results. A known murderer and escaped convict was loose on the streets of San Francisco. He was exceedingly clever, having escaped from the Las Chipas Maximum Security Facility during the night with no suggestion of the means by which he had done what only one other man, with a smuggled pistol, had been able to accomplish. He had deposited $60,000 in the Golden Gate Savings and Trust. That could represent the weapon with which to perform a great deal of mischief in the hands of a clever, ruthless man like Skardon.

Rivers sat at his desk, feet planted squarely on the floor, hands folded in front of him, staring at the blank wall. Some cops liked to do their thinking with their feet on the desk, toothpick in the side of the mouth, and a tobacco-juice-streaked wastebasket within comfortable range. Rivers thought better in a more formal posture: if his body was tense, ready to spring, his mind would be inclined to follow suit.

He remembered Skardon but had known little about him. Now, having read his file, he had some ideas how the man's mind probably worked. One: he had gone to some trouble to devise an impenetrable disguise. That meant he was still being wary, even after having not been seen for three years. Two: he had deposited $60,000 in a checking account. That was a lot of money. If he had a lot of money, he could conceivably have a lot more. But a con would, for safety's sake, spread it around. Ergo, it would be well to determine whether he had other accounts, in other names, with other home addresses. Three: that could be determined by comparisons of his handwriting with the information given for other accounts opened the same day and, if nothing was found, the same week.

Within four days his subordinates had located accounts in three other banks, and Rivers went personally to interview each of the tellers to see if they could agree on putting a face to the name. By means of an identikit, the tellers tried to remember what the man looked like whom Rivers sought. Their memories were handicapped by the very volume of business their banks did but aided by the recency of the event and the unusually large amounts that had initially been deposited. The three resulting reconstructions of the suspect's face were close enough for the staff artist to draw a composite that all agreed was the man.

Rivers then consulted a map of the city. He put crosses at the locations of the four banks. They formed a diamond in the rough. Slicing away at the problem with Occham's razor, Rivers reasoned that Skardon would most likely choose banks more or less equidistant from his home. He joined the opposite crosses with lines. That point, which happened to be the location of the local Perpetual Life Insurance branch office, would be the logical place to start the search. From that point the hunt would proceed in concentric circles. He had full confidence that he would flush his quarry, probably within a couple of days.

He ordered hundreds of copies of Skardon's mug shot and several hundred more of the artist's composite printed. Patrolmen on the beat distributed them to apartment building supers and shopkeepers in the neighborhood. Sure enough, before the first day had passed, a super in the Nob Hill area reported that the wanted man had rented an apartment in his building within the past month.

Rivers briefed his men and assigned them posts that covered all possible escape routes. Approaching the apartment building from several directions, the plainclothesmen took their stations and radioed their readiness to Rivers. The detective lieutenant, with two men, entered the building and knocked at the super's door.

"Are you the man who reported seeing this man?" Rivers said, showing him Skardon's mug shot.

The man studied the picture and shook his hand. "Naw, that doesn't look anything like the man in 4-H. The cop showed me another picture."

"Is this the picture?" Rivers held out the composite.

"Yep," the super said, shaking his head emphatically. "That's the guy, all right. H. E. Forsythe."

"You're sure? I don't want any mistakes. Take your time and study the picture carefully."

The super glanced at it and said, "Like I told you."

"What if I told you the two pictures are of the same man?"

The super took the pictures, held them at arm's length, and studied them feature by feature. Finally he looked up. "Well, I don't know. Maybe they could be. Why don't you take him in, shave his beard, and have a good look?"

"That's exactly what we propose to do," Rivers said.

He produced a document and flashed it at the super. "This is a search warrant."

"Right this way, gents." He led the way down the hall.

Had he not been absorbed in comparing the two pictures, the super might have noticed that the woman who had just passed them, going down the hall the other way, was the wife of the man they sought.

23. FIREBAUGH
11 AUGUST 2002

MRS. JOHN K. SKARDON WAS DOUBLE-PARKED DOWN THE street from the Santorini of Nob Hill, her eyes shifting from the street map on her lap to the entrance, getting more edgy by the moment, afraid that he had already come and gone. She had retrieved the white Pierce-Arrow from the garage, driven by the most direct route to the Santorini, and parked where Skardon, on emerging, could not miss seeing the antique automobile. But what if he had come back to her apartment another way and she had missed him en route? What if he were still with this man Pope and had dallied so long that the police dragnet had had time to include this area, only blocks away, in their searches? What if the tall spare man who had displayed her husband's pictures to the police had become impatient and asked for a description of their car and even now was looking for it? What if Skardon had not been able to gain admission to the great man, despite his painstaking disguise, and still sat, patiently waiting in the lobby for permission to "interview" the composer?

That was a possibility that she could, at least, check out. But on second thought, she could not even do that. The car was too long to fit in one of San Francisco's parking spaces even if one were empty. Besides, from the admiring glances cast at the automobile, and having read of the high crime rate of San Francisco in the year 2002, she feared it would not be there if she left it for a single moment.

Nevertheless, she had come to the decision that that was her only recourse when Skardon tottered out of the apartment house, glanced up and down the street, spotted her and, shedding his limp, came toward her in long strides. She switched on the engine and moved over to the passenger seat. When he reached the car, he opened the door to the driver's side and slid behind the wheel.

The old con's instinct for survival had been aroused by the sight of the Pierce-Arrow down the street, when it should have been in the garage. Emily would never have brought it there unless something was seriously wrong. And the only thing that could be seriously wrong was that the police had somehow discovered that he was still alive and back in San Francisco.

He gunned the automobile straight ahead. He knew he had to move fast. If Emily had been alerted, that meant the police had come to the apartment. And if the police had come to the apartment, and he did not return soon, they would send out a general alarm for the automobile. There probably wasn't a Pierce-Arrow outside a museum in the pristine condition of their car, and its distinctive sleek lines and fender-mounted headlamps would give it away in a minute.

"Take a left at the next corner," Emily said calmly, glancing from the street sign to the map. "It's the quickest way out of town."

Skardon shook his head grimly. "No time. Any minute now they'll have roadblocks on all roads leading out of town." He drove on until he saw what he was looking for, a large used-car lot. He made a left turn, swung into the lot, and drove slowly along the ranks of cars until he came to a space between a late-model Ford and a '95 Honda. He backed into the space and switched off the engine. As the salesman came out of the office, Skardon gave Emily terse instructions.

"Hello, there!" the salesman said, looking the part in a straw hat, striped shirt, and red suspenders. "My, what a beautiful car you've got," he said with a sincerity that he had not practiced in months. "Wouldn't want to trade it for this '95 Honda, would you? I make you a good deal—an even swap!'' He laughed at his jest. The Honda was worth maybe $14,000, the Pierce-Arrow at least $200,000 if it was in the mint condition it appeared.

''Just might do that.'' Skardon smiled, not joking at all. ''As a matter of fact, I brought my wife around to look at something along those lines, something to give our maid Maryam for Christmas.''

''Couldn't do better than this number,'' the salesman said, and launched into his spiel.

Skardon cut him short. ''I know the automobile,'' he lied. ''But we'll have to road-test it before we decide.''

''Be my guest. I'll get the keys.''

When he returned a minute later, Skardon handed the keys to Emily, who got in and started the car. Skardon motioned to her to pull the hood latch. As she did so, Skardon pretended to examine the engine, calling the salesman's attention to the timing, which sounded a bit off.

The salesman stuck his head under the hood, pulled on the accelerator rod a few times, and assured his customer that the automobile had been tuned before being put on the lot but that any adjustment required would be made at no cost to the customer once the deal was struck. At that moment, Emily pumped the accelerator a few times and Skardon pronounced himself satisfied. If the car performed as well as it should in the hands of his wife, it would be ideal for Maryam. ''Want to take it for a spin, honey?'' he said.

''Sure, climb in.''

The salesman held the door for him. He did not usually let his customers take a car from the lot unaccompanied, but with $200,000 worth of insurance in hand, his usual caution evaporated.

''Take your time,'' he said generously.

''Thanks. We'll do that,'' Skardon returned. ''And if we don't come back, you can keep the Pierce-Arrow.''

The salesman laughed.

* * *

They saw the roadblock two blocks ahead of them going southeast out of San Jose. The line was moving slowly but still fast enough to persuade Skardon that the search was not thorough. He climbed out of the car, nodded to Emily, and walked leisurely down a side street, like the last man off in a car pool on his way home from work. He went two blocks, turned left, and wound his way through the residential neighborhood for approximately half an hour, then turned back toward the main highway. When he reached it, he headed southwest in the growing darkness, alert for signs of police, until he saw the Honda parked at a fast food joint. He climbed in the car.

"Perfect timing," Emily said. "I've just ordered your dinner."

"Christ, the trouble you'll go to to avoid having to cook for me," Skardon said gruffly. "I don't know why I ever married you."

"Because you wanted company while fleeing from the police. Frankly, it's sort of fun, but I don't intend to make it a lifework."

"When I settle with that bastard Pope, we'll go wherever and do whatever you want. Deal?"

"Sounds good to me. Didn't you get in to see Pope?"

"Yes and no."

"That wasn't a yes or no question."

"I know it sounds crazy, but I saw Pope. Only it wasn't Pope, if you understand what I mean."

"Of course. Clear as mud."

"Well, the man I saw was Pope, all right, down to the last freckle. When I saw him he was a down-at-the-heels would-be composer, and in the three years since he has become an authentic genius. I know, because he improvised for me, showed me his latest scores, played recent recordings of his music, with his name on them."

Emily looked thoughtful. "I can think of an explanation."

"Shoot."

"He traveled back in time, stopped with Bach a couple

of years, with Beethoven, Brahms, and so on, and over a period of years nurtured a promising talent into what today seems mature genius."

"That's logical, except for one thing: It would take a couple of decades for Pope to acquire that kind of knowledge. But remember, even in time travel the aging process cannot be arrested. If your thesis were correct, he'd look fifty or sixty. But he's actually not far beyond his early thirties. There's something else: he seems to have an affinity for, and a knowledge of, Vienna. His German is native Viennese, and his dialect is distinctly archaic."

"So?"

"I don't know. But I'll find out. Meanwhile, where's that chow you ordered?"

It soon came. When it did, Skardon regretted having asked.

They put up at a motel on the eastern outskirts of Fresno that night. Early the next morning, having removed his disguise, Skardon asked the Fresno Comfort Motel manager the driving time to San Francisco and was told that it was a comfortable day's trip. Heading back west, he made a stop at a local bank and cashed in $50,000 worth of gold eagles from the sack Emily had transferred from the Pierce-Arrow the night before. It was a sum large enough to ensure that he would be remembered. Again he asked the driving time to San Francisco. An hour later Emily Ferguson had bought a sporty Elbati, paying $21,000 cash. A few blocks down the street she pulled up behind the Honda, whose plates Skardon had taken the precaution of exchanging with those from another car also parked at the Fresno Comfort the night before, and Skardon moved off.

Ten miles west of Fresno, Skardon found an untraveled dirt footpath leading off the main road. He followed it to a tributary of the San Joaquin indicated on the road map. Telling Emily to wait, he bounded off across the farmland bordering the stream. He was gone the better part of an hour.

"What took you so long?" Emily asked.

"Had to find water deep enough to drown it. Then I had to drag out the tracks for a couple of hundred yards from the river's edge."

"Well, I can still see tracks from here."

"Yes, I guess I'd better do something about them, too," Skardon said wearily, and went in search of another branch to efface the tire tracks still visible from the road.

Within easy driving distance of Fresno was the town of Firebaugh, and there Skardon found a furnished apartment for rent. He also rented a garage for the car. It was safe enough, for the moment. The police would track them to Fresno, learn of his inquiries about the mileage to San Francisco at the motel, find that he had asked the same question at the bank on Fresno's west side, and conclude that he was laying a false trail for them to follow. They would therefore concentrate their search toward the east. When that well ran dry, they would search in other directions—a futile search because not only had he changed cars, but the Elbati was now safely concealed in a garage and never driven. More probably, in the manner of difficult police inquiries, the search for him would be abandoned for newer and more pressing investigations.

For the next two months Skardon labored on a time-transference device. Before he began actual construction, he consulted the current literature in the fields of electronics and magnetism and was delighted to discover that the machine that had occupied some seven cubic feet in *Tempus Fugit* could be miniaturized, thanks to advances in electrical generation and microchip technology, to fit comfortably in the cavity beneath the back seat of the Elbati, with the controls under the dash. Parts mailed to Firebaugh from various high-tech companies were preassembled in the apartment in a mere two days. The magnetic element, consisting of approximately three miles of fine nickel-copper-cadmium-cobalt-niobium alloy wire strung on a rectangular frame welded to the bottom of the automobile, took considerably longer.

On 14 November Skardon, having come in the guise of an automobile mechanic on the job, quietly left the placid town of Firebaugh for San Francisco. There he rented a working-class apartment and immediately sought an underground contact he knew from prison.

"I want a key which will open a 1998 Toyota Midnight van—*any* Midnight van," he told the contact, a neatly dressed young man who could have passed for a bond salesman.

"No problem."

"Then I want half an hour without interference in the Santorini of Nob Hill, preferably between the hours of midnight and six."

His contact shook his head. "*That*'s a problem. The Santorini's where Justin Pope lives. If it was just Justin Pope, maybe it wouldn't be so bad. But he's attracted a number of the rich and would-be famous who want to rub shoulders with the great man. The apartment house is swaybacked from the crowds of senile old tycoons and their social-climbing chippies. A lot of the boys have had their eyes on that building, but they've never figured out a way to get through the cordon of heavyweights that occupy the whole ground floor. The usual gimmicks—delivery boys with an Uzi in the box of roses, the inside-man switch, the maintenance crew ploy—are out. The place is a regular Fort Kick-Ass."

"You said 'ground floor'."

"They've got the whole building covered, but the first floor is where the listening devices and television monitors and sleeping quarters of the guards are located."

"How about tunneling?"

"Yeah, I guess I could find somebody that could get you in that way. But you'd have to assemble a team that could strong-arm its way to the upper floors. The boys in blue would be all over you like stink on dog doo-doo ten seconds after you forced the door up to the lobby from the garage."

"I don't want to go up to the lobby. I want my half hour in the garage."

The connection chuckled. "Well, why the hell didn't you say so? Sure, we can manage that."

A fortnight later, Skardon entered the basement garage of the Santorini of Nob Hill through a narrow tunnel that had been drilled from a branch of the storm sewer through the basement floor. Skardon, as he had estimated, was able to do his work in slightly over half an hour. He then had departed, leaving behind the tunneling crew to grind the exit hole into a perfect circle twenty inches across. When they finished, they too would leave, lowering in place behind them the plug of quick-drying concrete they had poured as soon as they had broken through. Nothing had been visibly disturbed, and there was no reason to suspect that the plug, firmly cemented to the floor, would arouse suspicion or even be noticed.

For Skardon, there was nothing to do but wait.

For Detective Lieutenant Rivers, there had been nothing to do but wait, too. A methodical man and a proud one, he had been annoyed by the jibes of his associates about the ease of Skardon's escape. He had waited an hour for Skardon or the woman who was living with him to return and then bolted the barn door. Before the day was done, he had found the Pierce-Arrow, followed the Honda's trail to Fresno, traced Skardon to the motel and back toward San Francisco, decided that it was a false back trail, and sent his men eastward again. It had been a futile exercise. The trail was cold. Returning to San Francisco, he circulated Skardon's pictures again, in concentric circles from the apartment he had rented. Within three days he struck gold when the security guards at the Santorini positively identified him.

Rivers questioned Justin Pope, who had received Skardon. A blank. He checked out the credentials of "Hans Otto Graf" and found them, as he knew he would, spurious. Spurious but indicative of painstaking, expensive groundwork. Merely to get to meet with Justin Pope personally. Why? He had gone to a great deal of trouble and expense, involving among other things a trip to Vienna and a fairly long stay abroad. The interview with Justin Pope had been innocent enough, with no apparent threat of physical harm or any attempt to extract information from the famous composer that could form the basis for blackmail or indeed anything sinister. According to Dr. Pope, the two men had merely discussed his music.

"The impostor, you see," Justin Pope said, "was a music critic. I am a musician. It was natural."

"From what I understand from the security men," Rivers said, "it is not your practice to receive visitors—especially critics."

"Well," Pope said lamely, "I guess that is true. It was just that I took pity on an old man who had come so far merely to see me. Or so he said."

"And the visitors you *do* see," Rivers continued, unappeased by the answer, "you invariably see in the presence of your secretary, Conrad Karpiosky. Why not this 'Hans Otto Graf'?"

Franz Peter Schubert was in a quandary. To admit that it was because he was homesick for the accents of Vienna would reveal that he spoke fluent German, a fact unknown to anybody but Philipa Dedeny. It would open a Pandora's box of inquiry, and he didn't want to go through that again with Rivers. But then he remembered that he was the great Justin Pope, a genius, and genius need never explain.

"A whim," he said shortly, and stood up, ending the interview.

Rivers went, but the questions remained—and grew. Something funny was going on between Skardon and

Pope. Sooner or later Skardon would surface. If he kept watch on Pope, Rivers would catch him. He was a cop. Cops knew how to wait.

24. DOUBLE DUTY
10 JANUARY 2003

ARE YOU *SURE*?" A SHAKEN SCHUBERT ASKED.

"Absolutely, Dr. Pope," replied Lino Machado, Schubert's swarthy chief of security. "They watch in relays, a pair to each of the two cars at opposite corners of the block, and someone is on duty twenty-four hours a day."

"But how did you know they're watching *me*?"

"That was easy. Every time you left the apartment, they followed, usually with about three or four cars between us and them. They switched positions from time to time, presumably to avoid alerting us."

"Presumably?"

"Yes, it's a funny thing. If they were professionals, they'd have known that the tail would have been picked up by us sooner or later, their technique was that crude. They were practically *inviting* our security team to discover their presence. And we did, of course."

"If I was being followed all this time, I would have thought you would do something about it before now," Schubert said.

"We did."

"You notified the police?"

"No. You see, they *are* the police."

"What?"

"That's right, sir. Finding out who they were wasn't as easy as discovering that they were staking out the place. It seems as if they *wanted* you to know you were under surveillance but weren't quite so eager for you to know who was doing the shadowing."

Schubert was at a loss and suddenly apprehensive. "But I haven't done anything wrong," he protested. "I've committed no crime."

"No, sir. But there's more to it," Machado said, producing a set of eight-by-ten glossies. "Recognize this man?"

Schubert studied the pictures. They were all of a man of middle age with a cloth cap pulled down over penetrating dark eyes, with firm lips, strong jaw, and long straight nose. He looked somehow menacing. And somehow familiar. Schubert tried to put a name to the face.

Machado helped him out. "Try Graf."

"Of *course*. Hans Otto Graf. Without the beard and Tyrolean hat. And considerably younger."

"Also without the phony German accent. While my men were soft-shoeing around the neighborhood to see who else might be on the police surveillance team, we noticed that this guy seemed to spend a lot of time watching the police while they were watching you. A patient fellow, sitting in an Elbati behind a newspaper during the hours of darkness, but sometimes in the daytime, too—that's how we were able to get those pictures, by means of a 1000mm lens—and taking precautions not to be observed by the police."

"What the devil can he want?"

"Can't tell you that, sir, but his movements—or rather nonmovements—are peculiar. When you take the Rolls or another of the cars, he stays put. But when you go out for a drive in the van, he leaves his station, drives in this direction or that, and eventually loses us. We quizzed our police contacts, but the address on the papers is fake, and his name is phony, too. So we haven't been able to get a line on him, but rest assured, we will. Meanwhile, what do you want me to do?"

"Beats the hell out of me," Schubert said, employing one of the English colloquialisms he found so amusing. "Let me think about it."

He thought about it. So did Philipa Dedeny. Neither

could arrive at an acceptable hypothesis. As Justin Pope, as well as Franz Peter Schubert, he had led an unexceptionable life. He had never in either incarnation been in trouble with the authorities. He was, on the contrary, on the best of terms with everybody. He had received laurels from virtually every civilized country. He had become Sir Justin Pope, KB. Not to be outdone, the President had awarded him the Medal of Freedom. The French had made him a chevalier of the Legion of Honor, and the Russians had awarded him the Order of Lenin *and* the Order of the Red Star. Even so distant a country as Thailand had bestowed upon him the Order of the Elephant, and Japan the Order of the Rising Sun. And his bank account was as richly endowed as he was personally.

In fact, life had become an overflowing cornucopia of honors, wealth, adulation, good eating, comfort, and reverence. He found that he was spending more time receiving the plaudits of the world than working on his music. He was a living demonstration of the perils of having his wildest dreams come true. And, predictably, he was bored.

He had never been bored in that concrete home back in the mountain above Brig. When he was not writing music, he and Philipa were milking the goats that Pope had brought on one of his provisioning trips, or planting trees or tending the vegetable garden, or taking long walks through the winter snows, or making love. He had had all the advantages of civilization and none of the handicaps. There was no pollution, no war, no deafening street music, no drugs, no rapacious physicians and lawyers and impresarios, no muggers, no in-laws, no bills or debts, no automobiles, no newspaper propaganda, no television lies, no politicians, no crowds, no timetables. On the other hand, there were more books than he could ever read and more music than he could ever play on a five-foot stack of twelve-inch compact discs. He and Philipa were more than self-sufficient in food, most of it grown and canned with their own hands, and none of it was adulterated with dyes, preservatives, or fillers. Necessity provided him with exercise, nature with inspiration, and Philipa with a heart overflowing with affection. In the Swiss mountains, he now realized, he had spent the most carefree, most productive, *happiest* days of his life. He missed them.

Between the early 1800s and the early 2000s he had experienced just about everything that the world could offer, from the worst to the best. For that he was grateful to God. After so much living, he could retire to a quiet place, digest his varied experiences, and devote himself to that which God clearly intended he do—write music.

And where better to do it than Brig? It was free of all disturbance and conflict, yet each new day was an adventure in discovery—of adaptation to the virgin world about him, of new ideas from the tens of thousands of books and musical manuscripts contained in his stack of shiny silver discs, of new facets of the character of the woman he loved, of himself. Nor was he taking any chances: if he tired once more of that life or if curiosity about another time again possessed him, as it had three years ago, the *Fugit* would transport him there.

There was but one hitch: the occupation by the real Justin Pope of his home and hearth. Pope would definitely have to be removed. But that would pose no problems either physically or morally. In the unlikely event Pope refused to return to the year 2003 to enjoy the celebrity, honors, and riches Schubert had gained in his name, he would zap him with the stun gun. Lino Machado had instructed him in its use in case he was suddenly confronted with lunatics or kidnappers his bodyguards somehow failed to thwart. As to the morality of stealing Pope from the future, why not? Had not Pope stolen *him* from the past? Besides, the crime for which the police were pursuing him had clearly been committed by Pope, and it was only justice that Pope should pay.

Philipa sighed with relief as he described his plan. She had gone along with his return to the San Francisco of the twentieth century but had never been enamored of the idea. She had seen it all and knew that all the gloss and glitter, gadgets and gush, could mean something only to one who had never experienced it. For him the life of composer as cynosure had been exhilarating but had finally, inevitably, palled. "When do we leave?" she asked.

25. FUGUE
12 JANUARY 2003

JUSTIN POPE WAS UNDOUBTEDLY THE GREATEST COMposer of the century—perhaps *any* century, Detective Lieutenant Rivers reflected—but when it came to evading the police, Pope did not know a fugue from a fox-trot. On second thought, perhaps he was not a fugitive, after all: to be a fugitive, one had to be at least *accused* of a crime, and so far as Rivers knew, Pope had committed nothing resembling a crime, unless it was consorting with that known murderer and escaped convict, John K. Skardon. But did Pope know that the man in phony chin whiskers signing himself in the Santorini of Nob Hill guest register as Professor Hans Otto Graf was actually John K. Skardon?

Whatever the truth, Pope was taking elaborate if childish precautions to evade possible pursuers. He was definitely fleeing *something*. Rivers smiled to himself and shook his head as he drove down a side street parallel to the route Justin Pope was following at the moment. If Pope had wanted to advertise his departure, he could have done as well under the cover of a trumpet fanfare and a twenty-one-gun salute. Both he and his consort, the beauteous Philipa Dedeny, wore dark glasses, widebrimmed hats, and Burberrys turned up at the collar, but they had left the Santorini's garage in the gray van in the apparent belief that the men Rivers had stationed ostentatiously outside the apartment house were unaware of its existence. Babes in the woods.

For the next hour they drove aimlessly through the streets of San Francisco, making sudden turns and frequent switchbacks. Meanwhile, one of Rivers's four plainclothes surveillance vehicles always had Pope in sight, and they passed the van back and forth between them by radio until Pope's suspicions were apparently allayed and he shoved the van into overdrive and made a dash for San Francisco International Airport. There, after checking in the van as cargo on the same flight, they bought tickets, paying cash, and boarded the night flight to Geneva.

Rivers, boarding a police helicopter when it became clear where Pope and Philipa Dedeny were headed, arrived at the airport shortly afterward and took passage on the same plane. They booked a sleeping compartment forward; he took a tourist seat aft. At dinner hour, he took one look at TWA's ersatz food and handed it off without comment to a passing stewardess. He opened his overnight bag and took out a ham and cheese as tired and ragged as he himself felt, and masticated it without enjoyment. When the cabin lights dimmed and the movie, that old science-fiction standby, *The Ayes of Texas*, flickered onto the screen, he slipped on his raccoon disguise and within two minutes was lulled to sleep by the deep-throated sonority of the engines.

After a while he slipped into that recurrent old dream, as comfortable as his worn carpet slippers. In it, he was sitting at home in front of the television, trying to concentrate on the football game as his shrewish, dough-faced wife, dressed in a food-stained dressing gown, hectored him about his sleeping with Della, the cute secretary from the steno pool, and how she was going to sue him for a divorce and collect a fat alimony, on which she was going to move to Mexico and enjoy the good life, and if that included a hot-blooded young Mexican with the stamina of a stallion, so much the better. At the mention of hot blood, he calmly went to the kitchen, considered a long butcher knife before finally concluding that the meat cleaver was better suited to the work at hand, and painted her gown red. The pleasant scene faded, and he found himself standing on the steps of city hall to receive the departmental meritorious award from the mayor. He smiled in his sleep as he contemplated future wife-free afternoons with Della.

The two beers with which he had washed down the ham and cheese woke him up three hours later. The cabin lights were out, and most of the passengers were asleep. He trudged to a phone booth at the rear of the cabin, inserted his plastic card in the slot, and dialed a number from a crumbled piece of paper he took from his vest pocket.

"Hildebrand Hanser," came a voice from the other end of the line.

"Inspector Hanser, this is Lieutenant Rivers of the San Francisco P.D."

"Ah, yes, Lieutenant, I was awaiting your call. Did you get off in good order?"

"Fine. I gather Captain Catlin got in touch with you?"

"He did, indeed. He said you would be requiring a partner well acquainted with the local geography and language. As that description fits all of my men, there should be no problem. Have you any preferences as to special qualifications or physical type?"

"None at all. I leave it to your discretion, Inspector Hanser."

"Your confidence is appreciated, Lieutenant. I shall have an experienced agent, Estée Beaupré, meet you upon arrival."

Lieutenant Rivers had parked his rented car within view of the cargo gate, waiting for his partner. Twenty minutes passed, and still he saw no sign of the man Hanser had promised would meet him at that spot. He pulled the handset from its receptacle on the dash and dialed Inspector Hanser's number. There was no answer. *Somebody* had to answer, for Christ's sake: it was police headquarters. He dialed again. On the third ring the gray van drove through the gates, heading toward the main gate as fast as the law allowed.

Decision time. He had to either await Hanser's man and almost certainly lose contact with the van or follow it and hope he would not be detected, a fairly futile gesture in a country where, being totally ignorant of the street layout and local landmarks, he would have to follow close behind and risk discovery. Still, it was that or lose them. He switched on the engine and shoved the car in gear.

At that moment a red sports coupe pulled directly in front of him and stopped, blocking his way. He honked furiously, but the elegant raven-haired woman of forty-odd years who stepped out of the car merely waived gaily at him and walked around to his side of the car, as if she had taken him for an old friend. Meanwhile, the gray van was speeding out of sight in the dusk.

"Lady, get that goddamn heap out of the road!" he barked at her in English, regretting for the first time in his life that he had cheated on his exams and gotten thrown out of French class.

"Where's the fire?" the woman said in the same language, in a fair imitation of a traffic cop opening a debate with a speeder, showing that the influence of a thousand American B movies had not been lost on a benighted world, after all.

"I'm about to build one, under your shapely ass, if you don't get out of there. I'm on police business."

"My, *my*," she said with mock gravity. "Police business. Imagine that!"

"Come on, lady," Rivers pleaded, "*move* it."

"What for? By now they're halfway to Geneva."

"Don't you worry, I'll catch up with—hey!"

She smiled expectantly.

Rivers looked at her a long moment and laughed. "You're S. T. Beaupré."

"You need not be so formal—Estée will suffice. I understand that you Americans find it a mental strain to memorize more than one name per person and that the surname is an endangered species, particularly when preceded by an honorific. I suppose that sooner or later Americans will tire of even such elementary distinctions and simply follow the lead of their women of the night."

"Huh?"

"I understand they call *everybody* 'John.' Now, if you'll kindly move over, I'll drive."

Numbly, Rivers, still trying to unravel the woman's penultimate declaration, eased to the other side, and Inspector Estée Beaupré of the Geneva police department climbed in, took the wheel, and proceeded toward the city at a discreet pace. Rivers was unsurprised when she took from her lizardskin handbag an instrument roughly the size of a pack of cigarettes and placed it on the dash. She switched it on.

"Bearing 351, range 3,210, steady . . ." a mechanical voice intoned. It paused, and five seconds later it resumed. "Bearing 265, range 3,190, closing . . ."

"He's turned west," Estée Beaupré said unnecessarily. "I know a shortcut."

"Wish to hell we had those," Rivers said wistfully.

"You *don't*? Why on Earth not—they've been around for years."

"I know. In fact they were actually invented in San Francisco. By a Taiwanese refugee. But the ACLU won't let us use them."

"The who?"

"The American Crime-Loving Uplifters. They say they trample on human rights by helping us catch criminals."

"Thank God we're in Switzerland."

"Amen. Where'd you stick the beeper?" Rivers asked.

"I didn't. The customs man put it under their dashboard. You know the Swiss—no imagination."

Rivers cast an appreciative sideways glance at Estée Beaupré, whose dress had hiked up above the knee to reveal a stretch of quite shapely nylon-clad leg. He did not know about the Swiss, but there was nothing wrong with *his* imagination. It was growing dark, and there was no telling how far Pope would drive. Rivers hoped it would be a long, long way. He cleared his throat. "By the way, S. T., are you married? What I mean is," he added hastily, "it must be tough on family life, your being away from the home and kids on assignments like this."

"No."

"No what—not married, or not tough?"

"I'm tough as I have to be, and no—I'm not married. Are you?"

Rivers hesitated. "Not so's I've ever noticed."

"Are they still behind us?" Schubert asked.

"I guess so," Philipa replied. "They were the last time I looked."

"No danger of them losing us?"

"Not until I disable their beeper."

"What if they've somehow concealed more than one?"

"This gadget Lino Machado gave us," she said, looking down at the round instrument with the blinking dial on the seat between them, "is supposed to scan all beeper channels and give the bearing and distance in centimeters of each in sequence, just as Rivers's indicator does from the beeper signal itself. So far, we've got but a single reading, and that's of the beeper we've already located, stuck to the underside of our dash."

"I hope you're right."

"Don't you worry, darling," Philipa Dedeny said, reaching over and patting Schubert's hand. "When we're through with the inquisitive Detective Lieutenant Rivers, he'll never bother us again."

John K. Skardon and his wife, Emily, had brazenly boarded the same plane as Rivers and the man masquerading as Pope and the woman who lived with him.

Rivers had never seen Emily, nor had "Pope." Skardon was the last person in the world he would expect to encounter on the plane; therefore, Skardon's disguise, as a gray-haired episcopal bishop, and matching counterfeit passport were quite adequate to escape detection.

In Geneva, the Skardons were last to claim their car from customs and drove into the city some time after both Schubert and his shadow, Rivers, had left the airport.

Skardon's foray into the garage at the Santorini of Nob Hill had borne fruit when he had been able to conceal behind the license tag a transmitter that emitted a signal of such low frequency that no detector in the world other than the one Skardon himself had fabricated would pick it up. Nevertheless, the receiver/computer in his Elbati gave him information as to the bearing of and range to his target quite as precise as that registered on the monitor Rivers carried, and it was detectable over thousands, not merely tens, of miles.

It was night and pouring rain when the van—followed by Rivers and Estée Beaupré less than a kilometer behind and John and Emily Skardon only two hundred meters behind *them*—pulled into Brig.

And at that moment, the beeper receiver on the dashboard of Rivers's car fell silent. He looked at Estée Beaupré in consternation. "It's gone dead!"

"I noticed," she replied dryly, squinting through the downpour at the indistinct center stripe.

"Did you bring a spare?"

"No. This has never happened before."

"There's always a first time. Unless . . . unless . . ."

"They found the beeper?"

"Yes."

"It's one or the other," she agreed. "But right now all that's academic: we've lost them."

They drove on in silence toward the middle of the town, in the direction in which the van had been headed. Suddenly, Rivers gripped his companion's arm.

"I see it," she said quietly, and pulled over into an empty parking space.

The van was parked in front of a sweetshop, and

through the glass front she and Rivers could see Justin Pope and Philipa Dedeny at a booth drinking coffee.

"Well," Rivers said to his partner, "what do you think?"

"I think we're in a fix. If we follow them close enough not to lose them, in this rain we'll need our headlights, and they'll spot us, sure."

"You don't think you could brace the local police for a replacement for that receiver?"

"Of course. But it would take time, and what if meanwhile they came out of that coffee shop and took off, and it turned out that they had discovered the beeper, and there was nothing wrong with our receiver, after all?"

"Yes."

They were silent.

After a moment, Rivers found Estée Beaupré looking at him. He looked into her eyes. "Are you thinking the same thing I'm thinking?"

"Well, we've got nothing to lose but our next promotions."

"Let's go."

They stepped out of the car and hurried down the file of parked cars to the van. Fortunately, the back doors were out of sight of the shop window; unfortunately, they were locked. But not for long. With an ease born of considerable quasi-illegal experience, Rivers applied two thin tools from a leather kit he carried in an inner pocket to the problem, and a moment later, now drenched, they had secured the doors behind them. By light filtering in from the street, they took stock of their surroundings. On the floor was a pile of blankets in which they wrapped themselves, an empty picnic hamper, some plastic water jugs, a portable electronic piano/organ, tire tools, and a cardboard carton with cans of motor oil. Behind the driver's seat was a large steel box, apparently welded to the body of the van. It had neither opening nor apparent function and was separated from the driver's compartment, as they were themselves, by a sheet of transparent plastic as thick and unyielding as bulletproof glass. That was a break. So long as they were covered in blankets and kept their heads down, Pope and his woman would not see or hear them, even if Estée Beaupré suddenly sneezed, as she had several times already since they had concealed themselves.

In the sweetshop, Schubert glanced at his wristwatch. "We've given them half an hour."

"That's plenty," Philipa replied, rising. "If they haven't made their move by now, they might as well send in their resignations."

Schubert shed bank notes onto the table, and they left the shop. They climbed into the van, not even glancing back into its darkened interior, and drove off. For the next twenty minutes Schubert drove with silent concentration through the deluge, snaking his way up the mountain road. He met an occasional car on the highway but could discern nothing behind him. At last he pulled onto a turnout, stopped, and set the hand brake.

During the flight over the North Pole, Philipa and Franz had debated when to reappear in the lives of the real Justin Pope and Angelica Hunter. Franz argued that it should, for the sake of simple humanity, be very soon after 1 March 3919, the day they had overcome him and taken command of the *Fugit*. Why should they deprive him of his youth, warehoused in a future time, without the adulation he so desperately wanted? Allow him to go back to the twenty-first century and reap all the acclaim he wanted. After all, so long as they kept the *Fugit*, they could always reclaim their former preeminence if they got bored with their home in the mountains of Switzerland.

"I disagree, Franz," Philipa countered. "Remember, he has done us no real harm. Far from it, if you remember, he brought us together. Yet if we let him return to the year 2002, the Rivers investigation will still be fresh, and he will be subject to police harrassment, which will scarcely contribute to the enjoyment of his celebrity. But give him five years or so, and the police investigation will have blown over and he can pick up where he left off. Hell, you can even afford to give him, as a going-away present, those last two symphonies you haven't yet turned over to the publishers. He can always say he was holed up on a Pacific island composing them."

In the end, they split the difference and set the time dial to 15 August 3921.

Outside, the wind buffeted the van and rain poured down in a steady stream as Schubert fingered the lever that his puzzled security chief, Lino Machado, had installed some days earlier. At the time, Schubert had told him he feared that should a kidnapper somehow gain entry to the rear of the van when he and Mrs. Pope were enjoying one of their incognito picnics, a device that could put the felons to sleep without injury until the police could be summoned would be useful. He now pulled the lever, and a thin stream of gas filled the back of the van. Within seconds, Estée Beauprée and Detective Lieutenant Rivers were sound asleep, never having stirred from their recumbent position in the back of the van.

Schubert pushed the "Run" button on the computer panel, and an aura of a different sort, an electric purple, filled the compartment. After nearly twenty centuries of suspended animation, which lasted no more than two minutes, Schubert and Philipa found themselves on a rough dirt road at midnight. A balmy breeze stirred the leaves of the trees around them, but otherwise all was silent.

"How I've missed it," Philipa breathed. "Until this moment, I had forgotten how much—the peace and quiet, broken only by the most lovely music ever written." She smiled and pressed Schubert's hand.

He nodded and bent over to kiss her cheek. "I guess I have, too," he sighed. "But frankly, having had a bellyful of the nineteenth and twenty-first centuries, I don't care much *where* I am, so long as it's with you."

"Just try to get rid of me." She laughed. "Meanwhile, heaven can wait. Once more: how are we going to do this?"

"Nothing to it," Schubert said breezily. "Pope and company will be sleeping. After two and a half years, their guard will be down, so we'll take them by surprise. We hit them with the stun guns, stick them in the back of the van with Rivers and the woman who's with him, transport them back to the year 2004, and deposit the policemen on the road between here and Brig. We'll take the Popes to Brig itself, where they'll immediately be recognized and feted. As for us, we'll come back here to the thirtieth century. What could go wrong?"

"Nothing, obviously. Drive on, James."

The Skardons had followed Rivers's rented car into Brig, parked within three car lengths of them across the street, and watched with amazement as the policemen got out of the car, jimmied open the rear of the van, and climbed in. When the Popes emerged and drove off in the van, the Skardons, as before, lagged well behind. A full two kilometers now separated the two vehicles as they wound their way through the mountain valley toward a destination Skardon could not guess. But he felt, at least, that the Popes must be getting close to it. Suddenly the low-frequency receiver indicated that the van had stopped. Skardon, who had been following their progress on the map Emily had spread on her lap, realized that the ersatz Popes were near no present town or city. They had no reason to stop except because of an accident or a time-transfer. He, too, stopped.

If they had suffered an accident, he would soon know: he would give them two minutes, then overtake them and see what had happened, summoning help if necessary. If there was a time transfer, he would know that, too, for he had synchronized his own time-transfer device to slave off of Pope's by radio: where the Popes went, he and Emily would go. He—he suddenly went into deep freeze.

* * *

When he thawed out, he looked at the time dial: It was 15 August 3921, and outside it was as dark as Hades.

Skardon smiled, looking very much like a tiger shark that had just sighted a school of tuna. He put the Elbati into gear and roared ahead into the night. But only for a very short distance, for he felt that sudden, distinctive vibration known and dreaded by generations of motorists.

He had a flat.

26. SWAN SONG
15 AUGUST 3921

JUSTIN POPE WAS ASTONISHED AT THE SPEED WITH WHICH he had become acclimated to life in the thirtieth century, in a world totally depopulated except for him and Angelica Hunter (he guessed; he could not be sure, of course, that the general nuclear war had not left pockets of survivors in other parts of the world), a world without conflict and strife, a world in which the air was pure, the streams clear, the quiet almost overpowering.

At first he missed the life of a musical idol and social lion—or thought he did. Gradually he began to recognize how little the plaudits of the uncomprehending masses really meant, how his huge bank account was as much burden as blessing, how indulging a fawning public at innumerable concerts and recording sessions stole precious hours from his real love—composing—how Angelica Hunter, freed of the responsibilities of protecting his interests from a grasping world, had daily become closer, more responsive, more loving. Here, much as Schubert himself had done, he spent mornings at the keyboard, the rest of the day reading, enjoying long walks with his woman, music by the world's masters, the beauties of pristine nature, relaxed and fulfilling love.

So, then, what compelled him to harbor a burning, ineradicable resentment against Franz Peter Schubert, who had enabled him to experience both lives? It was a question he had asked himself many times, and he could never come up with a completely satisfactory answer. The closest he came was that Schubert, a man from a civilization two centuries behind his, had outsmarted him, made him like a country bumpkin. Made him look *ridiculous*. His face reddened every time he thought about it. Franz Peter Schubert, whatever his manifold virtues, whatever services he had rendered to Justin Pope, had deprived him of the vehicle with which he might explore a thousand worlds through time, and by God, he wanted it back.

Perhaps it would not be so difficult, at that. Schubert, as Pope himself had done in the past, paid periodic visits to the nuclear shelter at Brig to bring supplies: newspapers, magazines, videodisks, canned delicacies, new compact discs, spares for the various electronic musical instruments, new kitchen gadgets, good modern art to adorn the concrete walls, the latest fashions for Angelica. Usually he came at night, when the Popes would be sleeping, and he usually deposited his hoard of goodies in a pile at the entrance of the cave. But not always. When rain or snow would have damaged the supplies, he drove just inside the entrance to the cavern and left them there.

Before the end of the first year, Pope had contrived a large net made of tough nylon cord, which he suspended from the ceiling just above the point where the stacks of supplies would unexpectedly appear some morning, to be seen as Justin Pope and Angelica were emerging into the sunlight for their daily stroll with their German shepherds, Franz and Pete. The transparent nylon was virtually invisible against the gray ceiling, and he had jury-rigged a remote device, scavenged from a derelict television set, that allowed him to drop the net into place, even from a distance. He trained his dogs, using Angelica as a decoy, to nuzzle him into wakefulness instead of barking at the detection of an intruder.

And as a second line of offense, in case Schubert for some reason drove deeper into the cavern and came into their living quarters, he rigged a second net just above the entrance to their sleeping chamber.

As the months passed, the existence of his booby traps

almost faded from his consciousness. He was growing increasingly accustomed to life in the uninhabited Swiss mountains. He *loved* it there. In time, he could think of no other life except with a faint twinge of regret that he had wasted so much of his on pursuits of no importance. Pope was an intelligent and perceptive young man and knew a lot about the world, more, in fact, than he knew about himself. He did not know, for instance—until too late—that his instincts had been molded to obey the compulsion of the obsession to have satisfaction from Schubert, which possessed him that first year.

Detective Lieutenant Rivers awoke with a start as the vehicle jolted to a stop. Muzzy—from the sleep, he thought—he raised his head cautiously and peered into the driver's compartment. It was empty. He shook his partner by the shoulder until she came around.

Estée Beaupré sat up and looked about her blankly. "Where are we? What happened?"

"I don't know—to both questions. But wherever it is, I think we've arrived. Let's get out of here and have a look."

He opened the door carefully, and they crawled out into the darkness. But there was light at the end of the tunnel, and they moved mothlike toward it. Beyond the gates they stopped.

Rivers squinted at the bright sunshine and felt the balmy breeze on his cheek. "What the hell's going on here?" he exclaimed, walking into the knee-deep grass that bordered the concrete apron of the shelter.

"What do you mean?"

"When we fell asleep, it was raining. And cold. Does *this* look and feel like Switzerland in January?"

Estée Beaupré shook her head slowly, suppressing a shudder. "What the hell's going on here?" she asked in turn. "I *know* this place," she said, studying the topography. "I know these mountains. I've skied here a dozen times. Down in the valley is Brig." She pointed.

"Where?" Rivers said, following her finger but seeing nothing but a verdant, virgin valley.

"Exactly. Where is the city? Where are the farm-houses between here and the Brig that isn't there? Where are the roads? Where are the people?"

Rivers shrugged.

"Do you know what *that* is?" she said, turning and pointing at the cavern entrance twenty feet away.

"Potato storehouse, maybe?"

"*People* storehouse. That's an atomic-bomb shelter. We've built them all over the country as a refuge in case of atomic war. I've toured some of them as part of my official duties as reserve officer in the Swiss Army, although not this particular one. Typically, they have six floors, descending from ground level. They have huge double blast doors—you just saw them. They have thousands of tons of supplies—food, water, medical supplies, books, children's games—everything a community needs to survive. The biggest can harbor twenty thousand people for several weeks while the rest of the world kills itself off."

They looked at each other.

Rivers swallowed hard. "Are you thinking what I'm thinking?"

"No," Miss Beaupré replied firmly. "I'm Swiss. I won't allow myself to believe such nonsense."

Justin Pope awoke with a start as his German shepherd Franz thrust a hard muzzle into his ribs. He had time only to shake his head clear of the last wisps of the boring dream he was happy to see come to an end, when suddenly the overhead lights flashed on and his living reincarnation and Philipa Dedeny stood in the doorway, menacing black pistols in their hands. Philipa fired hers at Angelica, who had turned in her sleep when the lights had gone on, a fraction of a second before his double could take aim and fire at him. By then Justin Pope, his mind numbed by the apparition of an exact clone of Justin Pope but his body reacting with all its accustomed reflexes, slammed the palm of his hand against the remote control on the adjacent wall, releasing the net above the doorway, slithered out of bed, knocked over a table, and took refuge behind it, wondering what the hell was going on.

In the brief seconds it took for Schubert and Philipa to become completely enmeshed in the net, their frantic thrashing about only tangling them ever more inextricably, Pope was assailed by questions: who *was* that guy? How could he look *exactly* like Justin Pope? How had he gotten there? What was he doing with Schubert's woman at his side? Why hadn't he heard a report, only a reptilian hiss following a flash of brilliant light from Philipa's pistol barrel? Still, he had heard no further hisses since he had dropped the net on his assailants. He cautiously peeked around the table edge.

Whatever they were up to, they were too busy to cause any immediate mischief. Before they extricated themselves, he needed time to think things over. Even more important, he had to get Angelica, who was slumped unconscious, half on the bed, half on the floor, to a doctor. That meant time travel. Fortunately, the *Fugit* was available. It *had* to be; otherwise, how could their assailants have gotten there?

He scooped up the unconscious Angelica in his arms and raced for the cavern tunnel, her nightgown flapping in the breeze, Franz and Pete frisking excitedly at his heels. Silhouetted against the tunnel entrance was the *Fugit*. He yanked open the back doors and laid Angelica tenderly on the heap of blankets he found there. The dogs jumped in before he could slam the door. Well, at least *they* would not hurt her.

He slammed the door shut, climbed behind the wheel, switched on the engine, gunned it around in a tight half circle, and shot toward the mouth of the cavern. Just as he reached it, two figures appeared, doubtless alerted by the roar of the engine. He was going too fast to try to establish their identities, but the pistols that appeared in their hands demonstrated their hostile intentions beyond any reasonable doubt.

As he zoomed past them, Rivers loosed two shots into the air in the traditional policeman's polite request for the fugitive to stop. Hearing the shots and never doubting that they were aimed at him, Justin Pope mashed down on the accelerator. He tore down the mountainside toward the Brig that was and its hospitals, debating whether he should program the *Fugit* back to the twenty-first century with its smooth paved roads at once and chance the obstruction of other cars and pedestrians impeding his progress. Or should he carry on like this, down a bumpy path that might well cause more harm to Angelica than whatever kind of projectile that cursed Philipa Dedeny had blasted her with? He was undecided and his hand was still on the time-computer control when suddenly, around the bend, coming head-on at high speed, a sports car appeared.

Instinctively, Pope gave the time-transfer dial a single vicious twist, hit the "Run" button, and closed his eyes when he saw that he had not, as he had fully expected, been transported to another time and escaped the onrushing car despite a momentary flash of the familiar purple haze.

The sound of the vehicles crunching head-on reverberated throughout the valley. The fronts of the cars rose into the air like rams butting heads and fell back to earth with a crash. It was a crash from which nobody could have possibly survived without serious injury.

For three or four minutes all was silent save the low-throated growling of the dogs. Then through the sprung door of the van stepped a shaky Justin Pope, thanking God he had buckled up automatically when he climbed into the cab and switched on the engine. He staggered around to the back, pulled open the door, and saw that the mass of blankets must have cushioned Angelica

Hunter when the cars collided, for she was sitting up woozily, shaking her head. He helped her out of the van.

"How do you feel?" Pope said, his arm half supporting her.

"I feel like hell," she replied crossly. "How do you *think* I'd feel, hit by a bolt of lightening? And where the hell did you learn to drive?"

Pope breathed a sigh of relief. She could not be hurt badly if she was up to criticizing his driving.

"However bad she feels," said a voice conversationally behind him, "it's a great deal better than *you're* going to feel in about two minutes.

"Skardon!" Pope said, turning toward the man who was approaching him with fists balled.

"It *is* you, you son of a bitch! I *knew* it. I could *taste* it. But just for the record, before I tear your hair out by the roots, who is the other Justin Pope?"

"Other Justin Pope?"

"Don't act the innocent with *me*, sonny boy. The Justin Pope who speaks native Viennese German, who composes *real* music."

In spite of his aching ribs, several of which he thought might be broken, Pope laughed. "So *that's* who the mysterious gunman is!"

"Mysterious gunman?" Skardon echoed, mystified in turn.

"That's Franz Peter Schubert, Skardon. The *real* living, breathing Franz Peter Schubert," Pope explained.

John K. Skardon was silent, his brow wrinkled in a frown. Finally he figured it out, and his brow cleared. "Right. Now, before I forget what I came for . . . ." He cocked his fist and took aim at Justin Pope's chin.

Pope did not flinch. He stood his ground, smiled and whistled between his teeth. Instantly Franz and Pete took up their posts at his side and sat down, tails stilled, their ears thrust forward expectantly. "I don't think my friends here would like what you have in mind."

Skardon inspected the menagerie and decided that Pope

had a point. "All right," he growled. "But I won't forget."

"You've forgotten already—to introduce me to the lovely lady who is looking at you with marked disapproval."

"Emily, I wish I could say I'd like to introduce the real Justin Pope, when what I'd *really* like to do is kill him. Anyway, this is the guy we've been chasing. My wife, Pope, Mrs. Emily Skardon."

"I am pleased to meet you, ma'am," Pope replied, taking her hand. "I hope you'll forgive the pajamas. We didn't have time to pack. Allow me to present *my* wife, Angelica."

The women took each other's hands, then spontaneously embraced, as women do who recognize what a burden the other is carrying being married to such a beast.

"Okay," Skardon said, taking charge. "Before anything else, we've got to get out of here. But the first question is, Where's here?"

"We're near Brig, Switzerland," Angelica volunteered.

"I know *that*. I mean, where—in *time*?"

"Well," Pope said, "it must be sometime around mid-August 3921. At least it was the last time I looked at a calendar, sometime around a week ago."

"I know that, too. My time computer is slaved to the one in your van. Before I had the flat, it was the fifteenth of the month. But that's not the time right now."

"How do you know?"

"Because you changed it. I know—I saw the purple flash just before the collision."

"Say, that's right. But why don't you check the—"

"Computer read out? I already did. It's a delicate piece of work, that computer, and mine was destroyed by the impact. Let's hope yours isn't."

But it was—totally.

"So where does *that* leave us?" Pope asked.

Skardon shrugged. "Beats me."

"Come on. *You're* the scientific genius."

"I'm good, but not good enough to repair a microprocessor with a pair of pliers and a crowbar."

The four of them fell silent, contemplating a future in a world where they did not even know what century it was, although judging by the imminence of the impact from the time Pope had laid his hand on the dial, it could not be too distant in time from their starting point in August 3921.

They heard the sound of voices coming their way. A moment later a handsome young couple appeared, walking hand in hand.

The young couple stopped, surprised to see the four silent people in the middle of the road, standing beside the two wrecked automobiles. The girl bore a striking resemblance to Estée Beaupré. The young man was the pith and image of Justin Pope.

It was the young man who spoke, addressing Pope. "What are *you* doing here? I thought I just left you in the music room. And who on Earth are all these other people, Father?"

Neither Angelica nor Emily understood a word he said. But Pope and Skardon did: the young man was speaking German.

CODA
18 FEBRUARY 2088

THE AUDIENCE HAD RISEN TO ITS FEET IN HOMAGE TO the work of the great composer whose compositions it had just heard played by the New York Philharmonic in an all-Pope concert. Already, in the lobby, the music critic of *New World*, the most influential newsmagazine in North America, was holding court, surrounded by a small knot of sycophants.

"Maestro," said one acolyte, a pale young woman with her hair in a tight bun, "what did you think of it. I mean—*really*?"

"I thought it was a magnificent performance—really."

"And the choice of the final work on the program—did you agree with that?"

"Most certainly," the critic said emphatically. "Justin Pope wrote an astonishing number of great compositions in his tragically brief career, but there is no question that nothing else ever came close to that masterpiece of masterpieces, the first work he ever published—the *Malibu* Symphony."

ABOUT THE AUTHOR

FOR 30 YEARS DANIEL DA CRUZ HAS LIVED AND worked—as a diplomat, teacher, businessman, and journalist—in Europe, Asia, and Africa.

He spent six World War II years as a U.S. Marine volunteer, serving ashore, afloat (in 1941 aboard the *Texas*), and aloft in the three war theaters. A *magna cum laude* graduate of Georgetown University's School of Foreign Service, da Cruz has been variously a census enumerator, magazine editor and editorial consultant, judo master—he holds a second degree Black Belt of the Kodokan Judo Institute, Tokyo—taxi driver, farmer, public relations officer for an oil company, salesman, foreign correspondent, publishers' representative, vice president of a New York advertising agency, slaughterhouse skinner, captain of a Texas security organization, American Embassy press attaché in Baghdad, copper miner, and Adjunct Professor of Anthropology at Miami University.

Da Cruz has published seventeen books, among them an American history text, a monograph on Amerindian linguistics, and three suspense novels for Ballantine Books, the most recent of which, *The Captive City*, was awarded a special "Edgar." He has written five other science-fiction novels, *The Grotto of the Formigans* (Del Rey, 1980), *The Ayes of Texas* (Del Rey, 1982), *Texas on the Rocks* (Del Rey, 1986), *Texas Triumphant* (Del Rey, 1987), and *F-Cubed* (Del Rey, 1987).